THE MALLARD CONSPIRACY

BY SYLVIA HORNBACK

The Mallard Conspiracy

Author: Sylvia Hornback

ISBN: 978-0-9835120-5-9

Library of Congress Control Number: 2018939606

Edited by: William Greenleaf

Design & Layout by: Douglas DoNascimento

Published by: Briggs & Schuster
                 BSA.IM

Printed in the United States of America

This book is dedicated to

Dick Hornback, my partner and best friend, who

always believed in me.

Prologue

Nine-year-old Zahid coughed and choked on the ever-present exhaust fumes as he wove through the heavy city traffic with his plastic jugs. Most mornings, Zahid began his three-hour journey before dawn. It was imperative for him to be in the water line before the city hydrants shut down. He traveled through the polluted paved streets rather than risk the slums, where open sewage cut an insidious river of disease through the dirt paths. His mother had warned him of these dangers, and together they'd planned the safest route for him to travel.

The city water system provided only a few thousand gallons of potable water each day for the heavily populated city, where dozens died by the hour. Desperation had forced residents to drink groundwater contaminated with salt, or else the polluted water from the shrinking river. Water piped directly to homes from the city system had long since become useless. Either no water came out at all, or it dribbled out as brown drops of death. The only source of clean water had dwindled to a few large hydrants connected to the single city filtration plant. City trucks filled at the hydrants delivered water across the city. Even though the city effort operated around the clock, the few hundred trucks were vastly inadequate to serve the entire population.

Like many others, Zahid's family could not depend on the trucks for water. Sometimes the trucks reached them, and sometimes there was no water delivery for days. Those days bred frantic crowds that surrounded the delivery areas and waited, hovering to pounce on the vulnerable drivers. Angry mobs grew larger and became more volatile every day. Aggressive gangs targeted the weak and shoved them aside to take their places in water lines. A boy of Zahid's size was no match for men with clubs. Violence escalated with every delivery, and before long, the trucks stopped coming altogether.

When the trucks no longer came, the government sent soldiers to guard the hydrants and protect the masses that traveled there daily. News of the safe zone surrounding the city hydrants buzzed throughout Zahid's neighborhood, and everyone hoped for the possibility of clean water. Their only other option was the river, but it was an impossible distance from Zahid's home—much farther than the walk to the city hydrants. Zahid's family decided to chance getting water from this safer source, and Zahid was the one who would make the trip into the safe zone. The responsibility fell to the child, as it did in many homes, because he was the oldest male in his family.

Zahid had been making the trip for two months now, but he could only manage two gallons of water at a time, barely enough for his family to survive one day. His early start allowed him to get a place in line. Young and old, strong and infirm waited for the trucks to leave on their first run. No one knew where the trucks took their cargo each morning, but they could guess. They were certain of one thing: the water wasn't for them.

After the trucks disappeared, the crowds of people could fill their containers from water hoses that the uniformed guards attached to the pipeline. Twenty-four lines stretched down the city streets. Twenty-four human chains connected to lifelines.

However, on this day the hydrants shut down before Zahid could fill his plastic jugs. One woman near him collapsed on the curb and sat staring at the crowds. Another turned and walked back down the street, resigned to her circumstance. Zahid, along with many others, simply sat back down and prepared to wait until the hydrants opened again the next day. At least then, they'd be the first in line. They couldn't go home empty-handed.

~~~

Zahid's mother waited for him to return, worrying every minute he was away. She looked at the water jar in her kitchen. Her family only had sips remaining. When he hadn't returned by sundown, she knew the night would be a long one, especially for Zahid. She could only pray that he was waiting unhurt in the water line, and hadn't fallen victim to something worse. Stories of injured neighbors filled her with dread. Friends and neighbors had waited in the long lines to fill their containers. Then they were attacked and had their water stolen on their way home. These victims were adults. What chance did Zahid have? She couldn't sleep until her son made it home.

~~~

Zahid did not sleep either. Even though he'd tied the plastic containers to his waist with a strong rope, he was afraid someone would steal his jugs. Then what would he do? He would be ashamed to go home. While he waited, he draped his arms over the giant containers attached to his sides. Many coveted his lightweight plastic containers. Most had clay jars that were extremely heavy when full. He was vulnerable and he knew it. His vigilance meant life or death to his family.

Later in the night, when the crowds had settled for the long wait, Zahid scoured the sleeping faces around him, then pulled the chapati and onions from his pocket. His mother had given him a small portion of the flatbread that morning. He had been patient and watchful, waiting for the best time to eat. If someone decided to take it from him, there was nothing he could do to stop them, so he ate it quickly. Eyes around him popped open. The aroma of the onions betrayed him, but by that time he'd swallowed the last of his food. Eventually, the glares disappeared in sleep, but Zahid intended to stay awake. He didn't trust anyone.

Zahid's mind drifted, and he thought of earlier times when he'd been a foolish child and sat on the grand rock near his home. He'd looked out at the vast sea that licked the shore of his city. He still remembered his shock when his mother had told him that none of the seawater was fit for drinking.

"But there's so much of it," Zahid had said.

Chapter 1

Low rumbling nagged at Sam Stanfield's twilight sleep. He turned on his side and snaked the cool sheet over his long torso and onto his shoulder. Then he settled down to sleep a few more minutes before sunrise when work would begin on the Bar S Ranch. He remembered today was Georgia's day off from the hospital. She still slept beside him. Otherwise, she'd have the coffee on already. Sam had one day that he was the official coffee brewer, so he decided to get on with it.

The instant he put his feet on the floor, he felt a vibration that traveled through the walls and resonated through the hundred-year-old ranch house. Gracie began barking at the back door. It was an alarm, not her usual single bark to let them know she wanted to go outside. The Australian shepherd rarely barked outside and never inside the house.

"Do you hear that?" Sam asked. He reached across the bed and touched Georgia's arm. "Let's get up."

"I can feel it." Georgia was out of bed quickly, pulling on her jeans. "What is it?"

"Don't know yet," Sam answered over his shoulder. He responded in one fluid motion—up, dressed, and running through the house in seconds.

"Gracie's having a fit," Georgia said.

"I'm coming, girl. What's wrong with you?" Sam had barely cracked the back door when Gracie flew past him, and the blue merle became a blur of gray and white. Gracie raced toward the corral on the north side of the ranch in a burst of frantic barking. Sam followed. He could hear the cattle bellowing in the distance. The sound was unmistakable—they were stampeding.

"Can you see anything?" Georgia shouted from the back porch. "What do you think she's after, Sam?"

Sam turned at the edge of the yard and started back to the house. "It's a stampede. The strange thing is the cows sound like they're in two pastures. I hear some by the barn, but the main herd is stampeding from the east pasture."

"Can it be coyotes causing this kind of upheaval?"

"We need to check it out." Sam stepped into his boots and grabbed his keys. "I'll get the buggy and meet you in the driveway."

Sam didn't think the answer was as simple as coyotes. His cows were ferocious protectors of their young and wouldn't hesitate to chase off a runty coyote. He made it to the garage and was climbing into the Rustler when a muffled crack echoed through the rolling hills. He raced the buggy up the drive and slid to a stop.

"That was a gunshot!" Sam shouted. "Hurry, Georgia." He

was certain there was real trouble now. He couldn't think why some-one would be shooting on his land.

"I heard it, too." Georgia came running out the back door, hopping to get her boots on and heading for the Rustler. She jumped into the vehicle, then pulled her auburn hair through the back of a ball cap.

The minute Georgia sat down, Sam turned the buggy around and sped toward Gracie's relentless barking.

"I'll get the gate," Georgia said. "Slow down enough to let me jump out."

"Leave it open, Georgia," Sam said as he bumped over the steel cattle guard.

Georgia climbed back in the buggy just as the sun broke over the top of the hill. The glare blinded Sam. He slowed down until he could shield his eyes and look below the horizon. As he picked up speed, thick stands of sunflowers popped against the grill and slapped the riders as the buggy plowed through. Suddenly Gracie came tearing over the ridge toward them.

Sam stopped the buggy and stood to give hand signals to the shepherd. "Go, Gracie," he yelled. He pointed in the direction of the bawling herd. Gracie understood the familiar commands and ran in the direction of the gunshot. Sam followed, but rocks and inclines kept the buggy lagging behind the fast shepherd.

"It looks like something over by the cemetery," Georgia said, pointing south, as Sam quickly turned in that direction.

"I think we have a bad stampede on our hands," Sam shouted over the engine noise as he launched the buggy over the ridge.

A trampled swath of grass appeared in front of them and trailed forward. The herd had broken through barbed wire fences. Pounding hooves had cut tender new crops to pieces along the way, leaving scattered clods of dirt. Sam stopped to study the tracks. The ditches were hard to see on the west side of the hill. He searched for the source of what had frightened the cattle.

"What scared them, Sam?" Georgia said as she looked wide-eyed toward the destruction. "They went through two fences!"

"I don't see any signs here. I'm afraid they're headed for the cemetery."

The air was electrified, and Sam was uneasy. He felt an increasing sense of urgency to find out what had spooked his cattle.

"I hope the cemetery isn't ruined." Georgia stood to study the trampled fields.

"Hold on, Georgia," Sam warned before he stepped on the accelerator. He waited until she'd hooked her arm around the bar and leaned against the windshield. Then he stomped on the pedal, and the buggy jerked forward, bouncing over rocks and clumps of hard-packed balls of grass.

"The cattle have split around the cemetery," Georgia called into the wind. "I see Gracie on the top of the hill waiting for us."

Sam watched Gracie racing back and forth, continuing her desperate barking. The hair on her furry back was bristled, and her ears stood up straight. Sam manhandled the buggy over two more rough ridges before he reached the family cemetery. The five generations buried there made the cemetery a special place on the ranch, but Sam and Georgia forgot their ancestors when they topped the final ridge.

Sam slammed on the brakes and rose in the buggy to look over the top of the windshield. He surveyed the grotesque landscape. In all his sixty years, he had never seen anything so disheartening. "Who would do something like this?" he asked. His eyes darted from horror to horror as full sun bore down on the mutilated bodies of their cattle spread across the prairie.

Georgia cried out and covered her mouth, dulling a scream. She sat down hard on the seat, tears springing to her eyes.

Sam felt Georgia's hand clutch his shirtsleeve, and he reached across and put his massive hand firmly over hers. "Stay back here. I need to check to see if it's safe down there. Whoever has done this may still be around. Call the sheriff's office and talk to Ray if you can. Let him know what's happened and that we need him out here."

"Be careful." Georgia stepped out of the buggy and stood, trying to take in the scene. She looked at Sam. "Please, watch out for yourself."

"I'm taking my pistol." Sam removed his .45 from the console and strapped on the holster, then began walking down the slope. He kept his pistol in the buggy for rattlesnakes. He never thought he might have to use it on a man. He left Georgia punching in numbers on her cell phone. He didn't expect Ray could make it to the Bar S for at least thirty minutes. Until then, they were on their own.

Sam's steps were deliberate and cautious as he took in his surroundings. He held his firearm ready with the safety off and the clip fully loaded. He looked for movement across the fields. The cows left alive didn't move. They'd run until they'd reached the distant fence and stood there bunched together. Sam stopped to listen. Mesquite beans clacked in the persistent south wind. Tires rolled over the gravel road beyond the barn, and Sam saw headlights disappear over the horizon on the county road. But that could be anyone. He heard bawling calves calling for their mamas. Cows were bellowing for their calves. Some of them were dead, some lost.

Sam kneeled by the first carcass, his oldest cow, Lady Ruth. She'd born eleven calves, and eight of them had been show calves. Her latest calf was lifeless beside her.

Georgia's hand touched his shoulder. He looked up and saw the sorrow in her eyes.

"You shouldn't be here." Sam had a sick feeling in his stomach that something could happen to her. "You must go back."

"I wanted you to know the sheriff is on the way," she said. "I can't understand this. Lady Ruth probably walked up to them. She was so gentle."

"Yes, she would have."

"I have to see for myself. I can't stand up there and wait."

Sam couldn't deny her right to be there. He took her hand

in his gloved one, and together they walked through the death field. Sam and Georgia found at least a dozen cows massacred. They recognized them all and could call their names.

"I see more cattle on the ground by the barn," Sam said. "Let me go first. Outside looks clear, but I'm not sure about the barn."

"I don't think I can take any more right now," Georgia said as she walked back up the hill to the cemetery to check the graves.

By this time, Sam believed the intruders had gone. Still, he was relieved Georgia had gone back up the hill. If someone was there, she'd be out of danger.

Sam moved on to the corral on the far side of the barn. When he rounded the corner, he came to an abrupt stop. There in front of him, where the well had been, was a crater the size of a small car, filled with water. Now he knew what had frightened the cattle and what had bothered him in his sleep - this explosion. The pump house was gone. Sam walked the circumference of the hole. Everything was destroyed. The well, the piping, the pump: all gone. The concussion of the explosion had cracked the concrete watering trough.

Beyond the ruined well he found five show calves with their throats cut. The carnage was sickening. These barely weaned calves were trapped in their pens. They waited there for the high schoolers to come and feed them. The students trained the heifers for show calves. He'd have to call the ag teacher at the high school. The kids couldn't come out and see this.

In all, Sam tallied twenty-five cows, calves, and yearling heifers that were slaughtered. Sam looked back toward the silhouetted gravestones. Only a few were left standing. He replaced his pistol in its holster and walked up the hill to Georgia. As he drew closer to the top, he could see Gracie flat on the ground, her head down resting on her front paws. Georgia was kneeling. Her long red hair had come loose and was flying in the wind. When he reached his wife, she was holding the bloody paw of the other ranch dog, a lovable old hound named Hambone.

"They killed Hambone. They shot him."

Sam shook his head. "He was trying to protect the cows. This is senseless."

Chapter 2

Waggoner County Sheriff Ray Collins stood under the thick leaves of the oak that shaded the timeworn tombstones at the Bar S. He watched his deputies cover the massive crime scene. His men were soaked with sweat from the Texas heat. Spring temperatures could range from freezing to the nineties. This was one of those warmer days where it was cool in the shade and downright hot in the sun.

Ray had been downing his first cup of coffee when Georgia Stanfield had called. Instinctively, he knew the catastrophe she described carried a deeper motive than random violence. Ray made several calls to outside experts on his way to the ranch. He wanted them there as soon as possible.

When Ray arrived, Sam Stanfield was waiting for him at the top of the hill by the small cemetery. The tall, angular men walked toward one another with a solemnness that matched their surroundings.

"I'm sorry, Sam."

"So am I, Ray. So am I." Sam's piercing blue eyes stared at Ray.

Ray felt the anger emanating from his longtime friend. He watched the older man rub his forehead and cross his arms in determination. Ray knew Sam and knew he was gearing up for a fight. Ray looked over the countryside that smelled of death and blood and understood why. "Why don't you tell me what you know so far, Sam? Start when you got up."

Sam's voice began as a low rumble as he retold each moment of the morning. His clear baritone emphasized the details of the explosion, the gunshot, and when he and Georgia came upon the cattle. While Sam went over the details, Ray noted his sunken cheeks and the paleness beneath his tanned leather face.

"I'll need to talk to Georgia."

"She's back at the house. She took Gracie with her. They're in shock and grieving the death of the cattle and Hambone. He was still alive when we got here."

"Does Joe know about Hambone?"

"Georgia called him after she called you," Sam said. "He should be here soon."

"Lots of ranchers are going to miss ole Hambone."

The two stood quietly looking over the hillside, deep in their own thoughts until Ray broke the silence.

"I think I have everything I need from you for now, Sam, but I'll come by later to talk to you and Georgia."

"I need to get a bulldozer out here. Let me know when I can start the disposal." Sam nodded to Ray and walked away.

Ray watched the turkey vultures circling overhead, indicating for miles around that a fresh carcass was in the area. Earlier, only a couple of the raptors were riding the thermals, waiting to feast on the fresh kill. Now at least twenty birds had joined in the wake. More were joining the lazy cyclone by the minute. The large black birds forced a sense of urgency they all felt. Ray ordered the deputies to take pictures of the scene so they could leave the fresh carrion to the waiting scavengers. There was more than the whole kettle of vultures could carry away.

"Sheriff, I found a heel print in the cemetery," a deputy called. "Looks like a man's boot print." The deputy pointed to the partial but definite print as Ray approached and crouched down near him.

"Good find," the sheriff said. "The person who made this mark was in a hurry and fell on his way out. There's a fresh break in this section of this old hoop fence. See how the grass is flat here? We'd better go over this area again." Ray took his time surveying every inch of the cemetery. He looked more closely at the broken wire and found evidence of blood, possibly from the intruder. "Deputy, get this blood sample. It could belong to the man, the dog, or it could even be a transfer from one of the cows, but at least we have something to test."

"Sheriff, do you want us to bag these . . . body parts?"

"Mark them and photograph them for now. When Doc gets here, he'll instruct you how to handle the evidence from the cows and Hambone."

A small white Ranger pickup drove up on the nearest oil road. Shirley Talbot from the animal cruelty division of the ASPCA Texas climbed out of her vehicle. Ray had worked with her when he was a detective at the Houston Police Department. He had developed an extensive network of contacts nationwide during his time there. He had called for her help earlier that day.

"Hey, Shirley."

"Hey, yourself, Ray. I haven't heard from you in a long time. How's Margaret?" Shirley looked up and shaded her eyes as she talked to Ray.

"Oh, she's doing fine, adjusting to small-town life. She jumped in with both feet, though. You know how she is."

"Glad to hear it. How about you, Ray? How are you making it, after leaving HPD?"

"I'm all right. We stay busy. More to do around here than you think. We're too close to the metroplex not to get some overflow. Criminals think nobody will notice them if they're a few miles out in the country. They think we're all bumpkins."

"Now what do you think this is all about?" Shirley asked as she swung her arm in an arc that covered the entire pasture.

"Why don't you take a minute to look around?"

"When's your vet going to be here to look this over?"

"My guess is in about an hour."

Shirley began looking around and almost immediately called Ray over and pointed toward some markings on the ground. "See this arrow where the head is? They dug into the dirt on purpose. It's pointing to that tank of water over there. They wanted to make some sort of point to the landowner."

"That's what I was afraid of. I wanted to see if you agreed. Sam and Georgia Stanfield, the owners of this place, have a website about water rights that's gotten a lot of attention lately. They may be poking a hornet's nest they're not aware of."

"Ray, I've seen several other mutilations like this one, but they were all in South Texas. I have no proof of a connection. They are similar, though."

"I'm aware of the other cow killings and the possibility of cults and rituals. That's why I wanted you to come. I know this sort of practice is on the rise in our prisons, and we've even had a few practicing voodoo here in our county jail. But this doesn't look like voodoo to me."

"I don't think this is a ritual. They were pretty clumsy."

"Anything else you can tell me? I'm on my way to the ranch house to interview Sam and Georgia." Ray pointed west with the brim of his hat.

"As you know," Shirley said, "water resources are vital for the crops and for the cattle. Most farmers rely only on the rain God blessed them with to survive. Lately, farmers haven't been so blessed. Even this pond is almost dry. This has something to do with water rights, but I don't want to say anything definite until I get back to the office and make some comparisons."

"But you think there's a pattern here?" Ray pushed a little harder.

"Yes, I do. Be on the lookout for more of these cultlike crimes, and alert your neighboring counties, too. The first ones reported were south near Brownsville, and they've steadily worked their way up north to Waggoner County. I can't get anyone to take me seriously about my theory. But it's important." Shirley's brow wrinkled, and she squinted in the bright light of the day.

"I'll keep it in mind," Ray said. He'd mapped the southern counties himself. He'd add Shirley's details. If there hadn't been so many ranches that had animals killed, he might have thought it was environmentalists, but he'd ruled that out.

A vehicle roared up the gravel road, churning up the dust. Ray waved to Doc and motioned him over to park next to Shirley's little pickup.

The local vet stopped and gathered some papers and notebooks from the passenger seat, then slowly climbed out. "Mornin', Ray." Doc nodded. "I see you have some help here."

Ray introduced the two investigators and then excused himself. Shirley and Doc were already in deep conversation as they walked together to the cattle pens.

Another truck pulled in and parked alongside Doc's. This one was beat-up and rusted. Ray saw that Joe Weaver had come to see about his dog, Hambone. Ray sighed and walked down the hill to meet Joe.

Automatically, the men shook hands.

Ray said, "Up here, Joe." To Ray it seemed to take forever to climb back up to where the hound lay.

"That's ole Hambone, all right," Joe said.

"I'm afraid you're going to have to wait until Doc gets through going over Hambone. He'll take him into his office for a thorough examination. He'll call you and let you know when you can pick him up."

"I understand," Joe said. "How's Georgia? She was upset when she called me this morning."

"I haven't seen her yet. Sam says she was pretty shaken up."

"Most of these cows were like pets. Sam won't rest until the killers are found."

"This is personal," Ray said. He was talking about himself as much as for Sam. He had never seen anything quite like this.

Chapter 3

Nelson Jenson watched his partner writhe atop the thin blanket on the filthy bed. He knew this place had to be at least seventy years old, but it was the only motel in Waggoner with a back door. He'd searched all of J. D. Hood's belongings and found the pistol. He'd stored it in the pillowcase so he could get rid of it later. He wanted to write down the details of the night before while they were fresh in his memory, but he knew he couldn't. It was too risky.

The hard wooden chair cut off the circulation in his legs, but he paid it no attention while he sat and stared out the window, rethinking the ranch job. He'd watched Hood stagger along behind him across the rocky field as they left the Bar S.

He looked over at Hood again. His leg had swollen to twice its normal size. He had to do something soon. He sure didn't want a dead body on his hands. Jenson waited for his phone call. He had to report in, then he'd do something.

He and Hood had been partners since prison. After they met, it only took one beating to make Hood his lackey. The two men were extreme contrasts physically. Although tall, Hood was stooped and thin. His curved body gave his arms an apelike appearance, while his shock of unruly blond hair was buzzed close to his scalp and gave him a boyish countenance. Hood's look often confused people he met. People always seemed frightened and sympathetic at the same time. But Jenson believed they were well suited for each other, and for endeavors such as this. Without conscience they could butcher humans and animals alike. Even those who hired them didn't know the depths of their cruel nature.

Hood moaned and his eyes opened. "This ain't no hospital. You have to take me to the emergency room." He whimpered as he struggled to pull up his pant leg.

"Shut up and stop whining. We'll take care of it, but not before we hear from the boss."

"But this is bad! Please."

Jenson ignored him. He was still angry. "Why did you fire that pistol?"

Hood tried to sit up, but he cried out and fell back on the sweat-soaked pillow. His eyes squeezed shut. "My face feels numb, and see my arm! A big damn dog, I tell you. I threw him off, but he kept coming. I had to do it! You would, too, if you was being attacked."

Jenson was silent. He knew someone had heard that gunshot. The fiasco at the Bar S could really slow them down. They might have to lay low for a while until Hood got well. They could use a rest anyway. He dreaded talking to his boss. Hood's blood, not to mention that slug left in the dog, were trouble for sure.

"I tell you, I'm hurt. I don't feel good." Hood stopped talking, gagged, bent over the bed and vomited.

"Damn it, Hood!" Jenson screamed. He was going to beat the shit out of him. He'd just started for the man when the phone rang. "Damn it to hell! Not now!" One backhanded slap put Hood out again. The phone rang a second time. He ran both hands across his face and over his bald scalp. He must rein in his breathing. The phone rang for the third time. He was better. He answered on the fourth ring. He lowered his voice. "Jenson here."

"Well, it took you long enough," she said. "What happened last night?"

Jenson had planned what he was going to say. He would have to fix it before the next job. "Everything went as we planned. No problems. We left before daylight, and we're back in the motel. No-body saw us come in."

"You've been in that motel for two days. That's not good. Go somewhere else before the next job."

"Sure, we'll leave as soon as it gets dark."

~~~

Fifty miles south of Waggoner, Jenson raced to the hospital in Montgomery. He drove as far from the Bar S as he thought he safely could. Jenson didn't want any hospital records connecting him to the cattle crime. He couldn't have driven any farther though, or

Hood might have died right there in the van. Not that he cared, but he certainly didn't want him to die in the vehicle. Ever since Hood had stumbled into the van bleeding and moaning, Jenson knew this job had turned sour. From that moment, he'd been working out what he could do to smooth this over with his boss. What kind of explanation could he give?

Finally, he saw the red cross of the hospital sign. He drove in, slammed on the brakes, and jolted to a stop in front of the ER. "I'll come back for you, but we can't be seen together," he said as he pulled Hood from the front seat and pointed him in the direction of the automatic doors.

Hood blinked and nodded.

Jenson left him there and parked in a dark corner of the hospital parking lot. He'd go back in later to be sure Hood hadn't said anything incriminating. If Hood even told his own name, Jenson knew it would lead to him. He and Hood had served time together. They were linked. He'd be back in prison just as fast as Hood. Jenson was so uneasy he couldn't wait in the van long. He crept back toward the hospital to judge the situation for himself.

Jenson pulled a camouflage cap low over his eyes and waited by the ER door. He walked in behind a family rushing in with a baby in their arms. When the family gathered around the check-in window, he managed to disappear around the corner. He saw Hood making his way down the hall, then collapse on the floor.

A nurse yelled for help as she ran past him toward Hood's

crumpled body. "Sir, can you hear me? What is your name? Where are you injured?" She began looking at Hood's wounds and kept his head elevated.

An orderly ran to help lift Hood's limp body onto a gurney. Jenson kept following them as they rolled Hood into an examination room. He could hear them through the thin curtain cutting his sleeve away to expose a bloody arm.

"Look at his arm," the orderly said. "That looks bad."

"It looks like a dog bite, but that's not what's causing these other symptoms. We need help. Go get Dr. Richards." The nurse turned and shouted at the young man standing a few steps back from the bed. "Don't stand there. Move it!"

The boy turned and hurried out without even noticing Jenson standing there within arm's reach. The curtain was open enough for Jenson to watch the nurse check Hood's foot and ankle.

"Sir, your leg is so swollen that I'm going to have to cut your pants away so I can see what's wrong." She began to cut the tough jeans at his ankle and slowly made her way to Hood's thigh. "Sir, have you been bitten by a snake?"

Jenson inched over and stood in the doorway until Hood noticed him. He saw the fear on Hood's face. He heard Hood's incoherent speech, and he recognized the other man's terror. It was the same terror he remembered on Hood's face in prison when he'd made him his slave. He'd made his threat clear to Hood even in his almost delirious state. Satisfied, he crept back out of the hospital.

~~~

Jenson didn't know how he was going to get Hood out of the hospital without a fuss. He'd been waiting in the parking lot for two hours. He had called Hood several times, but there was no answer. His mind went crazy while he watched people come and go. Every siren made him jump. He went over and over the escape from the ranch that morning when he'd heard Hood scream. He still felt like the whole county could be onto them while he waited in the van outside the hospital.

Then Jenson remembered that he'd thrown his machete in the back of the van, still covered with blood. It lay next to the box of dynamite. What an idiot he was. He panicked for a moment. He'd planned to clean it at the motel, but that was before Hood started freaking out and sweating like a pig. Now here he was, a sitting duck in a parking lot. He had to get rid of the machete and the dynamite and get to Hood before he spilled his guts.

This fiasco would change their operation. It had been a sweet one while it lasted. Jenson's lips pressed together in a thin line, his jaw clenched. He scanned the hospital parking lot and decided to drive down the road to get rid of the dynamite. But instead of dumping the machete, he would clean it. It was just too nice of a weapon to discard.

Jenson was nearing the city limits when his phone rang.

"I'm going to walk out," Hood said. "If I can swipe a car, I will."

"Be careful," Jenson said. "Don't do anything to call attention to yourself. I'll pick you up at that roadside park near Waggoner."

"You think wearing a hospital gown and breaking into a car won't be an attention-getter?"

"Don't do anything stupid. You know what I'm talking about. No last-minute destruction, or worse yet, hurting anybody." Jenson decided Hood was on his own until he got to their meeting place.

Chapter 4

The shock of the morning was waning for Sam, but the importance of it wasn't. At first, he was physically ill, seeing his herd cut to pieces. Cows he'd fed, taken to the vet, given shots, rescued in the snow, now lay dead. Quickly enough, his anxiety had turned into grief. Now it changed to fury—pure, raging anger that burned inside. He got himself under control before he went inside to check on Georgia. He walked into the stillness of the ranch house and saw Georgia talking on her cell phone.

"I've been called in to the hospital. They're shorthanded. I need to cover for someone out sick."

"Working might help you forget about this morning for a while."

"Maybe," Georgia answered quietly and left to get ready for the afternoon shift at Waggoner County Memorial.

Sam stood on the meandering porch, hands in his pockets, staring at the seemingly undisturbed rolling hills of the ranch. He saw a car kicking up a trail of thick dust, speeding down the dirt road to the ranch. He recognized the county sheriff's emblem on its door. He walked outside to wait for Ray.

Sam had known Ray since he was a youngster—his dad was his best friend. He was glad Ray had decided to return to Waggoner after leaving the Houston PD. He couldn't think of a better guardian of the county than Ray.

"Hello, Ray." Sam walked out and extended his hardened iron claw. "Come on in. How about some iced tea?"

The men sat on the porch. The breeze cooled them in the late afternoon shade. After a few minutes, Georgia walked onto the screened-in porch and set a tray of tall glasses of iced tea on the table.

"How are you, Miss Georgia?" Ray asked.

"Still a bit shaken, I guess, but I'll be all right."

"Why don't you join us for a few minutes before you go in for work?" Sam asked. He wanted her perspective added to Ray's account.

Georgia looked at both men, sighed, and said, "Let's get started, then." She sat down, her thin frame almost melting into the high-backed chair. She was already in her nurse's uniform.

"Tell me about your blog, *Water Rights in the 21st Century*. I've heard you mention it before. I think that's a good place to start."

Sam set his glass down on the table and picked up a thick purple folder of printouts that he thought Ray might find useful. "This ought to do it." Sam placed the file in front of Ray.

Ray raised his eyebrows and looked down at the stack of

papers contained in the file. "The blog?"

"That and more," Sam said. "That's what I've collected over the past several months. Some are articles and some are e-mails."

"This is good. I'll take this and study it. But how did you get started on this in the first place?"

Georgia smiled. "Sam was fuming about a proposed water law that was in committee in the Texas legislature, so much so that I suggested the blog as an avenue to get the word out to others about the law's implications."

"It surprised us both when it instantly became a success, at least in farm and ranch circles," Sam said. "But water is always a concern for farmers. We hit a raw nerve with our topic. Those responding asked a lot of questions about the EPA and WOTUS, Water of the United States. This began to redefine terms in the Clean Water Act, and the new language significantly expanded the federal government's control. I've included all of that in my folder, Ray." Sam wondered if this had triggered the slaughter on his ranch. He had some contacts in the Panhandle, and he knew of other explosions there.

"In other words," Georgia said, "much of what is considered rainwater drainage over land has been declared part of a stream."

"Ranchers are fined simply because cattle cross areas where drainage has occurred. The EPA insists these drainage areas are waterways. On top of that, we are in the sixth year of a severe drought, and we have reduced our herd significantly, as have our neighbors. I know you know all of this, Ray. You have to, if you live in Waggoner County."

Georgia interrupted. "I'm sorry, but I have to be at the hospital in fifteen minutes. You know I'll be glad to answer any questions you have later on."

Sam watched Georgia leave, and he sipped his tea as he waited for Ray to begin his questioning again.

"How many followers do you have on your blog, Sam?"

"We launched the site in early January, and our blog had a thousand followers by the end of February."

He and Georgia had talked about what to post on the blog. She had told him that most people weren't aware that water could become a scarce resource, and it could put them in a life-or-death situation.

"I wanted to disseminate information and show both sides, which caused many diverse opinions to be posted."

"What about those opinions? Any threats?"

Sam knew this was where the interview eventually would lead. "Yes, some have been rather nasty. But most have given us accurate information and been helpful concerning other situations. We've had responses from all over the country. Some of the threats have come from extreme environmentalists."

"What kind of threats?"

"Mostly name-calling, but some were about property damage, and one threatened our lives."

"When did this life-threatening one come in?" Ray asked.

"About a week ago. The author threatened to kill us if we didn't stop letting cattle roam our pastures. It said they'd kill the cattle and then kill us. That's when they went into detail about coming to the house to attack us. The troubling part was that the person seemed to know a great deal about our personal lives. I made a copy of the message. It's in the folder."

Sam sat back and let Ray peruse the folder and scan the pages. He'd clipped the harmless responses together and placed the significant information in single sheets on the top.

"We'll investigate all the information you have here. I'll let you know if I find anything. You and Georgia need to take precautions here at the house. I'll have the deputies come out this county road more often."

"We will. Gracie is a good watchdog. I'm not worried if we're here, but what about Georgia at night at the hospital?" Sam had been giving the situation a lot of thought. Georgia was the most vulnerable. Nighttime at the hospital bothered him.

"I'll call and have security walk her out. They're competent over there."

Sam planned to take her handgun to her and discuss a plan of action if anything were to happen. He would go by at suppertime and give her the 9 mm pistol. She had a concealed carry license, but the hospital didn't allow weapons on the premises. No one could know. He'd have to insist she carry it.

"Here's the site," Sam explained as he showed Ray the blog. "Our first post was about ranchers' rights to drainage water. We immediately received responses from other ranchers and farmers who felt the same way." Sam slid the computer over to Ray, and he squared the laptop in his view and read the post.

WATER RIGHTS in the 21ˢᵗ CENTURY

Posted by Sam Stanfield
January 7, 2015

This blog discusses the importance of water and what we can and must accomplish to protect water and water rights. We know water is an essential element for our lives, and we all know that without water there is no life, yet sometimes those with clean water take this resource for granted.

My name is Sam Stanfield, and together with my wife Georgia, we want to establish this blog as a forum to discuss water concerns and water rights for the people of this world. First, we want you to know a little about us and why we've begun this blog. We are ranchers, and water is always a concern for us. We raise grass-fed beef, and we depend on the native grasses to feed our cattle. We also depend on Mother Nature to send us the rain we need for our water source. It has taken us ten years to work the land so that it's returned to its natu- ral state. We must work together to keep our water clean and available to everyone. Below are a few of the stats from the

United Nations World Water Day website.

- *85 percent of the world's population lives in the driest half of the planet.*
- *783 million people don't have access to clean water, and almost 2.5 billion don't have access to adequate sanitation.*
- *6 to 8 million people die annually from the consequences of water-related disasters and diseases.*

We urge you to visit the site and read more information for yourself at the following link: http://www.unwater.org/water-cooperation-2013/water-cooperation/facts-and-figures/en/

Sam considered Ray's reaction. The killings this morning had a motive much more complex than he'd earlier suspected, Sam thought.

"Thank you, Sam. I'll keep in touch." Ray stood to go. "Sam, why don't you come by the courthouse in a couple of days? I'll have some news for you by then." He collected the file, the first blog posting, and started for the door.

After Ray disappeared, Sam walked to the gun safe and retrieved the 9 mm pistol. He was on his way to the hospital. He was on full alert.

Chapter 5

Giant fracturing trucks sat silently, filling the sixteen-acre lot in central Texas. Iron trucks, absent the massive amounts of pipe. Semi-trucks, sand trucks, water trucks, and slurry-hauling trucks all were idle. The oil rigs and trailers sat watching from the adjacent lot as if waiting for the trucks to carry them to work. Drilling and fracking oil and gas wells were at a standstill due to overproduction. It was a ghost town of red and black, the colors of the W. T. Cox Oil and Gas Company. The logo was recognized around the world, but now the company was only creeping forward in its production.

However, the man behind the initials, William Tremble Cox, had plans for times of shutdown. The oil and gas markets had always surged and crashed. Most companies didn't survive this type of roller-coaster business, but his would. His new money stream would guarantee his success.

Cox wove a pattern in the evening twilight as he walked between vehicles, counting each one. He ran his hand lightly over the red-and-black logo and thought back to when he'd started his oil company in 1969. His stature was certainly different then, thick chestnut hair now balding, lean torso now fleshy and camouflaged with an expensive wardrobe. He had dressed in his ranch clothes tonight. He felt more in touch with his oil business when he wore his faded jeans and steel-toed boots. The worn black Stetson made him a bit melancholy for the old days, but he shook it off, knowing the challenges that lay ahead. He had long ago crossed the billionaire line that provided him with the power he craved. The truck yard he walked through was one of hundreds he owned around the world. He'd known the country was addicted to gasoline, and he had what they needed.

Cox paused and wondered if he'd live long enough to hold absolute power in his hands. It was within his reach.

In the soundless dusk, Cox finished his inventory and angled toward the temporary metal building at the back of the lot. He watched his appointment roll slowly by in his silver Mercedes, tires echoing the crunch of the gravel. Cox was in no hurry for the meeting.

He ambled over to another equipment lot. He knew every piece. Cox loved the technology he now used to fracture shale. That one thing had allowed the United States to become the largest producer of oil and gas in the world. And he was part of it. His country was fuel-independent. Then overproduction raised its ugly head and caused a glut in the market. The price of oil plummeted. Production and exploration screeched to a halt in the United States. The fracturing method was too costly to continue. One hundred thousand oil field workers were laid off with no hope of work on the horizon. The former president had blocked the building of the Keystone Pipeline when so many were desperate for the work. Of course, the environmentalists hated the fracturing process, and Cox as well.

The new president approved the pipeline, but was it too late? He thought not, although his foreign competitors who didn't use fracturing continued their production. Places in the Middle East, Africa, and South America didn't have to use the costly fracturing technology. Cox fumed that all they had to do was pump oil out of the ground. The pumping process was straightforward, and their resources were plentiful, a big advantage for them. Neither could his friends in Saudi Arabia afford to shut down for fear of losing their largest consumer, China. Other smaller countries lived on oil revenues alone and hadn't diversified. He knew they'd experience dire economic collapse if they were to stop production. Cox knew the statistics all too well.

Suddenly, he turned on his heel and walked to the tiny building to the west.

"Hello, Jimmy," he said as he shook hands with the man waiting inside the trucking office. James Baxter was a second-generation lobbyist, well worth the money Cox paid him.

"Hello, Bill. It's a little eerie out here with everything so quiet."

Cox watched Baxter's trembling hands pour a scotch for him.

He was amused that he could still strike fear in someone he'd known for such a long time. He sat knee to knee, facing his informant in the claustrophobic cubicle. He was purposefully silent to force the other man to speak first, so he could feel the control he had over him.

"I like it when you call me Jimmy," he said. "You're the only one who does. It reminds me of my dad."

"Me, too. He's the one who showed me the slick side of politics. He had something on everyone in Austin. You've done well, too. He'd be proud of you. You have tentacles reaching virtually all over the world." Cox smiled, knowing his words would put James at ease. "Now, what's the word in Washington?" He didn't like to spend much time on small talk. He wanted the information he'd paid for.

"Our contact in DC has met with the Pakistan prime minister," James said. "She says he's open to the proposal. He has to go back to his superiors before it's finalized."

"How long will that take?"

"Sandra says at least a month."

"I was hoping sooner. See if she can speed it up." Cox knew the government contact could make the meeting happen whenever she wanted. If James was worth his salt, he'd make it happen.

"I'm flying to DC tomorrow. I can set up a meeting with the undersecretary, but it won't be easy this late. She refuses to use the Internet or any traceable phones."

"That's why you're known as the top lobbyist in Austin, after all," Cox said. He watched James smile and nod his head like the good boy he was. "Now let's talk about something else."

"The Stanfields?"

"Yes, and this blog business." Cox sounded disgusted. "Why is this still going on?" Cox knew the blog was gaining readers every day. People paid attention when folks lost their farms and ranches, and that wasn't good for him. He wanted the damn thing shut down. Nobody was nosing around now, but that couldn't last long. The EPA had been doing their work for them. Fines, regulations, and their overreach had broken the backs of the small landowners. Then he could scoop up their land.

"I heard from the ranch bunch today. Our guys did a job on the Stanfield place last night, but there was a posting this afternoon about the whole mess."

"What do you mean 'mess?'"

"They shot a dog." James looked away.

Cox stopped his drink halfway to his mouth, set the tumbler down on the metal desk, and waited for James to finish telling the story. He hated the man's singsong, pandering voice. He guessed James' years as a sycophant had permanently ingrained his pattern of speech. Finally, he was running down and would shut up.

"They've dug in, and they're determined to pursue who's behind the slaughter at their ranch," James said.

"What about the group in the Panhandle?"

"That's just it, Bill. Sam Stanfield called a meeting of the ranchers up near Dumas. He invited people from Oklahoma, Colorado, and New Mexico to join them."

"Get someone up there to go to that meeting so we know what's going on," Cox said. "Put more pressure on Stanfield, where it really hurts. If he doesn't back off soon, we may have to bring someone else in. Talk to that girlfriend of yours. She'd better handle those two thugs. You may have to step in, and you know what I think about giving her this assignment in the first place," Cox smirked. He would have gotten rid of that piece of ass a long time ago.

After James left, Cox sat in the worn chair and nursed his drink. Before he called his partner in California, he wanted to be certain about bringing in the heavy artillery. He'd asked for Gonzales before, and he understood what he was doing. Gonzales made things happen, and Cox trusted he could take care of the problems in North Texas. He should have known there would be issues that would hinder his plan, but he wasn't going to allow anything to get in his way. He was so close he could taste it, the same way he tasted the whiskey in his tumbler.

He stood and walked over to the desk, swirling the glass. He tossed it back and punched in the phone number. He left his message and waited for the callback. It wasn't long. He issued his instructions. The man understood without any lengthy explanation.

Chapter 6

Sam parked amid a bevy of white pickups near the tracks of the Santa Fe & Burlington. The oilfield workers surrounded Woody's Café by dawn, their vehicles lining the highway for half a mile in either direction. Before heading out for a day of hard labor, roughnecks stopped at Woody's, filling up on bacon, eggs, and biscuits with sausage gravy. Sam had timed his meeting to catch the slight lull ahead of the next wave of hungry diners.

As soon as the first round of customers vacated the steamy café, law enforcement invaded the twelve empty tables. Another four counter stools were available for stragglers who were either late or in a hurry. Sam rolled by vehicles for Texas Highway Patrol officers, Waggoner city police, county deputies, constables, Texas Rangers, and even game wardens who were eating at the tiny café.

It had been three days since the ranch crime. Ray had finished his initial investigation and given Sam permission to bring in a bulldozer for the cleanup. He'd made this trip into town to set the rumors straight through the regulars at Woody's. As Sam had expected, the noisy chatter clicked off when he stepped through the narrow wooden door. Everyone had heard about the slaughter at the Bar S.

Sam saw one plastic-bottomed chair waiting for him. Buddy Gatwick was waving him over in an exaggerated way. Sam approached, and Buddy motioned for him to sit down. Compared to the understated men sitting next to him, Weldon and Jack, Buddy was definitely still immature. Sam could see that his friends were already on their second cup of coffee and had been waiting for him to arrive. The group had its regular table by the south window, closest to the kitchen. Two men sat on each side of the table. There was room for a fifth person to drag up another chair, but today Sam noticed that the others in the café were giving him space. But as soon as Sam's table began their conversation, the other voices switched back on as well.

"Sam, I'm sorry to hear about what happened out at your place," Buddy said.

Sam understood Weldon and Jack would wait for him to tell them what he wanted. "It was a terrible waste," he said quietly.

"I talked to Joe," Weldon said. "He's torn up about Hambone."

"I'll miss that ole cur," Jack said. "He ran the coyotes off a week ago at my place and saved one of my newborn heifers." Jack Barrett was Sam's closest neighbor. They'd been friends for fifty years, since they were boys. There was no one he trusted more or knew better than Jack.

"I'll miss him, too," Sam said.

The oldest daughter of the café owner slid a cup of black coffee over the Formica top in front of Sam. Out of the corner of his eye, Sam saw the other customers watching.

"Thank you, Marcie," Sam nodded. He watched a sympathetic smile cross her face as she turned and walked back to the counter.

"What did the sheriff say?" Buddy asked.

"Oh, he had a lot of questions," Sam answered. He knew Buddy would keep pestering him, but he wasn't going to reveal what he and Ray had discussed.

It rankled Sam that Buddy presumed to take the lead in asking questions. Sam had been close friends with Buddy's father, who was a rock in the community, but Buddy was a different kind of animal. Buddy had assumed the fourth seat at the café table belonged to him after his father's death. Out of respect for their friend, Sam and the others allowed it. The looks across the table reflected what Sam felt himself.

Buddy also had inherited his father's stock in the local Oak National Bank and had forced his way into a top job there, which didn't go over so well in Waggoner. Sam had seen the fiery red Corvette parked out front and knew it could only belong to Buddy. He sure wasn't frugal. Sam was certain everyone in the café had noticed the expensive sports car. That notoriety had not done the pudgy banker any good.

Sam decided to change the subject. "Weldon, did you get the grass seed ordered?"

"Sure did," Weldon said. "Are you going to pick it up yourself?"

"I will, and I'd like to get one of those box trailers, if you haven't sold them all to the oilfield guys."

"The trailer business has been good to me, but I may have one left for you," Weldon said, smiling. "I'm counting on the trailers to keep me going until I start selling more seed. This drought is hurting a lot of people."

"I'll come by this afternoon. I don't want Joe to stop plowing to pick up seed. I can unload the sacks while he finishes. It will save us about a week's time, so we can get the seed in the ground sooner." Sam finalized a plan in his head at that moment, thinking that he and Georgia could get away in a couple of weeks to head to the Panhandle meeting. The gathering was even more important now.

About that time, Marcie unloaded an armful of bacon and eggs piled high with fluffy biscuits. The conversation took a temporary recess, and the men dug in. As he chewed, Sam noticed a stranger at the counter in a camo cap. He heard the man order a piece of chocolate pie with his cup of coffee. He was a big man, with enormous shoulders and arms. When the stranger left and walked through the tables to the door, Sam noticed he was less than average height. The contrast surprised him.

~~~

After breakfast, Sam drove to the courthouse and angled his maroon Ford pickup into a space on the south side of the square. He decided to take Gracie in to see Maureen in the sheriff's office. Gracie had waited patiently in the truck while he was inside the café. She would have waited forever for Sam. He slipped on the leash, and Gracie jumped out. Before Sam had a chance to look up, people around the square started shouting greetings to him and Gracie. Sam took his time walking to the courthouse while Gracie calmly allowed people to pet her.

Finally, the two made their way to the magnificent granite building. The courthouse was the center of all activity in Waggoner and Waggoner County. The sheriff's office was in the courthouse basement, even though the jail was in a different location. Sam descended the basement stairs with Gracie and followed a narrow hallway to the door marked *County Sheriff.* There was no name on the door simply because the caretaker said names changed anyway, so why bother?

Sam stepped into a crowded reception area. He waved at Maureen, the office manager, and she waved back and spoke to Gracie. Gracie ran to her and sat down behind the desk.

"I'll let the sheriff know you're here, Sam." Maureen had to shout to be heard over the noise. Loud talking engulfed the long corridor as more people arrived.

"I'll wait out here," Sam shouted back. He inched out of the office and leaned against the wall in the hallway to wait out the commotion. A deputy exited Ray's office, held up his hand, and everyone momentarily hushed. The deputy motioned the crowd to follow him, and in a rush, the office and the hallway were empty.

"Are you still out there, Sam?" Maureen called. "You can come on in. He's ready for you now."

Sam passed through the lobby and into Ray's office. Sitting in one of the guest chairs was a stranger.

"Sam, this is FBI Agent Frank Wade," Ray said.

The men shook hands and Ray offered Sam the other chair.

"Sam, I worked with Frank many times back in Houston," Ray said. "I wanted you to know that I've talked with the FBI, and we think the incident at your ranch seems to be part of a string of crimes."

"A string? Do you know why?" Sam had his own suspicions, but he wanted to hear from the other men first, especially since he'd already given Ray the folder of his correspondence.

"Frank has been working with the National Center for the Analysis of Violent Crime. They've alerted Frank that these cattle killings are unusual enough to have been done by terrorists, and to-gether with some of your threatening blog responses could point to a conspiracy of some sort."

Sam knew the attack didn't have anything to do with foreign terrorists, not with the responses he was getting from his blog. This reeked of a land grab. Intimidation. The motive was the real ques-tion here. "Do you have a theory yet?" Sam looked directly at Frank, expecting an answer.

"Sir, I have several theories. One stems from a response to your blog in February." He handed a copy to Sam for his comments.

WATER RIGHTS in the 21ˢᵗ CENTURY

Posted: John Hager
February 11, 2015

As a landowner, no one is more concerned than I am with water conservation and the protection of our streams, rivers, watersheds and underground aquifers. I must share my experience with federal regulatory bodies in hopes of informing those who follow the Water 21C blog of the horrifying takeover of water rights from the states and individual citizens.

Our ranch needed additional water for cattle in certain pastures. We got rainwater runoff stored in a water pond. The cost of creating a water pond is significant, so before committing to build our pond, we checked with county and state water officials and obtained the permits necessary to proceed.

Now a year after we have completed the work, the EPA showed up at our door and told us that we had to take out the pond and restore the land to its original condition at our expense because it's illegal. We did everything our local government told us. No one said we couldn't construct the pond, *and now the federal government is fining us $23,000 a day for every day we leave it in place. Every day! If I had read about our situation in the news, I wouldn't believe it was happening.*

At first, I worried about the fines. I've always paid my bills. On the second day of fines, I realized we couldn't pay for one day, so why worry about it? Currently, our fines are over $4 million.

We are seeking support in any form to fight this water pond issue in court. I thought the Clean Water Act protected active streams and rivers, but in our case, it applies to rainwater runoff. We will fight, and with the help of others that may be reading this blog, we can and we will win.

John Hager

Rancher

Sam had reflected on this piece when he first read it. He'd exchanged e-mails with John as well as several other victims who'd suffered similar treatment from the EPA. He chose not to mention this until Frank revealed the FBI's position. Sam could see that Frank was uncomfortable with the silence, but he waited.

"Are you familiar with the 'color of the law,' Sam?" Frank asked.

Sam could tell the FBI agent meant the question to be rhetorical. Frank had assumed he didn't know. Though Frank's conversation began with a polite "sir," Sam now knew it was placating, and Wade was underestimating him. Not a good trait for an FBI agent, Sam thought.

He decided to address Frank directly. "Frank, I do know what the 'color of the law' means. But I don't want to think that government officials are abusing their authority." Sam knew he'd hit a nerve when Ray and Frank glanced at one another. "Was the FBI called in because it has enough proof to accuse the EPA of governmental overreach and abuse of power?" Before either could respond, Sam continued. "I also understand that we could be targeted by environmental enthusiasts, or be victims of hate crimes or even terrorists. Now, tell me Frank, after reviewing the evidence that you and Ray have, which theory do you think is the strongest?"

Chapter 7

Lynnette Wilkerson's foot tapped a staccato rhythm as she finished reading the blog. She clicked off her computer and contemplated how much damage the site could cause. The latest posting described in detail the carnage at the Bar S, and already dozens of outraged followers were responding.

This damn blog is going to complicate things, she thought.

Her nervousness was sending her into panic. This anxiety was a constant companion that she often let get out of control. Now was not the time to fall apart. She had to act, to do something to calm herself. This latest uproar would cost her. She had been on the fast path up the chain, but this wouldn't go over well. Jenson had lied to her. She had to get the truth out of him. She relied on her knowledge to give her power and recognition in this organization. If she was unaware of something this critical, she'd be of no use to James Baxter.

Lynnette rang Jenson.

"What?" he answered.

"What?" Lynnette was incredulous, then furious. "What the

hell is going on up there?" she hissed. She knew she had to get control of this incident. The news reporters and then Sam Stanfield's online communications were clear.

"It went like we planned it, but we have a problem with Hood. He fell and hurt his leg on our way out. It may slow us down some."

For half a beat, Lynnette was silent on the other end. "What are you leaving out, Jenson? You're sure Hood didn't leave any evidence behind?" She was relentless as she interrogated Jenson. She knew he was lying.

"I'm telling you there was nothing left behind."

"Then why is the news reporting that a dog was shot?" Jenson hesitated, and she pushed on. "Where is the firearm that was used?"

"I have it, and I will get rid of it."

Because he answered quickly, she knew it was the truth. "Tell me about Hood." She could barely maintain a civil attitude, and her anger was ready to surface. Not just at Jenson, but the whole situation she couldn't control.

"Hood picked up a car at the hospital. I picked him up on a dirt road behind a roadside park. No one saw us."

"Did he talk to anyone?" She always worried about leaks, or at the very least some careless action at the crime scenes.

"He said nobody came by, and he left before any cops came around."

"We need to meet so I can give you the instructions for the next job. It's a little more detailed than usual, and we've been on the phone too long already. It would be informative if you bothered to turn on the TV."

"We're getting out of here. Where do you want to meet?"

"Meet me at Billy Bob's tonight at eleven." Lynnette had calmed. Jenson and Hood were on their way to Fort Worth. She was more at ease with them being in the city, better for anonymity.

"Where?" Jenson snarled. "That's a big place."

Lynnette heard the torment in his voice and stepped up the condescension in hers. "I'll find you. Don't worry, Mr. Jenson. Fifty-two, five ten, two-hundred pounds, white horseshoe mustache, tattoos, and bald. It won't be hard. Hang out at one of the bars." Lynnette hung up.

Jenson stood there a moment before he shared the arrangements with Hood. "She sounds like she's trying too hard. I hope she'll be easier to look at. Get some sleep. I'm going to set up another job for us."

~~~

Lynnette knew there would be a big crowd at the famous nightclub. She was counting on it. Dozens of people were milling about as she picked her way through the entrance. She'd forgotten who was performing, but she'd dressed appropriately for a country concert—tight blue jeans with bling on the pockets, ropers with turquoise underlay, and a crisp white Western shirt with a tan suede vest with fringe. Although many other women were dressed simi-larly, Lynnette stood out. Her striking beauty caused a buzz as she worked her way through the crowd. She hurried to the darker cor-ners of the dance floor and found a table near the back.

Lynnette surveyed the saloon area and found her prey. Jen-son was camped out at the end of the long mahogany bar with one leg hiked up on the brass footrest. He was nursing a beer, and occa-sionally he glanced around the room.

Jenson sat on the side near the toilets. Lynnette supposed he was checking out the women on their way to and from the re-stroom. His eyes were following two young girls—too young for him—when he turned back to take a swig of his beer.

When he looked up, he stopped cold. Lynnette sat beside him, and she knew she was sexy as hell. She could see the stunned look on his face. She didn't know why she had tried so hard to im-press him. Why didn't she ever learn? She could see any fear in his eyes had dissipated. To him, she was only a woman and not a mys-terious voice.

He slowly squared himself with the bar front and looked at her in the mirror behind the stacked liquor bottles.

"Jenson," Lynnette said in a flat, quiet voice. She nodded her brunette head slightly and called for a shot of vodka. She shook her silky tresses and flipped them back over her shoulder as she leaned over the small glass. The drink would help her recover what confi-dence she'd just lost. She watched Jenson thud his elbows on the edge of the bar. His massive arms invaded her space.

"Go ahead," he said. "Tell me."

"You'll need a different vehicle. Money will be in the account." Jenson made her flesh crawl. She was glad to have people milling around them. The music, the glass clanking, and the human sounds roared in her ears. She could barely hear her own voice. "What condition is Hood in? Can he function?"

Jenson dipped his head slightly and took a long swig of his beer. He was on his third. Lynnette kept count. "He's still groggy from the drugs he was taking, and he ain't pleasant. His leg is still double its size."

Lynnette could tell the beer was doing its job. She pulled back on her drinking and straddled the uncomfortable stool. She'd done her research on Jenson and Hood. She knew they were connected through the Huntsville prison. Jenson was the driving force that had ruled the cellblock. Hood did whatever Jenson ordered. Jenson strong-armed offenders, but Hood was the sneak and could handle a knife with precision. They were a perfect combo, the reason she'd picked them. Jenson and Hood had been committing petty crimes here and there until Lynnette contacted them.

"Are you ready for this job?" Lynnette asked.

"We're gonna do it. I want the money. Hood will be all right."

The unlikely couple sat at the bar and talked for half an hour. By then, there was no more for Lynnette to say. Satisfied that she'd conveyed what Jenson needed to do in Waggoner, she eased off her stool and walked away. She felt Jenson continue to watch her as she melted into the crowd.

Lynnette remained in the parking lot and watched Jenson lumber out the door a few minutes later and amble to the van. She was still apprehensive about the job she'd charged him with. She was as responsible for the wrongdoing as much as the thugs she'd hired. She worried about the law firm where she worked, worried about James, and now worried about Jenson and what he might do.

~~~

Hood was still in bed when Jenson returned to their new motel. It was somewhat better than the last one, although it smelled of strong disinfectant. Jenson considered Hood's condition and whether he'd make it. He didn't care. He had been eking by when this job came along. Now they were making some real money, and he wasn't going to give it up. Jenson gathered his tools, fished the pistol and the few remaining bullets out of a crumpled pillowcase, and pitched all of it on the bed.

"This was a bad idea for us to keep this pistol so long." Jenson handed Hood a replacement weapon, folded up the bedspread, and carried it to the car. He'd get rid of the evidence alone. He didn't want Hood spilling his guts if they got caught.

On a country road, Jenson found what he was looking for—a pond glimmering in the fading sunlight, not too far off the highway. He turned down the gravel road and slowed to a stop. He climbed over the barbed wire fence, walked a hundred yards, and tossed the tainted weapon into the circle of turbid water. It fell into the tank with a satisfying plunk, sinking to the bottom of the cloudy watering hole. Jenson scowled and trudged back to his car, then headed back toward Fort Worth.

Chapter 8

The yellowed lampshade cast a pale glow in the Bar S Ranch office as Sam sat at his antique desk and stared at the latest comment from one of his blog followers. "Please help me," the man had written. "I'm desperate."

His was the fourth report this month of explosions on Texas farms in the Panhandle and the worst yet. *Another family ruined*, Sam thought. He quickly sent the man information about the meeting of Panhandle farmers and ranchers. Sam had started his website to bring ranchers and farmers together to solve problems related to the drought, but this was another crime against hardworking families. He couldn't let it go, even more so with the Bar S memories fresh in his mind. He could still see the land strewn with dead animals.

How can I help them? Sam thought as he added this latest information to his files. He felt he had to do something. He thought back thirty years earlier, when he and two friends had risked everything to get a hospital started in Waggoner County. The staggering financial burden from that venture was nothing compared to the lives endangered here. His chair creaked as he rocked back, thinking about motives for the attack.

"I see you're at it again," Georgia said. She had quietly materialized in the doorway, already dressed in her running shoes and sweats. "It's not even daylight, and it looks like you've been up for hours."

Sam swiveled his chair to face her, showing a worried scowl. "I think this water problem is getting worse. It's just a matter of time before someone gets hurt. These incidents go far beyond vandalism. The man I heard from today may even lose his farm. He has four children. Luckily, he and his family were away at the time of the explosion."

"Thank goodness for that. What about the ranch meeting?"

"It's in three weeks, and I just sent another e-mail about it." Sam stood his full six foot four, raked his thick hair back from his eyes, and handed several printouts from his early-morning communications to Georgia. Sam valued her opinion, and he watched Georgia's expressive face as she read about the latest disasters. "Let's talk about these postings over coffee. I know I could use a cup."

Georgia looked up and smiled. She put her arm around his waist, and he draped his lanky arm around her shoulders. Sam walked with her to the wooden table in the middle of the kitchen of the century-old house, grazing the top of her head with a kiss as she sat down. On his way to the sink, he retrieved the coffeepot and walked over to the cabinet, leaving Georgia to finish evaluating the latest blog information.

His mind wandered, and his movements were rote as he filled the mugs. "Ray doesn't want us to go to the landowner meeting," he said finally.

Georgia looked up from reading. "I guess it's just small-town, but Buddy stopped me at the hospital yesterday and voiced his concern, too. He said he didn't think it wise to leave the ranch without this crime solved. He asked me if I was worried they might come back."

"What did you say?"

"I brushed it off. I'm not worried. Should I be, Sam?"

"No. I'm not going to let anyone keep us from living our lives. Anyone who would do something like this is a coward."

"Well, that settles it. We're going. Do you want to fly us up there, or are you thinking we'll take the RV?"

"I'd love the chance to fly. It's been so long. But the ranch is remote, and I don't know if there's an airfield close by. The plane is in good shape and ready, but so is the fifth wheel."

"We'd be without transportation after we landed."

"True. Let's take the RV."

"I'll buy supplies today."

Sam handed Georgia a cup of steaming coffee and scooted across the bench until he faced her. He wanted to instill her with confidence so she wouldn't worry when they left the ranch. Joe would be here. Georgia usually didn't scare easily, but this was different.

"Look at this post from a farmer in the Panhandle," Georgia said, handing Sam the printout. "This Mr. Toomey is distraught. He says his mangled irrigation equipment and the destroyed water well could cost him his ranch."

Sam read over the page for the second time.

WATER RIGHTS in the 21ˢᵗ CENTURY

Posted: Jason Toomey
May 17, 2015
Gander, Texas

Folks at Water 21C, I read the account of the terrible mutilation at your ranch. It's hard to believe that anyone could slaughter animals that way. I'm sorry to hear of your loss. While I didn't have any animals killed, I wanted to share with you what happened on my farm because I think it may be related. You said the circle and arrow pointed to your water tank. My damage may have to do with water, and some of you out there will agree.

Two days ago, I went out to check the soil for moisture content and found my irrigation equipment ruined. Someone had broken off most of the new sprinkler heads and cut the piping. The pumps aren't working, either. It looks like someone took a sledgehammer and bashed the pumps to pieces. I'll *have to repair my well. The damage totaled around $150,000. I don't think we can recover from this. I already owe the bank money, and I don't know how I'm going to replace the equipment. This may drive me off my land for good. I may have to sell it.*

Thanks for reading this. Pray for me and my family.

Jason

"I don't know if there's any connection to what happened here, but I'll e-mail this to Ray. It couldn't hurt." Sam was thoughtful for a moment, then walked to the computer to post another entry.

WATER RIGHTS in the 21st CENTURY

Posted: Sam Stanfield
May 18, 2015
Waggoner, Texas

Jason,

You certainly have our prayers, and I know there are many others out there who support you, too. Don't give up hope. Let us know how you and your family are doing. I hope you come to our meeting.

To the other readers of Water 21C,

If you have any other information that could help stop these crimes, or if you want to share what's happened to you, please post your thoughts and details for all to see.

God bless you,
Sam Stanfield

"We'll see if we get any feedback," Sam said.

Georgia had moved closer while he read. She leaned over and kissed him on the cheek. "You're doing the right thing."

He patted her hand. They were in this together. He was grateful they weren't in the same position as Jason in the Panhandle. He and Georgia were debt-free and could withstand the loss, but the motive behind the attack remained a puzzle to him. Had the Bar S been targeted because of the blog?

~ ~ ~

Sam walked into Woody's Café and sat at the counter next to the pie case. He sipped a cup of coffee while he waited for Ray. He ticked off his mental to-do list while he waited. Buddy Gatwick had arranged their finances at the bank. Joe would certainly look after the ranch. Joe loved the place and the cattle as much as Sam and Georgia. He was drinking his second cup when Ray sat down. He'd watched Ray come in and glad-hand the whole café before he joined him on the seat beside him.

"Mornin', Sam." Ray slid in on the cash register side and signaled for a cup of coffee.

"Ray."

"So you've made up your mind to go?" Ray had already expressed his concerns about Sam and Georgia attending the Panhandle meeting.

"We're leaving in the morning after church. I'll call along the way."

"I'll go out to the ranch myself while you're gone."

"Thank you. I sent you some more information that came in on the blog. The crimes are escalating."

"Is there anything I can say to convince you to stay here?"

Sam figured Ray must know more than he was sharing—otherwise, why would he be so worried? "We'll be all right. We'll only be gone ten days. Two weeks at the most. Six of those days will be travel days. We're stopping to see Georgia's uncle, then on to the Panhandle for the meeting, and straight back. Believe me, I don't want to be gone long either."

~~~

Sam parked the fifth wheel in the driveway, and he and Georgia packed it with clothes and food while Gracie sat by the truck and watched. Sam lowered the tailgate and backed his maroon pickup to line up the fifth wheel. He kept an eye on Georgia until he made the connection in the middle of the truck bed. She stood to the side and signaled when the hitch lined up with the truck, then she squeezed in between the RV and the truck and closed the tailgate.

When Sam heard the hitch click into place, he climbed over the wheel well into the bed and connected the chains. "I'll be ready, Georgia, after I make my final check." He jumped to the ground and walked around the entire rig to ensure the steps were up, and all hoses, antennas, and vents were in, down, and latched.

~ ~ ~

The back of the parking lot at the church was clear, so Sam pulled in and turned the truck so it faced the closest exit. They'd arrived early so there would be plenty of room to park the fifty-three feet of truck and recreational vehicle.

A row of tall Photinias lined the edge of the parking lot and shaded the camper. They also provided cover for a lanky man who approached the vehicle from the alley as soon as Sam and Georgia disappeared. Within a few minutes, the man had attached a tracking device to the undercarriage of the truck and slipped away unnoticed.

Gracie walked with Sam and Georgia across the street and into the fenced-in playground area beside the church. Sam unhooked the leash, and Gracie trotted to her usual shady spot under a gigantic live oak, which was older than the church. Gracie stretched out on the cool green grass and crossed her front paws.

"Stay," commanded Sam, although he knew he didn't need to. She would be there when he and Georgia came to get her after church.

Friends greeted them and asked about their trip. They knew

a lot about their business, especially considering it had only been two days since Sam and Georgia had decided to leave. Buddy and his wife, Beth, were the first to approach them. Sam knew where the information had come from. Their banker liked to gossip.

After church, Sam and Georgia said their goodbyes and headed toward their first stop in West Texas. They planned to visit with Georgia's eighty-year-old uncle, who lived near Wichita Falls.

Not far behind them, a van pulled out from the church alley-way and followed the RV.

Chapter 9

Lynnette's voice was warm and caressing over the phone. "I need a favor," she whispered. Her face was passive and almost disgusted as she listened to his whining, pleading voice. She drove with one hand while she cajoled her mark.

"Anything for you, baby. Do you want me to come over there?" Buddy Gatwick asked, breathing deeply into the receiver.

Gatty hadn't changed since college, Lynnette thought. He was pliable and easy to manipulate, then and now. Pitiful, really. She knew he couldn't believe she'd called him. His youthful obsession for her had paid off. She intimated what kind of favor she needed. "Hold on now, Gatty. Let's talk a little first." She teased him with the pet name his fraternity brothers had given him.

"Go ahead and talk all you want, honey. My office has big windows so all the employees can see in, but I have my chair turned around."

"Gatty, do you know some people by the name of Stanfield?" she cooed.

"Yes, I do. Why?"

"What do you know about them?" she asked.

"I've known the Stanfields all my life. I know a lot about them."

"So you handle their finances at your bank?" Lynnette asked.

"Sure. All the important people in town do business here. And they have for a long time."

Lynnette could tell from his bragging that she had him right where she wanted him. He was trying to impress her. "Say, Gatty, can you meet me in Dallas?"

"M-m-meet you?" he stuttered.

"I'll let you know where. Can you come tomorrow?" She was pushing, but she wanted to get the plan moving as quickly as possible, and now she'd confirmed Buddy knew the Stanfields.

"Sure, sure, I can do that. You name the place and time, and I'll be there."

"I'll call you in the morning. Be ready." Before he could take a breath to answer, she was gone. Lynnette wondered what he'd tell his wife and coworkers. This conquest was too easy, she thought.

~~~

Lynnette watched through the peephole as Buddy popped a mint in his mouth and stood staring at the door to Room 625. His off-the-rack suit was rumpled and his tie crooked. Suddenly, he grabbed at his pocket, pulling out his phone. He turned his back, and Lynnette feared he'd chicken out and leave. She needn't have worried. She saw him turn off his phone, thrust it back in his coat pocket, and reach up to knock.

Lynnette made him wait. After he knocked a second time, she slowly opened the door and stood to the side. Lynnette's dark mane fell across her shoulders and flowed into the black fishnet teddy she wore. Five-inch Valentino pumps accentuated her perfectly shaped legs. She beckoned him into the room, and without a word handed him a drink. When he took it, she ran her fingers lightly inside the collar of his jacket and helped him out of it.

"Drink up, Gatty. Let's get started," Lynnette purred as she moved around him to sit in the only chair in the room. She slowly crossed her legs and leaned into him. She made every move count.

"You look amazing," Buddy blurted out. He took a seat on the end of the bed and sipped his drink.

"Here's to us." Lynnette smiled, then reached over and clinked his glass with hers. She made sure he didn't take his eyes off her.

"So should we talk about what business you want me to do for you?"

"We'll take care of that afterward. Do you really think I slipped into this little thing to talk business?" Lynnette smiled as the grown man turned into an awestruck teenager, his eyes roaming her body.

She filled his glass again and waited. His eyes began to lose focus, and his words started to slur. Lynnette moved out of the way when he reached for her, then placed her palm in the middle of his chest and gently shoved. Buddy sat back down hard. He looked up at her and tried to speak but fell backward, out cold.

Poor doofus Gatty, Lynnette thought. *Here you are on the king-sized bed with satin sheets that you'll never get to use.*

Lynnette had planned to shock her contemptible victim into compliance. She'd given Buddy enough drugs to keep him in the room until midnight. When he awoke, he'd need several hours to recover. Nausea, weakness, and a truly bad hangover would dog him. Eventually, he'd clean himself up and go home. But he would be frightened and do what she wanted. She was sure of it.

Lynnette draped Buddy's pants and shirt over the air-conditioning unit under the window. She kicked his shoes under the bed with his underwear stuffed inside, and she placed his wallet and keys in a neat pile in the chair where she last sat.

~~~

Lynnette called to let James Baxter know she was on her way to Austin. The guy she really wanted to spend the night with told her that he didn't think he could get away, but he'd try. She knew he was lying, but she kept driving anyway. She put up with canceled meetings, no-shows, and personal insults just so she could be part of his life. She'd told herself being with him wasn't worth it, but she couldn't let his influence slip through her fingers. She was a different woman with him than she was with anyone else. She hated that. She thought back to Gatty and wished she could be that detached with James.

Her psychiatrist had even told her as much. "Lynnette, you

keep telling me the same thing over and over," she'd said.

Lynnette had tried to explain why she couldn't just walk away, but failed.

"This man keeps making you promises he doesn't keep. I don't know why you put up with him. How long must he be a part of your life?"

"I don't know," was her pathetic answer. Lynnette was disgusted with herself, but she couldn't help it. She couldn't turn him loose. Not yet.

Lynnette pushed the conversation from her mind and focused on the highway signs. The apartment she and James kept together was in a suburb north of Austin. They'd never gone public with their relationship. They met when she was completing her internship for Justice Terry Maurice of the Texas Supreme Court, when she was in her early twenties. James was forty-two, and buzzed in and out of the Capitol constantly. She couldn't help but run into him, and often. She was young and wanted to climb the ladder of success.

Their age difference hadn't bothered either of them at first. They'd been on fire the first few years. But lately James was often uninterested. She'd moved on long ago in some ways, but here she was still, running the same emotional tapes again. She hoped her reasons for doing this were good enough.

When Lynnette opened the door, James was sitting with his back to her, nursing a rum and Coke. She rushed over and sat in his lap and kissed him long and hard. Her hands and body made her intent known.

"Everything isn't about sex, Lynnette." James pushed her away.

"No, it isn't," she automatically responded, disengaging herself. She stood and walked across the room to the sofa. He was in one of those moods. Her heart raced. His rejection always caused this terrible fear to suffocate her. How could this affect her so, when at this moment she actually hated his guts?

"You don't have to be so needy, Lynnette. Straighten yourself up and tell me what was so urgent that we had to meet again. It's only been a week since you were here last."

"I have what you wanted," she answered vaguely. She knew how to get him to talk, and withholding some of the facts made him ask more questions. She wondered why he hadn't figured this out yet. Probably because he catered to more powerful men and women every day. His talent and experience drove him to get the answers he wanted. He was a patient man. The tactic didn't apply to her.

"Did you have any trouble?"

"There were no problems. It was easy. I wore my black teddy."

"That would have done it for that poor hick."

"We were finished in less than an hour. It went like clockwork." Lynnette continued to explain, knowing James liked to hear the details.

"This is good news. When will you be able to put the plan

into action?"

"Next week. I doubt if he's even awake yet."

"You've done a decent job with this one, but we're bringing in someone else for the Stanfields."

"What do you mean?" Lynnette asked. She'd worked so hard to move up in the organization. Now this.

"It's out of our hands. Back off. Stay clear of the Stanfields from now on. Someone else will contact your man Jenson."

Chapter 10

Sam and Georgia pulled off the road to eat lunch at a treelined picnic area. It looked like rain, so they ate inside the RV. Georgia rolled out one of the slides and set the table for sandwiches and potato salad while Sam walked Gracie around the grassy area. Ten minutes later a van rolled in and parked near the restroom. It was still there when Sam and Georgia took off for Uncle Harry's.

Sam drove up Highway 287 until he exited at the town of Burkburnett. Oil country. Uncle Harry's home was nearby. Giant wind turbines flanked the RV as Sam drove down the gravel road. White windmills towered over the hammering pump jacks, Texas icons that stood like a herd of giant praying mantises sucking oil from the ground, cattle wandering among them. They were different from the two-acre gravel pads needed for fracking. Sam had oil and gas royalties himself and had used that money to fund the Bar S cattle operations. *Surely, we can coexist,* Sam thought.

"Turn here," Georgia said, guiding Sam down a narrow road that ended at a glade, lined with summer annuals. Sam angled in and parked. Mixed zinnias edged the pathway, and feathery mesquite provided a dappled shade along the walkway as they made their way to the house. Gracie was already lost in the underbrush chasing a rabbit. Beyond the flat green area where they had parked, a grand log home faced a man-made lake edged with cottonwood trees.

"Look at all these cars," Georgia said. "Who else could be visiting Uncle Harry?"

Harry was standing on the shaded wraparound porch of the enormous log cabin. "Do you want to drive around to the back?" he called to them. "I have hookups in the back."

"We will later," Georgia said as she climbed the steps and hugged the tall, slim gentleman. His perfectly coiffed white hair didn't move as he greeted Sam and Georgia.

"Gracie!" Sam called, and the shepherd bounded onto the porch, panting.

"Uncle Harry, do you remember the pup that was thrown out at our ranch a couple of years ago? She was about six months old when you saw her last." Georgia gave a silent hand signal for Gracie to sit by her leg, and Gracie obeyed.

"Well, she is beautiful!" Uncle Harry said. "And well behaved. Why would anyone not want this fantastic creature? Someone didn't know what they had. Let's take her to meet my labs, Rex and Josie. They'll all have a great time together while you're here."

"What are all these cars, Uncle Harry?"

"Come on. You'll find out. The guests are in the great room, and we are ahead of you by at least one cocktail. Please, do come in." Uncle Harry ushered them into his rambling, nine-bedroom log home.

Harry Reynolds had been—and still was—an important man across the state. As a young attorney, Harry had become famous when he won an almost impossible case involving a poor sharecropper. Tommy Williams was an innocent eighteen-year-old accused of killing a clerk when he robbed a store. The "townies" branded Tommy their scapegoat, reporting they saw him committing the robbery. Harry took the case and convinced a girl who was involved to tell the truth.

This case came to be known as the "Tommy Trial," and it launched Harry's political career. He was elected to the state legislature the following year and spent thirty-five years there, the last ten as speaker of the house. Twelve years retired now, Harry still kept his fingers in the Texas political pie. Those connections made Sam and Georgia especially eager to confer with him.

His guests would prove important, too, and reflected Harry's colorful career. Among those there that night was former governor Lyle Braden. Sam also had several in-depth conversations with Jim Darnell, the Texas commissioner of agriculture. He had only recently heard of the vandalism ruining irrigation systems in the Panhandle, but he'd been following the cattle killings across Texas. The commissioner assured Sam he'd keep track of the investigations. Sam liked Jim. He felt he could count on him.

After dinner the second evening, Sam and Harry sat on the

front porch. "I'll call some people for you tomorrow. There are no guarantees that I can find out anything else about the slaughters, but we can check the recent land sales in the area."

"I have a list of the ranches where explosions have occurred. We'll send the documents to Ray in Waggoner. I trust him, and that's important since we don't know where this trouble is originating. You be careful making inquiries. Make sure you can trust your people." Sam worried that Harry's former cronies might have formed new loyalties. He didn't want anything to happen to him.

"Don't worry about me," Harry said. "Just take care of yourself and Georgia."

"I will. We need to leave in the morning so we can make it in time for our meeting," Sam said. "I'll say goodbye tonight, Harry."

Sam's and Georgia's heads were swimming with the names of the many people who had come to visit. Georgia's father was the fifth of eleven children, and most of her cousins still lived in Texas. Uncle Harry was her father's youngest sibling and had at least six children who lived nearby. Every one of them had come to visit.

Sam and Georgia had insisted on staying in the RV each night. Being in a familiar place was calming for Gracie. They also needed a rest from the company.

"I think we've made great strides in getting help from across the state," Sam said as they got ready for bed. "Let's leave early in the morning so we can have some time for peace and quiet."

They lay there enjoying the events of the day again, trying to remember names, repeating stories, and laughing at Harry's antics. Gracie was lulled by the steady drum of their voices and fell into a deep sleep at the base of their bed.

"Harry never seems to age, and he has such a full life. I think we need to take a lesson from your uncle. Let's live in the moment." When she didn't answer, Sam smiled, kissed her on the cheek, and turned on his side. He was instantly asleep.

~~~

Jenson had lost Sam and Georgia going down the country road, even with the tracking device. He drove around the area until midnight before they finally had to stop the van and reconnoiter on foot. After an hour, Jenson spotted Hood limping back to the van. He flashed the headlights and started the motor.

Hood was breathing hard when he hauled himself into the front seat. "I found the RV behind a big log house over there. It's in a little circle at the end of the road. You can't see the house for the trees."

Jenson found an old oil road that led to a nearby pump jack, its head frozen in place. It had been idle for quite some time. The overgrown Johnson grass was waist-high and gave them the perfect cover to watch the comings and goings of the Reynolds place. They couldn't miss the RV when it left.

"How long do you think they'll stay here?" Hood grumbled.

"How would I know? You know we're supposed to wait. Besides, we get paid whether we're driving or sitting still. They're not leaving until morning, so I'm sleeping right here."

They'd been living in the van for three days without a bath or a change of clothes, eating only junk food from a gas station. They spent the next day copying license numbers and taking pictures of every visitor. After dark, Jenson sent Hood to snoop around, and he came back with more pictures of Harry Reynolds's visitors.

The next morning, Jenson had just gotten out to stretch his legs when Hood shouted that the RV was moving. Jenson scrambled back into the van as the couple turned down the road in front of them.

"Thank goodness," Hood exhaled. "Lynnette called while you were outside. Do you want me to dial her back for you?"

"Yeah, let's do it," Jenson said.

Hood smiled, dialed the number, and handed Jenson the phone while it was still ringing.

"Give me the report," Lynnette snapped. "The W21C Blog added another post this morning."

"They're on the move again," Jenson said. "They're headed north on Interstate 44. We'll follow and give you a report later in the day."

"You'd better call me twice a day from now on."

Chapter 11

Ray and his deputies gathered around the conference table in the courthouse basement. There were hardly enough of them to cover the 970 square miles of Waggoner County on a normal day. The county's population had doubled in the past five years, but its budget had not. Ray had some good people, but the Bar S case had overloaded his small team.

"Don't stir things up when you're asking questions," Ray instructed them. "But be persistent if you think they have useful information. Don't share any information with them. I know the people you'll be interviewing are your friends, but I don't want the whole county to have details before this office does."

The five deputies nodded their understanding, but Ray would remind them again about the importance of confidentiality at their next meeting. He wanted to keep a tight rein on security. He thought the Bar S crime was an outside job, but he didn't want to take any chances. This was the first investigation of this size since he'd taken office, and he wanted his deputies to learn how to conduct a thorough one.

Ray walked to the county map and pointed to the sections he'd divided. He covered his procedures and gave the deputies a checklist to follow during interviews. After his lengthy briefing, Ray sent them out to blanket Waggoner County.

He'd reserved the churches for himself. He wanted to follow up on what Shirley had told him about religious icons and symbols. Waggoner County had over seventy churches, according to the telephone directory. It would take several days.

"Maureen, I'm trusting you to handle the office while I'm out. You know to call me if there's an emergency."

"Sure, Sheriff."

"And if you get a call from Sam or Georgia, let me know right away."

~~~

A week later, Ray sat down to review everything from the Bar S case. He looked at the .38 slug, the size ten boot print, and the results of the blood sample, all spread out on his desk. Those were his only leads. The FBI hadn't contacted him, though the DNA report was due any day. Waggoner County didn't have its own lab, and getting forensics from outside sources was slow.

Ray's deputies reported several people had seen some strangers. There were always strangers traveling through Waggoner on busy US Highway 287. Everyone who journeyed to the Panhandle took 287 north, passing through Waggoner, Wichita Falls, and on to Amarillo.

Ray was reading the interview transcripts when Maureen walked in and placed a stack of the daily statewide bulletins on his desk. "Better look at some of these, sir," she said. "The important ones are on top."

The first bulletin described how someone had used dynamite to destroy water wells and irrigation systems near Dalhart. The sheriff there had no suspects. Ray noted the similarities and called Sam. He and Georgia were driving near that area.

~~~

Ray finished his interviews early the next day. He was down to the last two churches, with few results. At least he'd met more voters, he thought. He was a terrible politician, but he did enjoy talking to folks. His wife, Maggie, would be glad to know he'd been meeting some new people at least.

Ray's next church wasn't on his original list. He'd passed a hand-painted sign that sent him five miles down a dirt road. Peeling white paint covered a slender rectangular building. The cinder block foundation indicated the church had been moved from another location. The grass was neatly mowed, but the place was hard to see from the road. He read the name of the minister on a sign in the yard. A man was standing on a ladder scraping the crusty paint off the front entrance. By the time Ray had parked by the newly painted sign and gotten out of his squad car, the man had stepped down from the ladder and met him on the lawn.

"Hello, Sheriff. I'm the Reverend J. T. Sims, pastor here at

Cottonwood Free Will Church."

"Hello, Pastor."

"Sheriff, I know you from your posters," Sims said, smiling warmly. "What brings you over here?"

"I've been checking on all of the churches in the area to find out if anyone's had any break-ins or had any items stolen or missing."

"That's hard to say, since I've only been here for around two months. We've been doing inventory. I could let you know when we finish going over the equipment and furniture. Are you in a big hurry?"

"No rush really, but when you finish, please give me a call." Ray handed him a card with his contact information.

"Okay. But what's this about?"

"We've had some break-ins reported, that's all. But call me if you find anything missing in your inventory." Ray was evasive. He didn't want to have the whole county speculating about cults and slaughtered cows. "Looks like you've just moved your church building over here."

"Around three months ago. It needs some repair, but we already have fifty members and the work is going fast."

"Where was the church before?"

"We bought it from a group in South Texas near Kerrville and moved it here."

"Good luck on your repairs. Call me after you finish your

inventory."

That left Ray with only the First United Methodist Church of Waggoner, near downtown. It was the oldest church in the county and also where the Stanfields attended services. Ray had saved it for last intentionally. The minister there already had reported that twenty-seven crosses were missing. The Waggoner police chief had investigated the incident and given Ray the reports. But Ray still wanted to interview Bessie Gamble, the church secretary, himself. She worked at the front desk and would know more than anyone.

Ray walked two short blocks from the courthouse to the church. He admired a row of antique stained-glass windows as he approached the office.

The minister emerged at the same time Ray entered. "Morning, Ray."

"Hello, sir. I was coming to talk to Bessie about the missing crosses. Is she in?"

"She's right there at her desk. She can tell you all about it. I'm on my way to the hospital or I'd go back in with you."

"No problem. I'll call you if I have any questions."

Ray stepped through the heavy oak doors and into the calmness of an empty hallway. The quiet surrounded him. He closed off the outside world and walked into an ethereal one. His heavy boots only whispered footsteps on the thick carpet. When he walked into the front office, the fluorescent lighting seemed like a garish assault. Bessie was behind her desk, her back to the door, filing papers.

"Hello, Bessie," Ray said as he rapped on the doorframe.

The woman jumped and put her hand to her throat as she turned. "Oh, Sheriff, you startled me!" Bessie said as she rolled back to her desk. "Come on in. What can I help you with?"

"I wanted you to tell me about the burglary here at the church, if you could." Ray pulled up a chair and sat down.

"The ladies were really upset. I don't have any clue about what happened. Only that the crosses were gone from their class-room."

"I had heard you were very upset. That's understandable."

"Yes, I was. This is a church, after all. I couldn't imagine why anyone would come in and rip those crosses from the wall. Lots of folks are in and out of the church every day. That's why the trustees installed the camera."

"Camera? Do you have the video of that week?"

"I'm not sure, but I can check for you. The tape lasts for about a week, then we record over it the next week."

"I need those videos, if you have them, Bessie."

"Okay, Sheriff."

The choir director stood in the doorway. Ray knew the man had been listening to the last of the conversation.

"Ray, I can bring it to you after choir practice later this evening," he said.

"Thank you. I'll be in the office." Ray jotted down the names of the women who taught the Sunday school class and then stood to leave. Bessie gave a slight wave goodbye.

~~~

By dark, Ray had compiled the results of his interview notes and those of his deputies. He also had received the video from the church but hadn't had time to review it. He was tracking Sam and Georgia's blog information, which poured in daily.

His phone rang. "Ray Collins," he answered.

"Hello, Ray. This is Shirley. I'm faxing you some information regarding the other damaged properties and the animal crimes across the state. I wanted you to be there and personally pick it up."

"I'll head right to the fax machine. Fax away, and thanks, Shirley."

Ray retrieved the documents and read about the incidents in South Texas. Shirley had sent him copies of police reports, her notes neatly printed in the margins. Twenty head of registered Black Angus were shot while watering at a tank, the first crime Shirley investigated. Another herd in the hill country stampeded off a cliff. The rancher lost over a hundred cows and calves, and the rotting carcasses polluted the stream for weeks. Each account of the cattle killings was similar. All the details were right there in front of him. The last report covered the latest Panhandle explosion. This one was in the area where Sam and Georgia were holding their W21C meeting.

He picked up the phone and dialed Sam's cell.

Chapter 12

Sam and Georgia drove north on US Highway 283 into Oklahoma in drizzling rain. As the drops hit the remnants of the Texas dust on their windshield, Sam's view grew muddled. Although he encountered little traffic, the poor visibility and the slick road slowed him down. He watched Georgia take out her small shuttle and begin tatting. He couldn't imagine doing anything that delicate, but her slender hands seemed made for it. He took the drive time to consider the conversation with Ray earlier that morning.

When the rain stopped, Georgia asked, "What did Ray tell you?"

Sam glanced at her. He'd been so deep in thought that he hadn't noticed when she'd put her lace back in its travel case and turned to stare at him.

"Ray has the report back on the bullet they took out of Hambone. It was from a .38, like we thought. He also told me the blood they found on the fence was human. He has it in the system now to see if there's a DNA match. He called because he's concerned about us. There's been another panhandle explosion and one in Waggoner County."

"Where? Do we know them?"

"It's a place about ten miles south of us. Family by the name of Cunningham. Ray doesn't think it's the same as the others. They rustled some cattle and blew up a watering trough. The cows were all longhorns. They'll be caught easily enough if the rustlers try to sell them. The hides are unique. The owner had pictures of the steers."

"I don't know any Cunninghams," Georgia mused. "Should we turn back?"

"No. I already told him we'd be going on. I don't think who-ever is doing this will interfere with the W21C group. I told Ray we'd be camping in the Black Kettle Grasslands tonight." Sam wanted someone to be aware of their whereabouts. This whole mess was spreading farther afield every day. He was apprehensive about the motives behind all of it. But he didn't want to alarm Georgia, so they focused on something else, using the drive time to review ranch operations. Four hours later, they pulled into the national grasslands in northwestern Oklahoma.

"This peaceful prairie is a pleasant change from the past few weeks," Georgia said. "I'm glad to be here. The creek is right at our back door. We can sit out this evening and listen to the running wa-ter. That will be calming."

Sam drove the rig into the campsite. "This pull-through is

level. I don't believe I'll have to unhook tonight." Not having to unhook the RV from the truck saved time both setting up camp and preparing to leave. Sam was glad to have the extra time to plan the days ahead.

"Let's walk to the creek before we start the grill."

"Absolutely." Sam picked up his binoculars and headed to the creek with Georgia. Gracie halted her inspection of the surrounding grass and rushed to check the path ahead of them.

The couple held hands as they walked down the trail.

"I'm starving after that long hike," Sam said when they returned to the RV.

"I want to take a few more photos before we start cooking," Georgia said, snapping away. She always took a few pictures to remember their campsites. She walked around the RV with her camera.

A chilly wind picked up, but Sam had a nice campfire started right away. He sat watching the fire while Georgia continued to shoot.

"That ought to do it," she said a minute later. "The sunset was really beautiful."

"The fire is about ready," Sam said. "How about those steaks?"

"Coming up." Georgia placed a cast iron skillet on the grill and dumped in a stick of butter. Very soon, the yellow hunk began to sizzle, and she dropped in their campfire favorite—potatoes, onions, and secret spices. The aroma was tantalizing. Sam relaxed for the first time in days. He watched Georgia enjoying the time away from the stress as well.

"Georgia, I like this place. We could stay here another day, if we left early enough the day after tomorrow."

"Let's do it. I know that would be a long drive, but I can take the wheel for a while."

~~~

They headed into town the next morning for some supplies. The drive was short, but the crowded parking lot forced Sam to park far from the front doors.

"Sam, you can wait here. I'll run in and pick up a few things. I know you don't like to shop."

Sam grinned. He was relieved. He checked his reception and decided to listen to his messages while Georgia was inside.

She returned a few minutes later. "My credit card wouldn't work," she announced as she climbed into the truck. "I had to pay with cash."

"Did you have enough?"

"Fortunately, yes."

"I didn't let the credit card company know we were traveling. Maybe that's it."

"Neither did I," Georgia said.

"I'm sure that's all it is. I'll call Buddy and ask him to take care of it." Sam called the bank while they were still in the parking lot. Buddy answered immediately, and Sam put him on speaker.

"Hey, Sam. How's the trip? Are you having a good time?"

"We're having trouble with our credit card processing. I thought maybe there was a problem because we're traveling."

"Sounds like it. I'll fix that right away for you."

"Thank goodness," Georgia said. "I was worried."

"Nothing to worry about. Go ahead and enjoy your trip." Buddy hung up before either of them could say anything else.

"That was abrupt," Georgia said. "What's going on with him?"

"Good question." Sam thought it strange that Buddy spoke so lightly about their trip. He'd been there during the discussions at Woody's Café. He just didn't understand the controversy surrounding water rights. He seemed unaffected by the seriousness of the situation. Sam started the truck.

"Any other news?" Georgia asked.

"There's been another Panhandle attack."

"Oh no."

"Another terrible story. While a family was away from home, someone blew up their well and irrigation ditches. This time the explosion set the barn on fire. They lost their hay and the feed for next year. The authorities haven't found any clues for this one, either."

"It's about water. I just know it. This isn't the first destruction of irrigation equipment on property around here. First at our place, the other one in Waggoner, and another one in the Panhandle."

"You may be right, Georgia."

"What can we do?"

"We'll put it before the W21C group when we get there."

"I'm going to call Ray again and tell him about our credit card problem."

"Buddy's behavior was strange. It wouldn't hurt."

~~~

Jenson was on the phone with Lynnette when he drove past the entrance to the RV park. Lynnette told him to continue to write down who the Stanfields talked to and stay with them. He drove up to the entrance and got out to talk to the park ranger. "Can we drive around and look for a spot?"

"Sure. Just come back and let me know your number so I can mark your ticket. How many days are you staying?"

"One for now. Can we extend the days if we want?"

"That won't be a problem. Not too many people here yet. Wait a week when schools start letting out for summer vacation. Then it would be a problem."

"Thanks," Jenson said, walking away.

"I see you're dry camping in your van," the ranger continued. "You'll see the bathhouse and restrooms at the back. I'll have a map for you when you come back with your campsite number." The ranger walked into the station, and Jenson drove off in search of the Stanfields. It didn't take long. Jenson stopped the van and parked as far away as he could.

"Now what?" Hood complained. "We sit here?"

"Got to," Jenson said. "Orders. What we need to do is get that woman's camera. I know she took a picture of the van, and we need to search that RV."

"RVs are easy to break into," Hood said. "You just need the right tools."

Jenson watched Sam and Georgia walk down one of the hiking trails. "Come on, they're going down toward the water," he said. "They'll be gone for a while. Get in that RV and see if they have any plans laying around. Make sure to damage the computer. Don't grab it. I don't want to make them suspicious. Keep your phone on you. I'll watch for them to come back."

Jenson walked to the head of the trail that led to the creek. He leaned against the information sign, pretending to read the map. Few people passed by. The park was almost empty, and the folks who did stop just glanced at the sign, then walked down the trail. Jenson had a good vantage point.

Hood strapped on his scabbard and checked his hunting knife before he shoved it into the sheath, and walked to the Stanfield RV. There was no need to break into the RV. It was open. Hood entered swiftly and searched the entire vehicle in a few short minutes. He found Sam's laptop charging on the floor next to one of two large leather recliners. Hood turned it on. He was emptying a bottle of water over it when his phone rang.

"Yeah?" he whispered.

"She's coming back on another trail," Jenson hissed. "Hide. You won't have time to get out."

Hood closed the laptop, took out his knife and held it by his side. He crouched behind one of the recliners. Georgia climbed the stairs, opened the door, and walked around the counter to the refrigerator. The door swung open and banged into the arm of the recliner. The chair rocked into Hood. Georgia took out lunch, grabbed two bottles of water, and closed the door.

"Hello, sweet girl. You want to come in and get a snack?" Georgia let Gracie inside. Then she walked to the opposite end of the RV and climbed the three steps to the toilet.

Gracie smelled Hood. A low growl began in her throat and rumbled up to one loud bark. Hood poised his knife for an attack, but Gracie stood where she was near the door, between Georgia and the trespasser. She stayed there staring at the place where the strange face had just been.

Georgia came back to the kitchen. "What are you barking at? That's not like you." Georgia looked outside. "There's nothing out there now. Come on, let's go, girl." She grabbed the lunch and water bottles off the counter and held the door open for Gracie. Gracie hesitated, then ran down the steps.

Hood leaned back against the wall, lifted the corner of the window shade, and watched the woman and dog return to the creek. He was back at the van in minutes.

"Did you get it done?" Jenson asked.

"Sure. I also spotted a rifle and two handguns in there. They look like his and her pieces. This may not be as easy as we think."

Chapter 13

The day started earlier than usual at the Oak National Bank. Buddy Gatwick opened the door and walked in early, an extraordinary act for the president of the bank. The employees stared in surprise. Buddy's normal day began when he skirted in a minute under the nine o'clock start time, then made the rounds, speaking to clerks and other bankers in a condescending manner. He wanted to convey his privilege, his authority as the boss.

Not today. He walked straight to his office without a word to anyone. Even his secretary, Dena, watched him walk by silently. But Buddy didn't stay in his office for long. He marched out with papers in his hands and looked around the bank, searching for someone to harass. Those watching him quickly looked down. They didn't want to be singled out for his wrath.

Finally, he turned around and headed back to his office. "Don't bother me with this small crap!" Buddy crumpled a stack of papers in his fist and slammed them down on Dena's desk.

"Okay, Buddy."

Buddy had been in a mood for a week. Today was even

worse. It wasn't a secret that he'd made a trip to Dallas. Speculation was rampant, especially in a small town. Normally, his wife, Beth, came by the bank at least a couple of times a week. People noticed she hadn't been there, and they were beginning to talk.

~~~

Ray drove to the bank to talk to Buddy. After he'd talked to Sam and Georgia, he wanted to make some inquiries on his own. He parked and scanned the area before exiting his vehicle, as was his practice. He noted the cars parked around the bank and across the street. Then he entered the bank. All eyes were on him. Ray looked directly at each person and spoke. He felt the tension as he walked to Dena's desk.

"Good morning, Dena," Ray said. "I want to speak with Buddy."

Dena sighed and said, "Sheriff, it's good to see you. Why don't you go right on in? He's been on a tear this morning. Maybe you can settle him down." She shook her head and pointed her pen in the direction of Buddy's office.

"Has he now? What's wrong with him?"

"I don't know, but he's been this way ever since he made that trip to Dallas last week. Beth hasn't been in, either. Maybe the love-birds are having trouble."

Ray just nodded and walked toward Buddy's office. When he opened the door, Buddy had his back turned, looking out the window.

"Dena, you know you're supposed to knock!" Buddy yelled. "How many times . . ." He whirled around in his chair and stopped in mid-sentence. He choked out, "Sheriff, what are you doing here?"

"Buddy, I have a few questions for you. It seems you've been upset lately. What's wrong?" Ray kept his gaze steady across the desk.

Buddy broke out in a sweat, and drops of perspiration rolled down the sides of his flushed face. A man in distress if he ever saw one, Ray thought. But he was patient. He sat back and watched Buddy squirm.

"Nothing, Ray. Nothing at all. What would make you think there was something wrong?"

"People are talking, Buddy. About you and Beth."

"What are you saying? Beth and I are fine!" Buddy jumped up from his desk and started pacing.

"What happened in Dallas?"

Buddy jerked his head back before he answered. "Dallas was just business and had nothing to do with Beth. It was just business, I tell you." He raised his shoulders and started breathing quickly.

"What about Sam's credit card being frozen?"

Buddy stopped and stood perfectly still. "That's personal banking business. You know I can't talk about that."

"They're worried about their account. Is something wrong?"

"I can't tell you. I can't talk about it." He put his hand to his forehead and kept it there. Ray knew he was lying. Buddy was guilty of something.

"Will Sam and Georgia be okay?" Ray asked.

"They'll be all right. Don't worry. I'll take care of them." Buddy cleared his throat. "Ray, I've got an appointment I need to get ready for, if you don't mind."

Ray stood up and moved to leave. "Thanks, Buddy. I'll be back to talk to you later. I have some more questions."

~~~

Dena was gathering her things for her lunch break when the FedEx delivery showed up. "Mr. Gatwick will sign for you today, Grover," Dena told the courier on her way out the door.

Buddy walked out of his office and signed the pad. He instructed Grover to put the boxes and envelopes on Dena's desk. Then he stomped out of the office.

~~~

Lynnette didn't like what she saw happening across the street at the Oak National Bank. The sheriff had been in to speak with Buddy earlier in the day. And later she saw Buddy raising his arms and waving them around, ranting at the clerks. He returned to his office when customers came in, and emerged to start again when they left. The plate glass windows revealed it all. She was afraid he was falling apart. He was a liability she wouldn't tolerate, but she had to get what she wanted first.

She drove out of the parking lot to find another quiet spot to make her call and watch her plans unfold. She didn't want to stay in one place for very long.

~~~

When Buddy walked in after lunch, Dena was answering the phone and motioned him to his office to pick up a call.

"It's a woman," Dena mouthed. Buddy went into his office to answer.

"Yes? This is Buddy Gatwick."

"The Buddy Gatwick from Dallas last week?" Lynnette said in her familiar sultry voice. "You have unusual tastes, Gatty." She mocked him openly, knowing he'd fold.

"What do you want?" Buddy's voice was almost inaudible.

"Isn't that the question of the hour? What's more important is what's in that FedEx envelope you left on your secretary's desk at noon today. You don't want anyone else to open it, I assure you."

"What do you mean?"

"Better get it and check it out. Not so flattering, I'm afraid. I'll call you tomorrow at the same time." She tapped the red button and disconnected.

Lynnette picked up Buddy's movements through the bank windows when he rushed to Dena's desk to find the FedEx parcel. She watched him riffle through the stack of envelopes in the wire basket. He picked up a large white one, put it under his arm, and returned to his office.

She had enclosed two photographs that had white sheets of paper clipped to the front. The first page said, *FOR YOUR WIFE*. Lynnette watched as he pulled out the contents. She knew what he saw. In the picture, Buddy was naked and on all fours in the hotel room. A woman Lynnette had hired was riding him, nude, holding a whip in one hand and pulling on a bridle in his mouth with the other. His bright red lips puckered toward the camera, and his eyelids were taped open in a grotesque stare.

FOR THE WORLD was on the next page. The attached picture was vile. These photos gave her the leverage to get Buddy to cooperate and do whatever she wanted. Even if he proved the second picture was a fake, the first one wasn't. She knew that would put doubt in people's minds.

Lynnette drove out of the parking lot and back to Dallas. She had already been in Waggoner too long. Someone might remember her.

~~~

Buddy remained in the bank office until all of the employees had left. The approaching darkness and the bright florescent lights inside highlighted the slumped shape sitting at his desk. He stayed in the same position until Beth came and banged on the front door. Buddy stuffed the envelope in the bottom drawer. Beth waited there until he walked toward her. Then she returned to her car and left him standing there.

Chapter 14

The sun beat down on Sam and Georgia as they walked out of a computer store in Amarillo. Sam had found a parking spot for the truck and RV a block away from the strip mall. They followed the curb on their way back. Sam had the laptop tucked under his arm and Georgia had her phone out, ready to make a call.

"I thought it was taken care of," she said. "I never thought our credit card would be turned down again."

"Thank goodness it didn't take much to fix it. Again, cash saved our bacon."

"I'll call the bank while you check out the computer," Georgia said, punching in the number. It took three tries before the call went through.

"Buddy, Sam tried to use our credit card again, and it was declined. Why won't it go through? I want some answers."

"I'll take care of it. Don't worry. Are you going to use it again today?"

"Well, I don't know really. We're here in Amarillo. We stopped to have Sam's computer fixed and when he went to pay for it, the credit card was turned down. We were lucky we had enough cash on us. Would you like to talk to Sam?"

"No, no. Let me jump off the phone and get right on this," Buddy said. "I'll call you back sometime today." The call disconnected.

Georgia turned toward Sam. "Buddy was in a hurry to get off the phone, again. He didn't want to talk to you."

"Did he say he'd take care of it?"

"He did, but he sounded uptight. Maybe he's not cut out to be a banker."

They continued driving north. It was getting late, but they were nearing the Jackson farm, the site of their meeting.

"Don't worry. We can fix this. You know we have enough money in the bank, and our credit is good." Sam made a note to call again the next day and get it straightened out. Buddy hadn't called back, and Sam wondered what was going on.

"You're right, Sam. We can correct all of this mess tomorrow. The Jackson place should be coming up soon."

"There it is, just like they said. I can pull the whole rig up next to the barn, and we can hook up for the night."

Gracie felt the truck slow and jumped up to look around. Sam made a wide turn to get through the gate, and by the time he'd pulled in, the entire Jackson family had come out to greet them.

~~~

Early the next morning, more cars, pickups, campers, and vans poured into the Jackson farm. Those already there had tables set up for breakfast, and by nine o'clock the group had gathered in the sprawling side yard. Smaller cliques naturally formed, and intense conversations crackled in the air.

"The EPA should take care of its own business. What a crime! The poisoned streams and rivers in Colorado will be ruined for a long time from that mine accident," Sam heard a passionate man from Denver say.

But before someone could hijack the meeting with one topic, Sam stepped to the front of the group and began to speak. "Friends, my name is Sam Stanfield, and my wife, Georgia, is the spunky redhead standing by the coffeemaker. I want to thank all of you for being here. Georgia and I initiated the W21C blog, which many of you are familiar with. A lot of you have written to us on that forum. There is a lot to say here today, and everyone who wants to speak will have a chance to do so. But first, I want to thank the Jacksons for hosting us."

"Thank you, Sam and Georgia," Keith Jackson shouted as he waved. The crowd cheered, then settled down and turned back to face Sam.

Sam felt their expectations, and knew they needed encouragement. "This is an important day, not only for every individual here, but for our country. I am grateful to still have the freedom to gather and speak in our nation. I don't take this freedom for granted. This freedom gives us hope to solve problems in a peaceful way. I want to be clear that the W21C does not endorse violence in any way, but we do have the right to voice our opinions. As it stands today, we have two key issues. The first is government overreach and failure to follow through. While the purpose of the EPA is to protect our environment, politics have twisted the agency's mission. Those concerned about the consequences of unreasonable regulations can get together today to discuss ways to initiate change."

Sam heard a hum travel through the crowd. He estimated half the people there were interested in tackling the EPA. Sam knew this would be a sticky topic. As in any controversy, some would think the agency's regulations too strict, while others would think they were too lenient. His objective was to bring them together and provide a venue for discussion.

"We also are here to discuss the explosions, the destruction of property, and the cattle slaughters. This is a different topic, folks. While these incidents may seem scattered, I believe there is a connection. It is not coincidence that so many of you have lost your land."

The crowd rumbled loudly, seventy farmers and ranchers in all.

"Those of you interested in the mine incident gather around the table where Mr. Jackson is. The rest join me at the front."

A dozen people walked toward Sam. Most were victims with much in common. Georgia led the ranchers who wanted to help the victims get back on their feet. Sam watched as everyone's feelings of anger and frustration changed to determination and purpose. The giant human clock wound down as the afternoon moved on.

Sam and Georgia handed out cards until they ran out, then wrote down their information by hand. Sam never imagined that the blog he and Georgia had started would attract so many people and bring up so many issues. Sam was pleased the young people there were informed and would become dedicated activists.

The discussions in the small groups lasted well into the afternoon. Sam promised he'd publish the notes from each one. It was so late when the meeting was over, he and Georgia decided to stay with the Jacksons another night.

When they finally made it back to the camper, Sam contacted Ray. "Ray, the meeting went well. You can find a summary of the results on the blog tomorrow."

"Anyone seem suspicious?"

"I didn't notice anyone, but Georgia took a lot of pictures of the crowd. She can send them to you tonight. On another note, we're having trouble with our credit cards again. We've called the bank and talked to Buddy, but he seemed nervous and wanted to get off the phone in a hurry. We shouldn't be having any troubles with our finances at all."

"I can go by the bank and talk with Buddy. Will you and Georgia be starting back this way in the morning?"

"Not yet. We're driving over to New Mexico. A rancher near

Taos asked for our help, and we're going by there before we come home. We'll be back by the end of next week. We'll keep in touch."

~~~

The next morning, as Sam and Georgia headed toward the mountains of New Mexico, Georgia opened the laptop and checked the blog. The W21C group already had posted several comments.

"People from Colorado, Utah, and New Mexico who were victims of the mine leak have posted comments," Georgia read to Sam as they traveled. "One says, 'The EPA is supposed to protect the land, but they seem to go to the extremes. One minute they're issuing crushing fines to small chicken farmers, and the next minute they're negligent in keeping extremely poisonous toxins from leaking into streams. That blunder was catastrophic.'"

"It will be a long time before that mess is really cleaned up, probably not in our lifetime," Sam said. "I'm encouraged that the group was eager and willing to talk. That's a good suggestion to let someone else join in this fight and start writing some posts."

Georgia read on while Sam drove. Gracie put her front paws on the middle console and leaned toward Sam. She eased her muzzle close to Sam's ear and rested a moment on his shoulder. She gave him a quick lick on the cheek, then moved back and stared out the window.

"It's amazing how Gracie can read your mood," Georgia said. "She wanted to comfort you."

A soft smile moved across Sam's face. "She did make me feel better."

110

"Welcome to the Land of Enchantment," Georgia shouted, smiling, as they crossed the border. "I love New Mexico. It won't be long before we start seeing some mountains on the horizon."

"Let's stop in Santa Rosa for the night."

Georgia looked at the map. "There's a park that has 50-amp hookups. We could run our air conditioning. The temperatures are already in the upper nineties."

"That sounds like a good spot."

Georgia dialed the park number and reserved a pull-through. "We're to go on in and park in our slot since we won't get there until after five, and the office will be closed. Instructions will be on the bulletin board of the main office. The woman said we could put the money in the envelope there and drop it in the slot, or come by the office and pay by credit card in the morning when the office opens."

"Let's go ahead and pay tonight since we want to leave early in the morning. Then we can stop for breakfast in Las Vegas."

Chapter 15

Lynnette wore jeans, scuffed boots, and a loose blouse as she strode into the county fairgrounds in Dalhart, joining a lively crowd. This was a big event for the small Panhandle town. The arenas and barns buzzed with activity. Row upon row of used tractors, plows, bailers, and all sizes of cattle trailers were lined up for auction. Buyers and sellers from all over the state were milling around, hoping for a good deal.

The exception to hope was the forced sale. Two landowners were selling what remained of their farming equipment. Ruined farm implements and poisoned stock had driven them to bankruptcy. The families didn't have the money to buy new irrigation equipment or replace the cattle. The violent attacks had ruined their lives, and the distraught families stood to the side of the huge tent, waiting for their auction to begin. The edges of the awning snapped in the wind.

"Sir, do you know what time this is going to start?" Lynnette asked as she walked over to Jenson, who was facing the podium.

Jenson twisted his head to see Lynnette. He nodded his

recognition. Then he bent his head down and looked at his boots while Lynnette spoke.

The auctioneer began, but his voice receded into background noises as Lynnette and Jenson talked. People surrounding them focused on the sale and ignored them. The wind blew in their faces, and they instinctively inched closer to each other to hear. They moved toward the back of the tent to finish their conversation.

"Using explosives is not my idea of staying under the radar, Jenson. What were you thinking? It was all over last night's national news, with that woman telling her sob story. You're going to have to find some other way to get rid of the irrigation systems."

"Yeah, sure. We can do that. I'll think of something."

"Good. Now what did you learn at the meeting?"

"It's a lot worse than you think. There were lots of pissed-off people at that meeting, and Sam Stanfield is their ringleader. They're real stirred up."

"How many were there?"

"We counted more than a hundred. People were coming and going during the day, so it could have been more. We have license plate numbers. I'll send you the pictures. I'd be worried if I were you."

"We *are* worried. Jenson, expect a call from someone higher up. They're bringing in someone else. I read about the meeting this morning. More people are adding comments every day to that blog of theirs. Just the thing we were trying to avoid. We can stop two people, but if this blog spreads, we can't stop that."

"It looks like the auction is over," Jenson said, looking up. "The land auction is tomorrow at the courthouse in town. Are you going to be there?"

"We have others to take care of that. We have enough to handle as it is. Have you heard from Hood?"

"He's following the couple. They just left Amarillo."

~~~

Hood was driving a navy blue pickup he'd purchased in Amarillo. Jenson decided the van may have become too familiar, and the Stanfields might recognize it. Two vehicles also allowed them to split up and follow each person if they needed to. Jenson had updated Hood on the latest orders and planned to catch up with him later.

At twilight, Hood sat parked across the road from the Coyote Hills RV Park. He'd watched Sam and Georgia unhook the fifth wheel and drive the truck into town. He followed them to a café and parked outside. He knew he would have to wait until dark anyway before he could get inside the campground undetected. There were only a few shrubs scattered across the park. Cover was sparse.

It was midnight before the campground activity settled down. Hood sneaked onto the property through an unlocked side gate. The whole place was a quiet humming of air conditioners dulling the outside noises for the sleeping campers. After checking all directions, Hood walked past four spaces and slid under the diesel pickup that belonged to the Stanfields. Hood turned on his flashlight to locate the brake lines. Then he pulled his knife from its sheath and sliced partway through the braid and hose. The brakes would hold with moderate use. But in the mountains, they'd fail. The weak line would tax the brakes, especially hauling a 21,000-pound rig.

Hood eased out from under the truck and strolled back to his truck.

~~~

The next morning, Sam and Georgia spread their map on the wooden picnic table outside their RV. They came to an agreement and rolled up the map, hooked the pickup to the fifth wheel, and pulled out by 7 a.m.

Hood called Jenson. "They're headed west on I-40 again."

"Can you see them?" Jenson was worried about leaving Hood on his own.

"Shouldn't be hard to keep track of them."

"Get on that road right now," Jenson said, knowing Hood had stopped.

"All right, all right, I'm on my way. You can't lose something that big."

"I'm in Tucumcari. I'll leave in about thirty minutes. Don't lose them."

Nineteen miles later, Sam and Georgia turned off on Highway 84, heading north.

Hood dialed Jenson's number again. "Looks like they're headed to Las Vegas."

"Las Vegas!" Jenson exclaimed.

"Las Vegas, New Mexico," Hood said. "It's north of here, in the mountains. I've taken care of them. It won't be long."

"What are you talking about? What have you done, Hood?"

"Don't get your panties in a wad. I did it right so it would look accidental."

"Tell me what you did."

"I cut the brake line. Well, not all the way. It won't come apart immediately. It will take some miles and some hard braking. Nobody saw me, I swear. It will look like an accident."

Jenson thought a moment. If Hood's scheme worked, this chase would be finished. That would be a good thing. "I believe you. This could save us some time, and we can get back to Texas. I'll catch up to you by the time you get to Las Vegas."

Chapter 16

The bank was silent as a tomb, as empty as Ray had ever seen it. He'd hoped to catch Buddy when the bank was busy so his visit wouldn't encourage eavesdropping. But in a town as small as Waggoner, he supposed it really didn't matter. People would talk no matter what. At least the element of surprise would be in his corner. He walked past the occupied desks in the broad opening to Buddy's office and slipped into the high-backed chair opposite the startled banker.

"Sheriff, uh, you're here again. What do you want?"

"Even sheriffs have banking business, Mr. Gatwick."

"Sure, of course. What can I do for you? It's unusual, but I'm glad to help you. You know that. Do you need a loan? Let me get the girl to bring you an application."

Ray let Buddy prattle on. He could see the other man was anxious. He wanted to know what else was bothering him.

"Have you helped Sam and Georgia?" Ray asked.

Buddy looked away. He swiveled in his chair, stood, and walked to the window. "Helped them with what? I can't discuss people's financial affairs without a court order." Buddy remained facing the window.

Ray could see Buddy was frightened. He decided to push a little harder. "You know what I'm talking about. We've been over this. Sam called and told me all about it. He's concerned."

"He couldn't have told you. He doesn't know his accounts are frozen."

"Why are the accounts frozen?"

"Something with the IRS. That's all I know." Buddy walked back to his desk and sat down hard.

"What else do you know, Buddy?" Ray pressed.

"I can't say anything else. It has nothing to do with you. I'll talk to Sam, and I'll get it straightened out. I have another appointment, Ray." Buddy jumped up and hurried to the door to show Ray out.

"That won't work this time. You tried that before, Buddy." Ray could smell the fear radiating from the little man. What was he hiding?

"I'm under a lot of pressure, Ray."

"Tell me what's going on. I can help you."

"I wish you could, but you can't. Nobody can."

"What does this have to do with Sam and Georgia?"

After a short silence, Buddy said, "I can't tell you. I told you that. I can't tell you." His shoulders sagged.

Ray eased out of his seat and stared at the pitiful man. He

was convinced Buddy was connected to the Bar S crimes. "You can talk to me. Call me."

~~~

Lynnette closed the door to her office before she fished the burner cell from her purse and dialed Buddy Gatwick. He'd given her the Stanfield account numbers. She'd seen to it that deposits and withdrawals had already been processed through their accounts. Buddy had sent a letter to the IRS that had raised red flags for illegal activities. Today he'd call to get the IRS investigators out to the bank.

"This has to be the last time, Lynnette," he answered. "I've done what you wanted. Please, let me alone."

"Don't forget that I'll always have these pictures."

"I can't do this. Someone is going to find out. I don't know how much more I can take."

"Have you said something?"

"No, but the sheriff was in here, and he was asking a lot of questions. I think he knows something."

"Tell me exactly what you told him."

"I only mentioned the IRS. The truth about that will come out anyway. I didn't say anything else, I promise."

"Make sure you're available when I need you. Don't miss a day of work."

"I won't." Buddy hung up and left the bank. He drove out of town. He was going hog hunting.

Around 10 o'clock, Buddy pulled up and parked in a field alongside four other pickups. Wild hogs plagued the surrounding ranch, tearing up crops and eating several bales of hay a night. If the hunters were successful, they'd get rid of some hogs and help the rancher save his feed.

Buddy opened the back door of his new extended cab pickup and retrieved his .30-30 from the back seat. "Hey, Jack," he called to the grizzled rancher leaning against the fence post.

"Let's go set up our hidey-holes and give them hogs a chance to come on out," Jack said, grinning. "I think we'll get a bunch tonight. We got some powerful bait."

"What did you put out?"

"I put some strawberry soda pop on a batch of corn feed. Been lettin' it ferment for a week. They'll come from miles around to get that stuff."

"Which way should I go, Jack?"

"We need to spread out some." He pointed down the fence line. "You head north about a quarter mile, and I'll stay here. We'll be in a straight line so nobody gets shot. The other boys are off down south, and they're already in place. Good luck, now." Jack walked back to his blind and eased in to sit down.

Buddy walked in silence to join the hunt. He started off north and stumbled along in the dark. The .30-30 was heavy on his shoulder as he trekked through the thigh-high grass. A rustling noise startled him, and he pointed his Maglite beam toward the sound.

Nothing. He walked on to his spot and settled down and waited.

After a luckless hour, he decided to walk north a bit farther near some trees. On his way, he had to cross a barbed wire fence, so he placed the rifle butt near the bottom of an ancient cedar fence post and leaned the barrel near the top. Then he set the flashlight down near his feet and pointed the beam at the opposite side to see where to step. Snakes would be out on a night as nice as this. He looked for rattlers.

The fence wires were loose, so he parted the middle strands to cross through. He put his left leg on the other side of the fence and bent at the middle to guide his body through to the other side. He heard a swish and tried to look around to find the sound, but suddenly his rifle barrel jammed under his chin. He looked up in time to see a pair of dark eyes inches from his. Then he heard the rifle explode as the bullet ripped through his chin and out the back of his head.

A half mile away, Jack heard the shot and figured Buddy had already bagged a hog. He waited for thirty minutes, but when Buddy didn't come back to get the buggy to bring the hog in, Jack went to check on him. He followed Buddy's footprints to the barbed wire fence. There, he found Buddy facedown in the grass, one foot tangled in the barbed wire. Buddy's rifle was under his body, and half of his head was scattered in the prairie grass.

Chapter 17

Cox stormed across his Houston penthouse, glaring at a map of the plat where his pipeline should run. He needed that farm. It was perfect for his operation. "We have a family feud, three siblings fighting over their inheritance," Cox said. "At least two of them are ready to sell."

Cox showed James Baxter the elusive piece of land. He needed to blow off steam before he heard the man's report. He could make him wait. He was this lobbyist's most important client, and James had to pander to him. It seemed to Cox that the closer he got to finalizing his Mallard Project, the more his problems grew.

Cox slowed his pace and picked up a red marker to use as a pointer. "See these other three pieces of land?" He scattered dots over the acreage targeted for his pipeline in the Panhandle and in Oklahoma. Bold blue outlines surrounded the dots. He threw the marker across the office.

"Are the sales closing soon?" James asked.

"Not soon enough. I have people bidding on two pieces today. We'll see how we do. I have a state senator for you to talk to. He may come over to our side if the money is right."

"Have we worked with him before?"

Cox walked over to his desk and handed a folder to James. "I don't think you'll have any trouble convincing him after you see the pictures we have."

James glanced through the file. "Indeed, we won't." He sat down and slipped the file into his briefcase.

Cox sat down behind his desk and looked directly at James. "Tell me about the Buddy Gatwick investigation."

"The coroner believes it's an accidental death, a hunting accident. I talked to my contact in the highway patrol, but that's not the official word yet. The Waggoner County sheriff doesn't want to close the case. He's still investigating. Everyone else thinks it was an accident."

"Are we going to have trouble with that sheriff?"

"No, he's just small-town. Nothing to worry about."

"Have you heard from your friend the agriculture commissioner?"

"He doesn't give up much, but he let some information slip. He was visiting Harry Reynolds near Burkburnett, and he ran into a person of interest."

"You know I don't like games. Get on with it, James."

"Of course, Bill. Her name is Georgia Stanfield. She's the other half of that blog couple."

"What was she doing there?"

"Apparently, she's old Harry's niece. They spent some time at his house and filled him in on their crusade for water rights. The husband cornered the commissioner and gave him a firsthand rundown of what happened on their ranch. The commissioner has become a crusader for water rights. This could be hard to fight in Austin if Harry gets involved."

"See that he doesn't."

"I think I can keep it all quiet."

"Does the commissioner know about the auctioned land being contiguous?"

"He doesn't. He grew up in Amarillo, though. He said he was going to talk to some people up there. He might put it all together. Does this change anything about stopping the Stanfields, Bill?"

"Hell no. It doesn't change a thing. I hate that damned SOB Harry. He's always been a thorn in my side. If he gets wind that I'm involved in these ranch and farm takeovers, he'll dig in deeper. The quicker, the better, we get rid of those two. Then Harry won't have a mission."

"Do you still want to bring in the EPA?"

"Yes. Talk to your guy there. See what fines they can make stick. We need to discredit these guys. Cover all the bases. The messages from the meeting made Sam Stanfield a hero. We have to get rid of him."

Cox remembered how Harry had fought him when fracking was new. Harry brought the feds in to inspect his drilling sites. As a result, the railroad commission fined him heavily. With the help of James's father, he'd managed to keep it out of the papers, all because of Harry Reynolds. They had active feuds raging until Harry retired. He still wanted revenge. Harry's niece would be satisfying payback.

James picked up his cell and called his EPA contact. He was on the phone for only a few minutes. "Good news. They've already issued fines of a hundred dollars per cow, per day, against the Stanfields. They're charging them with potential pollution of streams from their gullies and ditches. That will cost them about twenty thousand dollars a day, and they don't even know, since they're traveling in New Mexico."

"Good. Then we can discuss the tank farm on the Gulf. Ask Albert to join us."

James walked to the door and asked the receptionist to show in Albert Martin, Cox's financial adviser.

~~~

Lynnette listened to the intermittent complaining that was Jenson's latest update. She'd found him disgusting at first, but she was beginning to depend upon him. The new player coming in changed everything. The new man could be in the field and direct matters from there, cutting her out. James told her a man named Gonzales had authority to do whatever he deemed best. That was all James would tell her. Gonzales, if that was his real name, answered to someone other than Cox. She figured Cox had either called in a favor or paid for one. The threat was real to her, and she intended to stay out of the way.

"Who is this guy?" Jenson asked. "He sounds like a scary dude."

"He is. He's going to meet you in New Mexico. Then he'll tell you his plans." Lynnette tried to emphasize the danger the unknown man posed. She knew her thugs wouldn't stand a chance if they challenged him. The bits of information she'd gleaned from James hinted that Gonzales came from farther up the chain, even above Cox.

"Who is he?" Jenson pushed.

"I can't tell you. For one reason, I don't know. And you're right, he is dangerous. So, watch yourself. Asking questions will get you killed."

She was apprehensive, and she knew her tone was out of character. She was afraid Jenson recognized the difference in her voice. She wasn't the woman she'd pretended to be the night at the bar. She knew her voice trembled.

"You sound spooked," Jenson said. "Are you ready for what's involved here?"

"I am, and I guess we'll find out." Lynnette was acutely aware of the mistake she'd made. Jenson had heard her fear. He'd pegged her as weak.

"Will you still be my contact?" he asked.

"This will be over soon, and we can get back to our original plan. Just do what this guy says."

"Got it."

Lynnette hoped she'd gotten her point across. If Jenson caused any trouble, they'd blame her. Her good looks wouldn't help at all.

Chapter 18

An early start put Sam and Georgia in Las Vegas by eight o'clock, in time for breakfast at a great little café they knew. The place had a large parking lot where Sam could pull the rig in easily. They sat in a booth and took the time for an extra cup of coffee.

Sam picked up the bill. "Ready?"

Georgia nodded, and they walked together to the cash register at the front of the café.

"Sir, your credit card won't go through. Would you like to try another one?" The young woman was polite and waited for Sam to decide what to do. Georgia slipped some bills into his hands, and he gave her a quick nod.

Back in the truck, Sam said, "Let's call and find out what's happening before we go one more mile. This has been going on for more than a week." Sam dialed Buddy's number, but voice mail picked up. He left a message at his house as well. "No luck. We'll try again later in the day. We'll have to call Ray if we don't get a call back from Buddy."

Georgia watched the traffic as they pulled away from the café. "Did you see that van across the street when we pulled out? I think we've seen that same van before. It looks just like the one parked in the campground at Black Kettle."

"I doubt if it would be the same one from Oklahoma," Sam said, but he kept an eye in his rearview mirror. A blue pickup pulled out, and then the van drove out behind the big RV. All three vehicles began the scenic mountain drive.

"We'll call Ray when we reach Mora," Georgia said. "There should be phone service in the village. I think we should try Buddy again, too."

"Yes, let's talk with them before we go across the mountains to Taos and can't reach anyone."

Less than an hour later, adobe buildings appeared around a curve and framed the quiet community that was the crossroads to the Sangre de Cristo Mountains. A few businesses were open in Mora, and Sam pulled into a gas station to get a cup of coffee and make his calls. He had to pull alongside the building to accommodate the entire rig without sticking out into the street.

Georgia was already getting out of the truck when the van drove by the front of the station. Sam took a good look at it. He was checking out every person who passed by and every vehicle parked around them. He saw a blue pickup in a space in front of the tiny store attached to the gas station. Sam watched the truck, but the driver didn't emerge. Sam felt the need to keep an eye on Georgia when she walked into the convenience store. He saw the man turn his head away from her, tug down the bill of his cap, and look at something in the passenger seat.

By the time Georgia returned with drinks and snacks, Sam was deep in conversation with Ray. "Do you know when the funeral is? How is Beth holding up?"

Georgia whipped around to face Sam. She sucked in her breath. "Whose funeral? What happened?"

"Hold on a minute, Ray. Let me explain to Georgia." Sam caught her up on the news about Buddy's death, then put the cell on speaker so she could hear the rest of the conversation.

Georgia clutched the sack of drinks while she listened to Ray explain what he'd learned from Buddy the day before about the IRS.

"I also made some calls and found out the IRS has frozen your bank accounts. They've taken most of your money. That includes freezing your bank cards."

"Why would the IRS freeze our accounts?" Sam asked. "That doesn't make any sense."

"I'm driving into Fort Worth to talk to the IRS face-to-face," Ray said. "I'll let you know something as soon as I find out."

"We'll come back home so we can straighten this out. We'll drive over to Santa Fe and come back on the interstate. If you can't get in touch with us, it's probably because we don't have any cell service in the mountains. We'll be back in range by tonight, and we'll call when we have service." Sam's mind was racing, and he wanted to get home. Their world was falling apart.

"Do you have enough money? Do you need me to wire you some cash?"

"Yes, that's a good idea. You can go to the ranch and get some money from our safe. Joe will let you in the house. Georgia will text you the combination before we leave Mora. You can wire the money to the nearest Western Union. That may be in Taos. We'll check there first. We have money for a day or so, but you're right, we need to have some cash to replace what we've spent so far."

After Sam hung up, the couple sat in dazed silence for a few moments, trying to make sense of everything. Finally, Sam started the pickup and drove around the small convenience store to the street. He pulled out and headed down the mountain road toward Taos.

Chapter 19

Ray crouched by the cedar post alongside the imprint of Buddy's rifle butt. It was a perfect match. There was no doubt he'd placed the rifle there. But why had he picked it up as he crossed through the fence? It didn't make sense. Ray searched the area himself but found nothing. He shook his head.

If this wasn't an accident, it's going to be hard to prove, he thought. Too many boot prints surrounded the body to tell if anyone else had been there. The hunters had even rolled Buddy's body over to rest him on his side. Everyone assumed it was an accident. Old Jack suggested a hog came up while Buddy was crossing through the fence, and he grabbed his rifle. Ray supposed it was possible, but he didn't feel right about calling the death an accident.

"May I take the body now, Ray?" the coroner asked. "Beth is distraught, and I want to get this autopsy completed as soon as possible. I'll call you as soon as I can confirm the cause of death."

"Go ahead," Ray said. "I have everything I need."

Ray remained at the scene, still puzzling over the details. He wanted to question Beth and the people at the bank. He'd also go by Woody's and check with the folks there. Ray started walking concentric circles where Buddy had fallen, looking for any sign that someone else had been there. He'd reached about thirty yards when he noticed some bent grass near a fallen tree. He walked closer to find the pointed toe of a boot print, barely visible. He took a picture of the print with his phone from different angles. He investigated the rest of the area until it was too dark to see anything, but he only found crushed grass. He had no proof of anything.

It was late Saturday when Ray finally returned to his office. He sat at his desk and looked at the notes and messages Maureen had left. Atop the stack was a message from Frank at the FBI. He'd have to call him first thing in the morning.

Ray glanced over the other papers and pulled out a picture of a man identified as Jefferson Darrell Hood. His DNA matched the blood sample from the Bar S Ranch. Hood was known as J. D. and had spent time at the Wall, the high-security Texas prison in Huntsville. His closest known associate was Nelson Orville Jenson. Jenson was known as Mr. NO at the Huntsville prison. He and Hood had been cellmates.

The next morning, Ray called in his deputies. "We have a hit on the blood sample at the Bar S. Here's a picture of him. His name is J. D. Hood. He has a known associate, his former cellmate." He passed the information to them. "Maureen is calling Huntsville to find out more about this associate, Nelson Orville Jenson. She's getting a picture of him as well."

Ray told one of the deputies to cross-check the footage from the Methodist church video for Hood or Jenson.

"Here are copies of Hood's picture. Start passing them around town this morning. We'll add Jenson when his picture comes in."

Ray dismissed his deputies and left to question Beth Gatwick. Maybe she knew why Buddy had been acting so suspiciously the afternoon before his death. In less than five minutes, he was at Beth's front door.

"I'm sorry for your loss, Mrs. Gatwick."

Beth looked as though she'd drop at any minute, so Ray ushered her to the sofa. She practically fell as she sat down on the edge of the cushion. "Thank you, Sheriff. I've been a little confused and light-headed since . . ." Beth drifted off, gazing through the window, unfocused.

Ray took his time but finally moved to the questions he wanted to ask. "Was there anything that was upsetting Buddy in the past few months?"

Beth began sobbing, and Ray knew something more than Buddy's sudden death was the cause. He gave her time to calm down.

"Sheriff, I don't know where to begin. I need to talk to you before my family gets here." Beth took a deep breath and started sobbing about Buddy and another woman. "He told me there were some terrible things that had happened to him. He wouldn't tell me what they were. I do know he was scared."

"Do you know who the woman is, Beth?"

She shook her head wildly. "I don't know who it was."

"Why do you think he was scared, Beth?"

She sat on the sofa silently crying and shaking her head. She shrugged her shoulders. "I wish I knew, Sheriff."

~~~

The next day, Ray combined his investigation with lunch at Woody's Café. After he'd finished eating, he headed toward the back to speak with the owner. "JoAnn, I have a question about some customers." He smiled and nodded to the other ladies cooking in the tiny kitchen.

JoAnn picked up a cup towel as she walked around the stove, wiping her hands on the way. "Sure. You know I'll always have an answer for you, Sheriff. It may not be the one you want, but I'll do the best I can."

"Have you seen either of these two fellows in here?" Ray held up pictures of Hood and Jenson for JoAnn to inspect.

"I'd like to help you, but I don't recognize them. I'm always back in the kitchen, though. Marcie would be the one to ask, since she's at the counter and cash register most of the time." JoAnn called Marcie back to look at the photographs and then excused herself to get back to cooking.

"Hello, Sheriff," Marcie said, smiling and taking the pictures from him. Ray figured she already knew why he was there. He'd been all over town already that day, showing the pictures to everyone. Word spreads fast in a small town.

"Have you seen these men, Marcie?"

"This one I haven't seen, but this one I have." She identified Jenson without hesitation. She described his size and her surprise at his height compared to the enormous bulk of his shoulders and arms. "He wasn't very friendly, but he sat at the counter so I got a good look at him."

"Thanks, Marcie. If you see him again, call the office immediately. I'll leave you both pictures. Pass the word to the others."

"What have they done? Are they criminals?" Marcie stared at the photos.

"Nothing you need to worry about. We just want to talk to them. That's all. Thanks for your help, Marcie."

~~~

Ray walked inside the Oak National Bank. He needed to interview the employees and search Buddy's office before the bank closed for the visitation at the funeral home that afternoon.

"Hello, Sheriff," Buddy's secretary said. "What can we help you with?"

"Hello, Dena. I came to look around Buddy's office. Open it up for me." Ray knew he could get in without any trouble, but he always took a positive, assertive approach, which got most folks to do what he wanted. Dena was no exception. She opened the vacant office and left him to look over things uninterrupted. Ray noted the atmosphere in the bank was livelier than usual, but he had found people were more animated when a death interfered with their daily routines. People were relieved to be alive. Some also were struggling with their guilt over not liking Buddy in the first place, Ray was sure.

Ray searched the credenza behind the desk but found nothing. The drawers were almost empty. He wondered if Buddy had cleared it out recently. The desk was messy, with papers stacked in several piles. Ray sat in the desk chair and cranked it up as high as it would go to match his long legs, only to smash his kneecap when he moved closer to the papers.

Ray meticulously reviewed each stack. The only interesting thing he found was a scribbled note that read, *Sam and Georgia Stanfield*. Ray thought it could have been a doodle during a phone call, or a reminder to do something. Next, he moved on to Buddy's desk drawers. All seemed to hold normal office supplies. The last one was locked, but it took only a second to find the key in Buddy's container of paper clips.

Not very creative, Buddy, Ray thought.

He inserted the key and opened the door without much hope. Inside was only a blue-and-red FedEx envelope. Ray tugged on it to get it loose, finally wrenching it free. He noticed one end was burned black and brown—a failed attempt to destroy it, Ray thought. He pulled out the two photos inside and stared.

Dena opened the door and stuck her head in. "Want some coffee, Sheriff? I made a fresh pot."

Ray scrambled to cover the images. "No thanks, Dena, but

do you have some big manila envelopes? I have some personal effects of Buddy's that I want to take."

"Sure thing." Dena scurried off and in a few seconds returned with two large envelopes.

"Thanks. I'll let you know if I need anything else." Ray waited for Dena to leave before he slid the scorched FedEx envelope inside the manila one. He'd wait for the privacy of his office before he looked at the photographs again.

Chapter 20

Sam shifted into a lower gear to slow the big rig on the sharp mountain curves. The terrain began to change immediately after Mora. Although the road was good, Sam had to concentrate on his driving as he negotiated the curves and steep inclines.

Even with the driving challenges, he couldn't help thinking about the trouble with the IRS. He knew there was nothing to it. He needed to know what evidence they had that was strong enough to freeze their accounts and take their money.

"I wish we could enjoy this drive without that IRS problem hanging over our heads," Georgia said.

"I was just thinking that very thing. I'll be glad to get to Taos so we can call and find out more."

Georgia nodded, then turned her head to stare into the side mirror. "Sam, that blue pickup from the convenience store is behind us. He must have left at the same time we did."

"He must be too close. I can't see him now." Sam watched the large side mirrors, which normally allowed him to see traffic behind the trailer. Some vehicles did, however, follow too closely, and he couldn't see them.

Georgia leaned out the window. "He's coming up closer. He wants to pass you on the right-hand side! There's no shoulder! I can't believe he's trying to pass."

Sam watched the pickup barreling along beside the RV on the edge of the mountain. Then Sam spotted an oncoming car. He had no place to go. "Brace yourself. I think he's trying to run us off the road."

They were barely moving up the mountain, but Sam could see the summit, and soon they'd be heading down the other side. The danger would be worse. The oncoming car passed as they reached the peak and headed down. Sam could see that the road ahead was empty.

"Sam, there's a turnout. Can you get over?"

"He's blocked access, and I can't outrun him." Sam saw the blue pickup move up beside the fifth wheel gooseneck. The man could maneuver the pickup more easily than the monster Sam was wrestling.

"He's trying to kill us!" Georgia shouted.

"There's a road off to the left. I'm taking it. I don't know how long these brakes will hold. Maybe I can stop on that road." Sam was already riding his brakes hard, trying to slow down.

"He's coming up the right shoulder."

"I see him." Sam gripped the steering wheel and gradually turned the lumbering RV. It screeched across the highway and tore down the gravel side road.

"He's coming with us!"

Sam smashed the rig left when the blue pickup slammed into them. Georgia screamed, and Sam tried to keep control. "What's he doing now?"

"He's coming up again." Georgia instinctively held on to the door. The blows from the smaller blue truck kept striking just below her window. Sam straightened the rig and kept it from jackknifing as he completed the turn. Georgia looked around frantically to find the blue pickup and spotted it directly behind them.

"I'm pulling over before we get killed." Sam stepped on the brakes. A loud pop came from underneath the truck, and nothing happened. Sam pumped the brakes. Still nothing. He felt sick in the pit of his stomach when he realized what had happened. The truck and RV began to pick up speed. Sam pumped harder on the brakes. He looked over at Georgia. She understood. He tried to guide the truck to the middle of the road and downshift the gears. He reached over and pulled on the emergency brake. The rig began to shift down slightly, but it didn't hold for long.

The road was a switchback, and Sam was making the first turn when the back end of the RV swung out, hanging over the edge of the mountain road. Sam held the wheels straight and began to pull the RV back onto the road. Then the gravel under the front tires made the entire rig slide sideways.

Sam lost control, and the couple heard a loud crack as the truck broke through the barriers on the edge of the road. The giant rig jerked forward and plunged down the side of the mountain.

The jackknifed rig was an arrowhead, pointing downward. The vehicles banged into tree limbs that cracked the windshield and poked the rig like a pincushion. The crashing finally halted, and the truck emerged from the pine forest onto a small clearing covered with loose rock. The RV rotated and passed the truck on its downward race. Then the rig banged into a pine stump that sent Gracie flying through the broken window. She hit a small spruce and began to slide down with the surrounding debris.

The sudden change in direction twisted the RV so the entire rig moved as one large piece of metal. Smaller trees popped and slapped the truck as it continued to slide another hundred feet, stopping at the edge of a cliff. There, the mangled pieces of metal lay trapped between evergreens that grew near the edge of a sheer, thousand-foot drop-off. The sounds of the wreck continued to reverberate across the mountainside. The dust finally settled, and quiet returned.

The man from the blue pickup stood above the wreckage, smiling at his handiwork. He watched for a long time for any sign of life. Jenson walked up beside Hood and looked down at the path the rig had taken.

"If they're not dead, they soon will be, especially if no one finds them," Jenson said. "Help me roll these rocks over."

"I see what you're doing. You want to cover this up and make sure they won't be found." Hood grinned and put his back into getting some large boulders pushed up on the side of the road to camouflage the broken barriers.

"It's getting dark. We can come back tomorrow and wipe out any tracks that you can see from the road. Let's get out of here for now."

Hood grunted acknowledgement and headed for the pickup.

"Before we leave, I want you to know something," Jenson said. "We now report to a man named Gonzales in Santa Fe."

"No more Lynnette?"

"For now, anyway. Follow me. I know the place where we're supposed to meet." Jenson climbed into the van and turned toward Santa Fe.

Hood followed in the blue pickup, its left side now showing deep dents its entire length.

Chapter 21

The phone call interrupted Lynnette at work. She didn't like to mix her two lives, but it was inevitable at times. She closed her door and then picked up. From the thirtieth floor, Lynnette could feel the Dallas high-rise sway slightly in the strong southern wind. She clutched the edge of the desk to steady herself.

"Are you positive they're dead?" James Baxter asked.

Lynnette hoped no one was listening. Her assistant hadn't eavesdropped before, but there was always a first time. Lynnette knew it would be a miracle if the Stanfields had survived. After all, they were both at least sixty years old. But she also knew James would want visuals of the bodies and positive identifications.

"Gonzales will have to take care of the details. I can relay a message to Jenson, but Gonzales should be talking to him directly by now. There are too many layers for me to know firsthand. You know that." Lynnette was impatient to get off the phone, a first for her when speaking with James.

"Of course, but how are you going to manage this? Can you

handle the pressure? You seem edgy."

"That's because we're on my office phone." Lynnette stood behind her desk. Her feet steadied. She was aware she was posturing for conflict. She wasn't going to let the prod from James distract her. She was in too deep to back down. There was too much at stake. She formed her answer carefully. "You know I can handle this, James. I've done this dozens of times. Just let me get on with it."

"Before you call anyone, wait for me to get back to you."

"You have to check in with your boss?" Lynnette wanted to goad James, but she didn't push too far.

"I do. He's the one who pays us. Don't forget that."

"When can I meet him? I think I've proven myself."

"That's for him to say."

~~~

Lynnette buried herself in research at her law firm. That was what she did best. Not the least was a thick file on the man himself, Bill Cox, James's boss. She wanted to know all she could.

She opened the file and spread its contents across her desk. Cox had started as a roughneck, then purchased a drilling company and began to really make money. Lynnette had uncovered several shady deals Cox was involved in, but nothing ever stuck except for some federal fines, which he easily paid off.

She lined up pictures of his four wives and studied their bios. Sherry was the first, but their marriage only lasted a few months. The next was more strategic. Cox had targeted Janet, a rich girl from

Tyler whose daddy was in the oil business. Cox's association with her family opened many industry doors for the ambitious young man. Unfortunately, she died of breast cancer after four years of marriage. She left Cox with a daughter, Marcia. Lynnette had done some digging and found Marcia lived in Europe. She hadn't spoken to her father in twenty years.

The third wife, Patti, was an attorney in Houston. After three years, they'd mutually called it quits. Cox's last wife wasn't much different from Patti, except he'd been much older when he married her. It hadn't taken him long to get rid of her, either.

Not a good track record with women, Lynnette wrote in the margin of the newspaper article. A lesson she'd remember.

Lynnette dug into Cox's financials, and one name kept popping up—Albert Martin. He and Cox had worked together since 1973, when the United States had gone into a panic after OPEC countries manipulated their oil production to control world oil prices. Oil prices had quadrupled. That was when Cox and Albert Martin had hooked up. Cox's oil profits allowed him to diversify, and Albert's financial genius made them both wildly successful, super rich in fact.

Lynnette wanted to know what Cox's latest project was. She knew that at least two people had the details—Cox and Albert Martin. James had to know something, but she hadn't been able to get at it. She thought that if she could get a face-to-face with Cox then she'd learn something. She knew James had been making a lot of trips to Washington DC. She had to learn more about that, too.

~~~

Cox paced the length of his luxury penthouse, considering strategies to move his project forward. He'd named it the Mallard Project after the beautiful green-headed duck, a common water bird, and the first bird he'd known as a boy. A family of mallards had lived on the pond in his backyard in East Texas. Every year the mallard pair raised a family, and he'd watched them with great interest. That was, until his family had moved to West Texas. There he only had sand and mesquite trees behind his house.

Cox smiled. That move to the Permian Basin oil patch had opened doors for him. He grew up thinking oil was the avenue to wealth, black gold. And no doubt, it had made him a rich man. But the Mallard Project would make him the most powerful man in the world. He just had to eliminate the last few obstacles.

"Mr. Cox, James Baxter is here to see you." James had followed the assistant into the office and stood behind her.

Cox waved her away. "What do you have for me this afternoon, Jimmy?"

"Good afternoon, Bill. I have good news for you. The Stanfields have been killed in a highway accident."

Cox pointed to a small circle of chairs. "Let's sit and talk."

"Lynnette told me about the accident. One of her guys called her. Jenson, I think. Gonzales may not even be necessary. She's told them to get a photograph of the bodies for confirmation."

"What happened?"

"The brakes went out, and they went down the side of a mountain. They may not even be found for a while. I understand it's a remote area."

"Let me know when you have confirmation."

"Sure." James paused for a moment. "Bill, I think we have a problem with Sandra in DC." James squirmed in his chair and shifted positions.

"What makes you say that?"

"Mainly, it's her attitude. In the beginning, she was eager, but the last time I saw her, she was flippant and sarcastic. I think we'd better watch her."

"Your girlfriend has always been eager to help out. Why don't you let Lynnette take your place? You need to back away anyway. If Sandra gets nervous, Lynnette can take the blame. We can take over the other country contacts from here. You know the names, and you're a better negotiator. Let's cut out the middleman."

"All right, I'll talk to her tonight. You're right that she's been wanting a chance to do more."

"Should she come to the ranch to see you?" James knew this was part of the vetting, a tradition that Cox savored.

"You bet. I wouldn't miss having her on my home turf."

Chapter 22

The wreckage was a giant pendulum, balancing atop the sheer cliff. The mangled steel cocoon creaked and rocked the bodies inside.

Sam forced himself to remain motionless until he could think clearly and understand their situation. The cab was on its side, and Sam was hanging by his seat belt.

"Sam, Sam. Are you hurt? Please say something, Sam." Georgia's door was digging into her side, and she could see Sam above her.

"Don't move, Georgia. Don't move. I'm okay. This truck is about to go over the edge." Blood covered half of Sam's face, and he began to feel it trickle down his neck. He checked his head and found the cause, a deep gash near his ear. The truck screeched and shuddered sideways.

"Take it easy, Sam." Tears trickled down Georgia's cheeks.

"It's just a cut on my head. It's not too deep."

"Check over the rest of your body, if you can. We may not feel anything right now. We're in shock. Make your movements slow."

"My knee hurts, and my left wrist may be sprained."

Georgia rubbed her leg, and her hand returned covered with blood. "There's a gash on my calf, but I think it will stop bleeding on its own. I'm sure I have some cracked ribs. Let me look at that cut on your head."

"My head doesn't seem to hurt, but my knee sure does." Sam leaned slightly toward Georgia. His seat belt was cutting into his hip. Georgia's door was on the ground. Dirt and pine tree limbs protruded through her broken window. She checked the cut on Sam's head and found a large knot. The bleeding had stopped.

"There's a first aid kit in the glove compartment, if it isn't jammed shut." Sam slowly turned his head to look at the cab. The damage to the truck and trailer shocked him to the core. He didn't know how they were alive.

"I can get to it. I have to move over a little." When Georgia moved, the whole rig began to shake and screech.

"Stop, Georgia! We have to get out of here!"

As Sam frantically looked around, the rocking eased for the second time, and the truck felt more secure in its perch.

The glove box had popped open in the shake-up, and the first aid kit fell into Georgia's lap. She applied a small amount of antiseptic to Sam's wound and her leg.

"That's about all I can do for now," Georgia said. "I can't do anything for my ribs. I'll have to wait until after we get out."

"It's enough for now," Sam said. "Our only chance to escape

is from my side. Can you move at all? If I release my seat belt, I'll fall on you. It will be too hard to open the door, but there's no glass in the window. We could get out that way."

"What's on the other side, Sam? It's getting dark, and we need to know that before we try this."

Sam pulled himself toward his door and looked out to discover the evening sky. He could see that the fifth wheel was anchoring them for now.

"It looks like we'll have to climb over the top of the roof or the windshield. We're hanging over a cliff."

"I'm ready."

Sam twisted to get his legs out from under the steering wheel. He bent his knees and pushed up through the window. When he did, the fifth wheel began to move, taking the truck with it. The force of the movement threw Sam back into the truck and over on Georgia. The cab of the truck slid forward and light came through Georgia's window. Below them was a narrow ledge, three feet below the cab. With Sam's weight bearing down on Georgia, she fell halfway through the window and hung from her waist.

"I'm going to push my weight off you, and then you drop to the ledge below," Sam said. He put one hand on the doorframe and pushed his weight back, and Georgia fell to the ground. Sam curled up as much as possible, squeezed through the open window, and followed Georgia to the ledge.

They clung to each other and sat horrified as the entire rig eased over the rocky overhang and fell into the canyon below. They were shaken and breathing hard but managed to move back against the inner wall of the stony shelf. They looked out across the New Mexico landscape into the fiery sunset. They sat there breathing in the night air, waiting for feeling to come back and the shock to wear off.

"Doesn't seem as though we've disturbed the world very much," Georgia whispered.

"Rather calming, isn't it?" Sam moved to straighten his leg, and he saw that Georgia had her arms wrapped around her rib cage.

"Oh, my heavens!" Georgia said. "Where's Gracie?"

"She must have been thrown out on the way down."

"I don't even remember the windows breaking, I was so terrified." Georgia began to cry. "I don't want to think about what happened to our Gracie."

"We survived. Maybe she did, too, and she's looking for us." Sam tried to be comforting.

"I hope you're right. I hope you're right."

"It's almost dark. Let's see if we can get off this little piece of dirt. We can't stay here. I'd be afraid we'd fall off in the night."

He stood and inched his way to a spot where he could get solid footing with his one good leg. He climbed over the edge several feet beyond where the wreckage had fallen over the cliff.

Georgia followed, and they stood at the edge of the cliff, looking at what might have been their death sentence. When they began their trek up the mountain, they realized the trailer had cracked open on the way down and left a trail of debris behind them. Supplies and equipment lay scattered over the mountainside. They searched for any provisions that could help them.

"I found a blanket and my backpack. Be careful where you're walking, it's a dark moon tonight." Sam pulled a flashlight from the backpack and hurried to find as much as he could before it was completely dark. His knee was beginning to throb, but he tried to ignore it while he searched for anything to help them survive the night.

"I found my jacket and the big first aid kit," Georgia said. "But there's not much left in it. Not much food around here, either."

"We need to find the sleeping bags."

"I'll keep looking."

Sam had a nice fire going by the time Georgia returned. She'd found one sleeping bag and a box of cereal.

"Roll up your pant leg, Sam, so I can see what's happened to your leg."

"I think my knee jammed into the steering column."

"You have a bad bruise, and the skin has been scraped off your kneecap. No wonder it was hurting. How's it feeling now?"

"It's not too bad. It will be stiff in the morning, though. We can go for help then."

Sam had built the fire inside a thick copse of trees. The low branches protected them and the small fire from the relentless wind.

The backpack proved to be a real boon. Sam had filled it with the essentials for a safe hike. He put the items on the ground.

"We have a compass, another small first aid kit, a map, two water bottles, four protein bars, and my ever-trusty roll of duct tape. I'd say we were very fortunate." Sam checked the side pockets of the backpack and found a Swiss army knife and some water purification tablets. "Thank goodness."

"We're blessed for sure. No doubt someone up there was watching over us. Anyone who saw that wreck would think we were dead." Georgia took a gauze roll from the kit and, with Sam's help, wrapped her ribs and secured it with the duct tape.

"Let's have some cereal and water tonight," Sam suggested. "We can save the protein bars for tomorrow."

Georgia opened the box of mini wheats, grabbed a handful, and passed the box to Sam. Sam passed one of the water bottles to Georgia, and they crunched away on the dry cereal.

Georgia gathered pine needles to cushion the sleeping pad and for insulation from the cold ground. Sam filled in openings between the brush and trees with branches to protect them from the wind.

"I'll unzip this sleeping bag, and we can both lie down on it and cover up with the blanket. You sleep next to the fire, Sam, since I have my jacket to wear."

"I need to keep this fire going through the night. I'm afraid the temperature could drop into the thirties at this altitude."

They gathered enough wood for the night.

"Let's get settled in," Sam said. "The temperature is dropping, and we need to use our body heat to keep each other warm."

Georgia nodded and pulled her hood over her head and lay down. Even with the pine needles for a mattress, the cold penetrated immediately. But the familiarity of two bodies melting into one another was comforting, and soon stress and exhaustion gave way to fitful sleep for them both.

Chapter 23

At midnight, Jenson and Hood rolled to a stop in the parking lot of the motel in Santa Fe where Gonzales was staying. The door to his room silently opened before they could knock.

At first, Jenson let Hood talk so he could watch Gonzales. Jenson studied his new boss while Hood bragged about the cut brake line and how he'd run the Stanfields off the road.

"That's enough." Jenson shut Hood down and told Gonzales everything he knew. Gonzales studied every word he said. Jenson gave the newcomer all the information he needed.

Gonzales finally nodded. "We only have two hours before we must leave here. One of you sleep on the floor." Before Jenson could object, Gonzales sat on the bed fully dressed, leaned against a stack of pillows and was instantly asleep.

Jenson tossed Hood a pillow and a blanket from the closet. He was spending the two hours on the sofa. When he sat down, he wasn't sure the sofa was any better than the floor where Hood was already sleeping.

Two hours later, Gonzales was awake and ready to go. "Get up." Gonzales kicked Hood in the side, picked up his backpack and was out the door.

"What the . . . ?" Hood rolled over and raised to all fours to try to stand. He rubbed his eyes and found Jenson standing in the bathroom doorway.

"Come on. You don't want to piss him off." Jenson followed Gonzales outside.

"What time is it, anyway?" Hood stumbled out of the room to catch up.

Gonzales was standing next to a black Suburban. "Drive the pickup to a grocery store parking lot and leave it there. Both of you ride in the van to the site. Paint transferred to and from the pickup and the vehicle you ran off the road. You must get rid of it. Meet me back here in ten minutes." He abruptly climbed into the front seat of the Suburban and shut the door.

Jenson and Hood followed their orders and made it back in their allotted time. Jenson pulled into the motel parking lot and coasted out the other exit without stopping. The headlights of the black SUV behind them blinded Jenson the entire trip. He was edgy and regretted his involvement in the whole thing by the time they reached the site of the accident. The two vehicles pulled over to the side of the road where Jenson and Hood had positioned the rocks the previous night.

Gonzales spat out orders. "Smooth out the tracks around

these rocks and search this entire area. I see debris from the rig as it went down. Get it all."

Jenson and Hood began shoving the rocks back enough to smooth out any trace of tracks on the edge of the road. They were inching down the side of the mountain when Gonzales spoke again. He was looking at the path the RV had cut to the edge of the cliff.

"I can't see the truck or the RV down this slope. Are you sure we're in the right place?"

"Of course we're sure!" Hood answered, bristling. "I watched it go all the way and stop before it went over the cliff."

Jenson elbowed him. "Shut up." He knew Hood was steaming. Hood pulled back, and Jenson understood that he could control him for only so long. Gonzales was ruthless, and Jenson respected his skill. Their only possible advantage over Gonzales was that he might underestimate them. Jenson wanted him to see them as inferiors.

"Looks like it's gone over the cliff," Hood said. "There's nothing there now."

"Come on, Hood, let's walk down and see what happened." Jenson took Hood's arm and shoved him toward the swath the wreck had made. After they'd walked a reasonable distance, Jenson turned on him. "Are you crazy? I saved your ass back there. Now get on down the mountain before you and I are the ones going over that cliff."

Hood glared but tromped down the wooded incline toward

the wreckage. He slipped on the loose rocks and tumbled until he reached the forested area. "You go first now!" he screamed. "I'm tired of this!"

Jenson picked up a duffel bag full of clothes and kicked the pieces of a broken camp stove. As he looked around, he knew they'd have to spend a lot of time clearing all the evidence.

Jenson took the lead as they continued and was the first to look over the edge and spot the wrecked RV at the bottom of the canyon. "That takes care of that. There's no way anyone could live through that. They've both got to be dead. Let's go tell Gonzales so we can ease his pain." Jenson was relieved. Now they could go back to Texas and not have to see Gonzales again.

"Oh, he'll find something wrong," Hood snarled. "He didn't even appreciate the fact that I ruined those brakes, or that I was able to push them off the road."

"Don't tell Gonzales that," Jenson warned. "He likes killing better than you do, and he'd just as soon gut you like a fish and leave you to suffer."

"I get it. I'll be okay by the time we get back up the mountain."

The men hiked back up, and Jenson approached Gonzales.

"They went over the edge, and it will be a long time before anyone discovers that wreckage."

Gonzales frowned. "I need to find a way to get down there. I've got to have proof that those bodies are at the bottom of the canyon."

"That's impossible," Hood said.

Gonzales ignored Hood and addressed Jenson directly. "After you get rid of everything from the wreck, take the van back to Mora and wait for me there. Don't contact anyone."

Reluctantly, Jenson and Hood began to trek back down while Gonzales made a call. Jenson heard him say that he could verify the death of the Stanfields. He wondered who Gonzales was talking to. He knew it wasn't Lynnette—she was out of the loop for this deal. Besides, he'd already told her about the wreck.

Jenson watched Gonzales finish the call and drive away in the opposite direction. Then he caught up to Hood and they began chucking the remains of the accident over the cliff. They didn't go too far afield in their search, and thus overlooked several pieces.

"Man, I'm ready to go," Hood complained as he picked up the last piece in sight and looked at his watch. It was noon. "I'm hungry."

"I think we're done here. Let's go," Jenson agreed, and they made their last trip up the mountain, climbed into the van, and headed back up the gravel road. They hadn't gone a hundred yards when Jenson threw on the brakes and slid to a stop, inches short of hitting something in the road. "Damn! What is that?"

"Hold on. I'll look." Hood jumped out of the van and ran around to the front.

There in the road sat Gracie, staring up at him with her gray eyes.

"Well, I'll be. How did you live through that? It's their dog. She must have been thrown out or jumped out before the truck went over the cliff." Hood bent down, and Gracie licked his hand.

"Is it dead?" Jenson yelled from the van.

"No, I think she's all right." Hood felt along Gracie's sides and checked her legs. She had blood on the side of her jaw from a tear on her left ear where the blood had already begun to congeal.

"You better put her in the back. We don't want anyone else to find her."

Hood picked Gracie up and set her down in the back of the van. She never whimpered and didn't bark. "She sure is a quiet dog. Most dogs bark all the time."

"Hurry up and get in. Let's stop in Mora and get some real food. We'll figure out what to do with the dog later."

~~~

Gonzales descended into the canyon along a park road and pulled into a hiking trailhead. He left the marked trail and walked through the brush toward the cliff and the crash site. An hour later, he found the wreckage. He climbed over a large boulder and stepped carefully on the hood of the truck to take pictures. There was blood and remnants of first aid supplies scattered around the cab.

There were no bodies. The Stanfields had survived.

"What is it?" Jenson answered his phone. He was in the middle of eating tamales and beans. The food was good, and they had a plan to get rid of the dog. He was irritated that the partnership with Gonzales wasn't finished.

"Get back to the site and keep an eye out for the Stanfields. There were no bodies in the truck, and it looks like they escaped before it went over the cliff."

"They couldn't have!"

"Do what I told you. I'll meet you there."

"We're on our way." After Jenson hung up, he quickly explained the situation to Hood. They gobbled their food and drove back down the mountain road again. They had tied Gracie to a post behind the café and left her there.

Jenson parked the van nose-to-nose with the SUV and got out to talk to Gonzales. Hood waited in the van. Jenson thought it was safer that way.

Gonzales stood silently for a while even after Jenson approached. "I found their tracks and where they spent the night," he finally said. "They both appear to be injured, and they're headed toward the road, obviously to get help. Let's hope they haven't already found a ride. You and Hood patrol the road from here back to the highway, then check the road east and west. You know what to do if you see them."

Jenson nodded. "Are you going to track them?"

"Yes. It will be better if I find them here in the forest. There are many ways to die in the wilderness."

Jenson pulled a sharp U-turn, and the partners began searching the road.

"We can look all night, but we have to get back and get that dog," Hood said. "We can't leave her in Mora. Someone will find her, and they'll remember us."

Jenson knew he should have just shot the damn dog. He was a fool to have let Hood keep it. Finally, he turned east onto the highway toward Mora.

Fortunately, Gracie was where they'd left her. Customers commonly left their dogs outside the café, and Gracie was keeping company with a hound when they pulled up. Hood jumped out of the van and loaded Gracie. Jenson turned the van around, and the two men continued their search on both sides of the road. They covered the area several times but found no trace of Sam or Georgia.

Chapter 24

The flames were gone, along with the heat, when Georgia shivered awake. "Sam, we have to get the fire started again," she whispered through chattering teeth.

"Let me see if I can move," Sam inched closer to the fire pit and dropped a handful of pine needles into the smoldering fire. A scattering of live coals flickered under the ashes. The dry forest kindling flamed quickly and gave them light.

Sam discovered that he wasn't as sore as he'd feared, so he straightened out, stretched his limbs, and took in the dim surroundings. Georgia and Sam stood together with their arms wrapped around each other. They didn't speak and remained motionless, listening to the sounds of the forest. The wind continued to sigh in the pine boughs and disguise softer noises. The fire popped and crackled. The glow was comforting. Birds were beginning to move about with the approach of daylight. Everything seemed calm and natural.

"Sam, that man in the blue pickup intended to run us off the road. Why would he do that?"

"There's no doubt what he was trying to do. Someone wants us out of the way. The ranch, and now this wreck. It's not a coincidence. Right now, they think we're in that wreckage that went over the cliff. They have to think we're dead."

Georgia shivered, though not from the cold this time. "It's truly a miracle we survived."

"At first light, we'll climb up the mountain and get help."

"I'm still freezing. Maybe walking around will warm me up. I can't do much with these broken ribs, though."

While Georgia ambled around nearby, Sam rolled up the sleeping bag with the blanket inside. He hoped they wouldn't have to sleep on the ground again. He expected they'd be able to walk up to the road and get help.

Georgia wasn't gone long before she eased back through the opening in the trees. "Look what I found." She dropped four more bottles of water beside Sam. "There are a few more bottles out there, but I couldn't carry any more. I can go back in a bit. That must have been from that case of water we had stored underneath the RV. Now we can drink a whole bottle and have a protein bar." She handed him the water and sat on the log Sam had pulled near the fire.

"Georgia, we need to talk about the possibilities of who that might have been."

"I know. I'm positive the man in the pickup is the same one I saw in the van at Black Kettle. I know he was in a pickup yesterday, but it was him."

"That means he's been following us for a while. The connection is the blog and the controversy it's causing. You've seen the threats, and several people have said they'd kill us, but I never took them seriously." Sam rubbed his brow, thinking, and winced when he touched the cut on his forehead. "We need to get out of here and contact the police."

"I'll pack what we need to get us to the road."

"It's getting lighter. I want to get those other bottles of water." Sam exited through the small opening in the evergreens and made his way toward the accident debris. He didn't find the water but did pick up three cans of tuna.

He was still foraging when he heard two vehicles drive up and stop at the top of the mountain. Sam started walking toward them but then recognized the man from the blue truck. Sam quickly eased back into the brush. He could see there were three men now.

Sam hurried back to camp. "Georgia, the man in the blue truck has come back, and he has two others with him." He was out of breath from the high altitude.

"Where are they now?"

"On the road where we went over the edge. They're coming down here."

Before Sam could finish, they heard voices. Two of the men were approaching their campsite. Sam and Georgia moved back into the shadows of the trees, against the backpack and the bedroll. Sam had extinguished the fire earlier so there was no smoke, but they could be found easily enough, if the men looked their way or followed the footprints from the ledge. Sam and Georgia didn't move and hardly took a breath. The men were so close that the terrified couple heard every word spoken.

"Man, look at that," Hood said as he leaned over the edge, staring at the wreck. "It's like a toy smashed with a hammer. Nobody could survive that. They're dead, and I made it look like an accident. You should've seen it when the brakes went out. No chance then. Straight down the mountain."

"If you hadn't done it, Gonzales would have. They'd be dead, one way or another."

Sam and Georgia watched as the men searched for wreckage and threw it over the cliff. They weren't there long before they climbed back up the mountain and disappeared in their van. Sam noticed the men had missed several things.

"Are they really gone?" Georgia whispered.

"I think so. Stay here. I'll check." Before Georgia could protest, Sam had slipped out of their camp to look around. He came back in a rush. "They drove off in different directions. There's one man by himself, and he's gone below to find our bodies. We don't have long before he'll be back. We have to get out of here. If that Gonzales they mentioned is as dangerous as we think, he'll come back here and easily find us."

"Let's go, then."

Georgia and Sam exchanged a meaningful glance and quickly grabbed their belongings.

"Georgia, I've made a strap on the bedroll for you to carry. It's much lighter than the backpack, and maybe it won't hurt your ribs."

"I can manage that."

"We must be careful when we approach the road because we don't know where they may be waiting."

Sam and Georgia prepared to leave, both limping as they walked through the trees. After they picked their way across the rock slide, Sam and Georgia hiked parallel to the forest road. They kept looking for a safe way to get to the road and check for any travelers. Sam picked up a straight limb that would suffice for a walking stick. He handed it to Georgia.

"Thank you, sweetheart. Look for another one for yourself."

The lack of oxygen at that altitude was taking its toll on Georgia. She gasped for breath in shallow gulps, trying to avoid the pain in her ribs. She stopped every few steps. They both knew how slow their progress was, but it couldn't be helped.

"Here's a place to rest for a moment." Sam sat on a flat-topped stone and rolled up his pant leg. The wound had begun to bleed again, but only a little. Georgia applied another bandage, then they moved on.

"Take the walking stick for a while and use it to help put less pressure on your leg. It hurts my ribs. I can't pull up with my arms, either. I'm using my legs mostly, and I'm getting shaky. The aftermath of the wreck must be setting in."

"Wait here and let me check out the path before you try it." Sam was reluctant to leave Georgia, but he took the pole and started up an animal trail that he hoped led to the road.

Sam quickly returned. Small stones rattled down the trail ahead of him as he maneuvered through the low-growing scrub oak. "There's plenty of cover by the road, and we can wait there out of sight. You go first, Georgia, and I'll come behind you so you won't slide backward." Sam placed the palm of his hand in the small of Georgia's back to steady her, and they inched their way to the top. The climb was hard for both of them, but they made it. Then Sam found a brushy hiding place where they could see in both directions down the road. They sat back-to-back on a fallen log, leaning on one another.

They'd been there for an hour when the pale van came crawling down the road. It rolled slowly by, making Sam and Georgia feel as though the two men inside were looking right at them. Instinctively they crouched down, but the van moved on without incident.

"I think they've discovered we're not down in the canyon with the truck. They're looking for us, and we can't chance going on the road now." Sam was whispering even though the van had moved on.

"They'll find our tracks and eventually come this way. We can't wait here, either." Georgia was whispering, too.

Chapter 25

Bill Cox measured the depth of the water in the thirty-year-old cistern on his South Texas ranch. Most people wouldn't recognize him in his work clothes. He looked like any regular ranch hand, a bit grizzled and red-faced in the heat.

The water level was the lowest reading he'd ever seen, and he didn't know whether to celebrate or swear. He was okay with the drought striking a blow to other ranchers, but not to him, even if it did serve his purpose. The temperature nudged 100 by midmorning and would be pushing 110 by afternoon. Sweat crawled across his scalp and ran down his neck. He decided to go back to the ranch house and cool down.

Cox strode down the narrow cow trail and stood for a moment under a live oak, wiping his head with his bandana. The scorching day would have his cattle crowding under any available shade, just as he was now. He wished he were as resilient as they were. He couldn't stand this heat.

Cox walked on and climbed inside his Jeep. The high winds made him drive with one hand and hold his salt-stained Stetson with the other. He raced back to the ranch house and slid to a stop on the gravel driveway. James and Al were standing on the front porch, waiting for him.

"You should have been out there, James. You'd appreciate this porch and cool breeze more."

"I spend too much time in the air conditioning in Austin to go out there in this heat." James handed Cox a giant glass of iced tea as he walked over.

"Gonzales reported to me about an hour ago," Cox said. "It looks like we may have a problem in New Mexico. But he says he'll have the Stanfield situation taken care of within a day."

"I thought they died in the accident," Al said.

"Apparently not," Cox answered. He walked over to the cushioned chairs and sat directly under the ceiling fans. His face remained beet red, partially from the heat, but also from anger.

"Do you think Gonzales will find them?" James asked.

"He has to. Update me about the property acquisitions, Al."

Al shifted in his seat and stared at Cox. "The land purchases are about to close in the Panhandle. We completed the sales before the W21C meeting. The recent postings from that meeting have caused a surge in interest from all over the country. We're in a 'wait and see' mode before we move onto anything else. Interest may diminish on its own. If Sam Stanfield is out of the picture, there will be no one to hold things up."

Cox moved on. He was waiting on Gonzales to take care of

Sam and Georgia. "What about the Rio Grande property?"

"Four of the five siblings have signed off on the sale. The last one is scheduled to sign the contract this afternoon, and that deal will be final," Al said. "I should hear from the attorney in about an hour."

"And Washington?"

James leaned in. "Pakistan is ready. The minister came to Sandra this time. The government and the rich are suffering because of the water shortage. The minister is under a lot of pressure. They want a delivery by the first of August." James paused. "Sandra says they're desperate. She wants to up the price."

Cox fired back. "Not for the first purchase. We'll make a successful delivery, then we'll negotiate. She doesn't get to make that decision. Sounds like she thinks she's indispensable. She's going to be a problem, James. Have you set up her meeting with Lynnette?"

"It's in the works now."

Cox was seldom wrong in reading people. Sandra would be a problem down the line, he knew, but he needed her now. People in Washington thought they were in control because they made the rules. They didn't know that only good guys followed the rules.

"I'll keep an eye on her. She's under surveillance. I get a daily report."

"What about your other contact?" Cox asked. "How close are you to making an arrangement, if the deal with Sandra goes south?"

"I meet with him tomorrow in Austin. It's very promising."

Cox stood, signaling the end of the discussion. "Jimmy, call me when you get word from Washington."

"Of course, Bill."

"If this all goes as planned, we can begin the final pipeline connections next week. Stay for supper if you like, boys. Have a drink. I'm going to get cleaned up."

Cox surged with energy. He rarely felt this good. His seventy-three-year-old body usually betrayed his determination, but not today. The Mallard Project was coming together.

~~~

After dinner, Cox returned to the porch alone. He watched his Black Angus standing belly deep in the water tanks, trying to stay cool. He thought about his inspiration for the Mallard Project, when he'd traveled to Africa in the early 1990s. He'd been in his late forties then. He'd realized that water could be the ultimate weapon of mass destruction. Most people thought of chemical warfare or of a nuclear threat. Let the leaders of the country worry about that.

He remembered his hunting trip in Botswana. Several Bushmen were hauling water into the Kalahari Game Reserve. Soldiers halted them, poured the water on the ground, and beat them. He watched them run the injured men off at gunpoint. He asked one of the soldiers what had happened, and the man told him they had orders to keep the Bushmen from carrying any water back to their homes inside the preserve.

The man had laughed, called the small reddish-brown people scum and said, "Without water, we will eventually eradicate the vermin. Let them find water in their precious desert plants."

For years after this encounter, Cox followed the plight of the Bushmen in their quest to regain rights to a land that had belonged to them for tens of thousands of years. They were at the mercy of the powerful. Cox collected thousands of documents from all over the world about the abuse of the powerful and the water rights of their people. Desert lands in the Middle East and Africa, Asian countries with vast populations, third-world countries without sanitation systems were all at risk of massive loss of human life, all due to the lack of drinkable water. It was clear to him that enormous power would come to those who controlled water rights. He had spent ten years putting together the Mallard Project, so he'd be the one to have that power. Oil was his foundation and the springboard for his project. Water would be his crystal gold, just as oil had been his black gold.

Chapter 26

Sam and Georgia moved away from the forest road as soon as the van disappeared. When they stopped, they could still see the road but had plenty of cover. Sam took out a map and traced their location from the wreck.

"We've only walked about a mile. Let's go north to the main highway to Taos. We'll have a better chance of getting help. The van is the only vehicle we've seen on this forest road."

"I need to wrap my ribs again before we go anywhere. The bandages are loose. The support helps. We're a fine pair. You're limping, and I can't breathe."

"Yes, we are. But we're going to make it."

"Ray will be worried. We didn't call last night, and he'll know something is wrong. He'll remember we stopped in Mora. But even if someone comes looking for us, it might be too late. You're right, our best chance is the highway. How far is it?"

"As the crow flies, not too far—close to five miles. But this map doesn't show elevation. We'll run into some obstacles—canyons and streams we'll have to cross, I expect. In the end, this is going to be much more than five miles. In our present condition and considering our age, we're not going to move very fast."

"We don't have a choice. Our cell phones went down with the truck. We have to get to other people for help, and the highway is the answer." Georgia reached out and took Sam's hand. "Please help us and protect us, Lord. Amen."

Sam put his arm around Georgia's shoulders and pulled her close. "We'll make it, Love. I'm sure of it. I'll lead going down. Put your hand on my back." He wanted to sound strong and sure, even if he was afraid of what they faced. He and Georgia had to outthink the men stalking them. Their lives depended upon it.

The van made a second pass back up the forest road a few minutes later. The couple started north immediately afterward. The game trail they followed ended in a wide, smooth path that lasted half a mile. Sam knew they'd be easily tracked on this path, but the easy walk outweighed the risk. They needed more time to recover from their injuries before they started climbing.

Unfortunately, the path ended at the edge of a steep incline, and the route north had them going downhill. The rocky trail made their path harder to track but more difficult to travel. At the bottom of the stony hillside ran a mountain stream, deeper than usual from the melting mountaintop snow. The couple had to walk several hundred feet to find a spot narrow enough to cross.

"Sam, let's take off our shoes and socks. It's so close to nighttime. We must have dry feet to stay warm."

The water reached to their knees, and the sharp rocks ripped their feet to shreds. By the time they sat down on the opposite bank, their feet were bleeding and numb with cold.

"Let's hope we don't have to do that again," Sam said.

Georgia took out the last of the bandages and wrapped their feet to stop the blood. Sam knew they were giving up their head start to the men behind them. He kept looking at the sky to judge the time of day and to watch the weather.

"There are dark clouds to the west. We may be in for some rain." Sam shifted his pack and walked on, hoping his feet would warm soon.

Georgia looked upward as she followed. "I guess rain could be a good thing. Maybe it will wash out our tracks."

Sam was panting within a few minutes and slowed down to catch his breath. "I can tell we're climbing. Breathing is getting harder. The spaces between the rocks and boulders are getting tighter. We'll have to climb over some of them to get to the summit so we can get down the other side."

"Let's rest a minute. We should drink some water. We really can't afford to become dehydrated." Georgia stopped and leaned against a wall of rock.

Sam touched Georgia's arm, and she froze.

"Be still. I thought I saw movement."

They squeezed closer to the boulders, watching the opposite side of the stream through a crack.

"What is it, Sam?"

"We must remember every time we stop to be sure we're concealed like this. We were lucky this time. Something in the distance caught my attention. It was a flicker. I'm not sure if it was anything."

"I saw it, too," Georgia confirmed.

Just then, a deer jumped into the clearing across the canyon and darted back into the forest, near the location where the couple thought they'd seen movement.

"Look at that, over by the tree that's been struck by lightning, a little to the left." Sam saw a man dressed in camouflage looking in their direction. "He has binoculars, He's searching this hillside. I wonder if that's Gonzales. I think he's looking for us, whoever he is."

"Let's go, Sam. Let's get out of here."

"Wait until he turns. He'll see movement before anything else."

Sam held on to Georgia's arm until the man turned. He wanted to run as well, but he knew it would reveal their hiding place. As soon as the man moved back into the woods, Sam and Georgia hurried up the mountain trail again. The sight of their would-be assassin pumped them full of adrenalin.

"This has turned into a switchback, and we're still climbing," Sam said after a few minutes. "We're getting closer."

The ponderosa pines had disappeared, and a few white spruce and aspen grew among the boulders. The ground was rockier. More open spaces exposed them. As sundown approached, a pale light gave them cover but dimmed the path. Georgia stumbled on a loose rock and fell toward Sam. She grabbed his jacket. He reached behind his waist and steadied her. They took a moment to rest and then moved on.

At the summit, distant thunder rumbled across the mountaintops as Sam stopped and dug out the last of the protein bars. It began to rain—not a pouring or hard rain, but a gentle, relentless rain that would eventually soak everything. Georgia's jacket was water-repellant, and Sam took a rain poncho from his backpack, still in its plastic envelope. The early evening was even darker with the gray clouds above.

"Let's keep going," he said. "Maybe we won't be cold if we keep moving."

On the back side of the mountain, the trees were thicker and hundreds of aspens were interspersed with spruce. The view was breathtaking, but Sam spent his time searching for hiding places at every turn. Thickets of scrub oak covered what could have been open places to leave the trail and find shelter, but the low-growing shrub created a wall that blocked any passage. Anxiety drove them forward. The evening was growing darker, and they were desperate to find a place to rest for the night. The only relief came when their path turned downhill.

"My calves are cramping. I need to stop for a minute. Georgia, take the lead."

She inched by Sam on the narrow path and headed onward.

She reached the bottom of a shallow ravine and waited for Sam to catch up. "I know we have to keep moving, but if we can find shelter for the night, we can get some rest." Georgia sat next to Sam, rubbing his calf to ease another spasm.

"Thanks, Georgia." Sam took over rubbing his calf, then began walking again. "Let's search for a break in the underbrush."

The surface leveled somewhat after a bit, but the brief stop had let exhaustion catch up with them. They both knew they couldn't continue much longer.

"Look at that cluster of huge boulders," Georgia said, pointing. "Is it worth a try to get off the path and look for shelter there?"

"Absolutely, it's worth a shot." Sam stepped off the path and inched his way into the giant rock maze. Some of the huge stones were so close together that it was difficult to squeeze through. On the far side, a large rock balanced against another boulder with a dry space underneath. The boulders and the stunted oaks mixed together offered protection from the weather. Only a hint of light crept through the narrow spaces. Shadows and deeper shadows were their guide. As they drew closer, they saw a stone leaning against the back side, creating a three-sided enclosure.

"Georgia, we'll be protected from the wind and the rain in here." Sam bent over and used an oak branch to brush the inside.

They crawled in on all fours and sat leaning against the stone wall. The angled roof was only a few inches away and made the hollow tight. They'd be able to lie down for the night. Georgia stuffed the holes in the rear with brush, then put the backpack there to block the cold. Sam cut down a couple of scrub oaks with his knife and stuffed them in the front opening. His army green poncho was the perfect background to hang on the branches and break the cold wind.

Sam and Georgia stretched out on the dry sleeping bag. With barely enough room to turn over, they huddled together and listened to the rain trickling down the sides of the stone guardians around them. Blessed sleep crept over them as darkness covered the mountain.

~~~

Gonzales finally got a call through to Jenson. "Hang out in Mora in case they show up there. If they do somehow get to the highway and catch a ride, I want you to be waiting for them. That's the closest town, and the logical place for them to go."

"I'll be there," Jenson assured him. "They won't get by me. We'll have this finished tomorrow." He was as eager as Gonzales to finish this job. It didn't feel right. Gonzales was too confident, and Hood was too careless. Jenson didn't like it.

"Have Hood keep patrolling the roads, even after dark. We have them on the run, and I don't think they'll get away. Remember, I'll be out of any service area tomorrow, but I'll come back to the road so I can call you when this is finished." Gonzales took out his rain jacket and checked his weapons when he reached the end of the path. He had his rifle and a 9 mm sidearm loaded and ready.

Chapter 27

Luther Brown walked into the pink granite courthouse in Waggoner, his son in tow.

"Maureen, I need to give this to the sheriff," he said as he clunked a plastic bag down on her desk. "My son, Cody, found this pistol in our cattle tank yesterday. He tried to fire it. I need to talk to Ray."

"Just a minute, Luther. I'll get him." Maureen hurried away and returned quickly with Ray.

"Hello, Luther," he said as he picked up the plastic bag and looked at the .38. "You said this came from your place?"

"Yes, sir. The tank is dry now. That pistol doesn't look like it's been in the water long."

"Come on in my office. Where is this pond?"

"You know we call them tanks here in Texas, Sheriff. I thought you were a native."

"I am, but I slip sometimes. After being in the city for so long, you get into some bad habits."

"It's the one on the north side of my ranch. It's by the road that runs perpendicular to the Fort Worth highway."

Ray knew exactly where the road was. He'd check it out later for himself.

"I'm sorry, Sheriff," Cody said quickly. "I shouldn't have tried to fire it."

"Your dad was right to bring it in. It could have blown up in your face."

"Yes, sir."

Luther walked to the door. "We'll leave you to it, Ray."

After the Browns left Ray's office, Ray reviewed his deputies' reports. Several people in town had positively identified Jenson and Hood. Chances were high the men were behind the statewide cattle killings.

His next step was to involve the FBI. He called Agent Frank Wade. Ray gave Frank the information they had on Jenson and Hood. "Frank, can you come to Waggoner? I have more information I want to show you. It would be better to do it face-to-face."

"Yes, I can come over, Ray, but maybe not until the end of the week."

After Ray hung up, he called one of his deputies into his office. "I want you to look at the videos you've collected from around town to see if you can identify anyone Jenson and Hood may have been with. These guys are working for someone."

The deputy nodded and left. Ray gave the bagged pistol to Maureen.

"Take this and have ballistics run on it. I think we may have the gun used at the Stanfield ranch."

"Yes, sir. I'll call someone to come in and cover the phones while I'm gone."

After Maureen and the deputy left, Ray started making calls. The first was to Sam Stanfield. He hadn't heard from Sam the night before, and he grew more concerned when the call went straight to voicemail. Ray estimated Sam and Georgia should be in Taos by now. They'd had plenty of time to pick up the money he'd wired to Taos Western Union the day before. He made a note to call Western Union to see if the money had been picked up yet.

But first Ray walked across the street to meet Joe for coffee. He'd called earlier and wanted to talk to Ray. By this time of the morning, traffic was thick on the square, and Ray walked to the corner stop signs to make it across the street. The cloudy day kept the heat at bay for a while, and people lingered on the sidewalks. Ray stopped several times on his way to the café to chat.

Ray arrived first. Most of the early diners had gone already and patronage was sparse. Ray walked by the counter and ordered a cup of black coffee. He surveyed the remaining customers on his way down a row of booths, then took a seat against the back wall.

When Joe walked in, Ray could tell he was worried. Twisting his cap in his hands, he approached slowly, then slipped into the booth opposite Ray and ordered a cup of coffee. Ray was already on his second cup. The men acknowledged each other but sat without saying anything until Joe's coffee arrived.

Ray looked at the server and asked, "Could we have some privacy?"

"Sure thing, Ray, I'll see to it." This was a normal event in the Courthouse Café, and every employee knew the drill. The high-backed booth afforded some privacy, and the wait staff seated other patrons as far away from the sheriff as possible. He'd found the lull between the morning and noon rush was the perfect time for meetings.

"How are you doing, Joe?" Ray sat back and gave Joe space to relax.

"I can't get in touch with Sam. I tried several times yesterday and last night. The calls go straight to voicemail. He would have re-turned my calls. He would know my calls would be about the ranch. Something must be wrong."

"I talked to them yesterday. They were in Mora and heading to Taos. I haven't heard from them since then."

"Also, I think this letter is important." Joe took an envelope from his shirt pocket and slid it across the table to Ray.

Ray examined it. "This is from the EPA. When did this come in?"

"Yesterday. I've been picking up their mail, and I had to sign for this one. I didn't know what else to do, so I called you."

"You did the right thing." Ray tapped the official envelope on the table, thinking. "Why don't I take this back to my office for safekeeping? I'll tell Sam about it when I talk to him. I'm sure he'll call when he can."

Ray knew a fine from the EPA would be unusual. Normally the EPA would have a representative meet with the party involved and discuss any problem concerning the property first. Then they'd negotiate the cleanup.

"I've never seen a case where the EPA jumps to a fine before a talk," Ray said. "I want to see whose name is on this letter."

"Sure, that's all right with me if you keep it. Let me know if I can help with anything when you talk to Sam."

"One more thing, Joe. I need the make and model of Sam's pickup and the RV."

Joe wrote the information on a napkin and handed it to Ray. "You're worried, aren't you, Ray? You don't know where they are, either."

Chapter 28

Bill Cox leaned back against the cream leather upholstery of his black stretch Mercedes. It was Tuesday, and he had a two-hour drive into Houston. He watched the landscape turn from the arid prairie of his ranch to the lush green coastal plains that surrounded the fourth-largest city in the United States.

As the car merged into the heavier traffic of the freeways, Cox began to work. If he could have avoided one thing, it was having partners. And he had three, none of whom knew about the others. Partners afforded him additional funding, critical contacts, and geographical ease for the pipelines. Partners were a necessity in an enterprise this massive. One partner lived on the East Coast, one in California, and one in the Pacific Northwest.

Cox's pipeline from the East Coast paralleled parts of the Little Big Inch, an oil pipeline that dated to World War II and ran from New Jersey to New Orleans. Cox laid his water transmission pipeline within the same rights of way. Back when the line was built, most oil traveled by barges up the Eastern Seaboard. During World War II, officials feared this made them susceptible to German U-boat attacks. That was when they turned to transporting oil via pipeline.

The route proved perfect for Cox's eastern line. His East Coast partner, John Hart, was ideal as well. He was only involved financially. Hart had earned his money quickly through early software development for the personal computer and the Internet revolution. Cox had convinced Hart that he was helping third-world countries get clean water, and Hart let him work out the details. Hart believed water sanitation for the poor was the first step in improving their lives. The guy thought Cox believed the same. Hart wanted his money to make the world a better place.

Every Tuesday morning, eight o'clock Eastern Daylight Time, Cox made a call to Hart. This time the call came from the back of his limo in downtown Houston.

"We're on schedule, John," he said. "Your first shipment of water will go directly to Africa. I guarantee it. Until next Tuesday." Cox knew he'd have to change his strategy for Hart next week. He didn't think John was as enthusiastic as he had been in the past. Cox thought about flying up to see him. He needed to keep him happy. He'd send him some sympathetic pictures. That should do it. He had fooled John before and now he needed to keep him from causing any trouble.

Cox's other partners were under no such illusions. They wanted to make money, simple as that. That was fine with Cox. Babysitting Hart was growing tiresome.

His western line ran from central Canada to Port Metro, Vancouver, where the massive port exported thousands of gallons of oil. Water shipped in oil tankers would pass through undetected. However, the central line was to be the first water line to become operational, and all stakeholders would be evaluating the results. It ran from the Great Lakes through Texas and into Mexico. The central line would become the model for the other pipeline operations to follow.

~~~

Later that afternoon, Cox and Al Martin hovered over a Texas map in Cox's penthouse office. The gigantic conference table dwarfed the two men standing there, but no one else ever filled the spaces when they discussed the Mallard Project.

"Is the Mexico tank farm ready for the water transfer into the ships?" Cox asked.

"We're waiting on the pipeline connection about ten miles from the farm." Al pointed to the tank farm off the Gulf Coast in Mexico. He traced the map northwest along a red dotted line that followed the route to the Rio Grande. "You can see here, we have it going all the way to the Texas property we closed on yesterday. Funding will clear today."

"When will the team start the directional boring under the river?" Cox asked. This part of the operation was tricky. The property was relatively secluded. However, with all the attention about the border wall between the United States and Mexico in the news, he was nervous. The last thing he wanted was attention.

"The trucks are ready to drive on the property and start when I give them a call," Al said. "And before you ask, it will take about a week to get the pipe to the Mexican side. The lights, the generators, the oil rig, it will look like we're fracking an old well. It's the perfect setup."

"Can they reduce the lighting at night and still do their work?"

"The superintendent has assured us he can. He's being paid very well to do this job, but he doesn't get the money unless he succeeds. If the authorities come out, he's on his own. He doesn't have a name or face to implicate us."

Cox nodded. He had transformed an oil tank farm on the Mexican Gulf to store the water. He planned for tankers from around the world to dock at the port nearby and get their water loaded from the tank farm. Tres National Oil Company, a Cox holding and a Mexican company, owned the tank farm. The storage tanks had been emptied and cleaned, and now they waited for the first water delivery coming through the supposed oil transmission line. The tankers were on schedule to dock in the Mexico port and loaded with water. The ships would be on their way to Pakistan within forty-eight hours.

Cox walked to the liquor cabinet and poured himself a tumbler of single malt whiskey. He could think better with a drink in hand. He didn't offer any scotch to Al, knowing he suffered from ulcers. He paced, then sat on the windowsill, looking out at the Houston skyline. "Al, I'm almost there. Of course, there are always a few hiccups, but that's what makes it fun. Tell me about the offshore accounts."

"The two DC accounts are up-to-date, and the Pakistanis sent half of their payment following their inspection of the tank farm. When they had proof that we could deliver the water, they wired the funds at once. They seemed eager to get this deal under-way."

"That's what I'm counting on, the desperation factor." Cox didn't mind reiterating the obvious. Going over his mental check-list was essential. He avoided mistakes that way. He noticed that Al paused before finishing his answer.

"I sent the DC two their share of the partial Pakistan mon-ey to keep them moving forward with the next contact in Africa. Sandra has been complaining that she's taking all the risks with no benefits. I think it's worked out so far. At least I haven't heard from them lately. But you know me, I'm always suspicious. I'm waiting on your friend in California to let me know when to pay Gonzales, and all of the Austin payoffs are contingent upon the Gonzales report."

The phone buzzed on Cox's desk. He pressed the speaker button. "Jimmy, Albert and I are alone in the office here. Tell us the latest in Washington."

"Ms. Sandra Kowalski is right on target with her assess-ments," James Baxter replied. "The Pakistanis are ready to send the first ten tankers to pick up the water. The first shipment is going directly to the highest officials there. They want to secure enough potable water to last a year for themselves before it goes to the people. The water near the coast becomes more contaminated every day. Circumstances are dire. It's only a matter of time before citizens start rioting and dying. They told her they'd take as many deliveries as we could provide."

"Any other interested contacts?"

"Yes. She's had contact with some of the sub-Saharan countries through the Bureau of Oceans and International Environmental and Scientific Affairs. No one questions her meetings with them. The secretary has personally appointed her as basically a liaison between countries for the worldwide water crisis. The department understands water can be a weapon of war."

"Do you think they're ready to come on board?" Al asked.

"They're very interested in our proposal," James said. "Much of their water is stagnant and has become polluted. They have foreign relief money coming in from the United States and Russia. They'll use that to make a deal with us. So far, the governments haven't changed administrations, but as you know, we'll have to act fast. We can charge an even higher price per gallon of water because Sandra believes they're going to use the water to control their citizens. They don't have the capacity to deal with water emergencies, and they know the faction that can provide water will rule."

"My God, this is going to happen," Al said after the call was over.

"Why are you surprised?" Cox asked. He raised his glass and saluted the Houston skyline.

Chapter 29

During the night, Sam and Georgia had shifted their positions and now lay facing one another. Sam was awake, and his senses were on full alert. He was listening to footsteps outside their stone cocoon. Crunching and rustling noises had awakened him. The noises eventually moved away from their hiding place. Sam gently touched Georgia's shoulder. He put his finger to his lips. She blinked and nodded. Neither of them moved.

"If someone's watching," Sam whispered, "we need to wait awhile longer."

The crunching sounds gradually faded, and the steady murmur of the forest returned. The sunlight crept across the opening, and Sam and Georgia began to shift in their cramped quarters.

"We need to move now," Sam urged as he pushed the brush away from the opening and crept out into the sunlight. It was difficult for him to stand. He ached all over, and he knew Georgia felt the same. Sam stretched and checked his knee. He took Georgia's hand as she crawled from the small cave.

"I don't hear anything," she said, scanning the area for movement.

"Stay here, Georgia. I'll look for tracks. We don't know what we heard."

Sam found boot prints ten feet away. He crouched behind a rock close to the trail and inched around the corner to check the pathway. No one was there.

They threaded their way through the scattered boulders and back onto the trail. Immediately, they saw the footprints of the person they'd heard pass. The prints seemed nondescript. They could have been anyone's, but Sam and Georgia took no chances. Without a word, they stepped gingerly on rocks and tufts of grass to minimize any signs of their own footprints. They'd followed the prints only a few yards when the path split. The boots continued down the right fork of the trail, but the left pathway seemed untouched. Sam and Georgia decided to cut back perpendicular to the left trail and loop around to it farther down. Sam hoped the detour a quarter of a mile would protect them, though it would cost them their lead time.

"I hope this effort is worth the trouble," Georgia gasped as she climbed over a fallen tree. The elevation continued to challenge Sam as well.

"We're nearly back to the path, if my calculations are correct. Stay here a minute, and I'll go look." Sam trudged on and discovered the faint markings of the animal trail just where he'd hoped it would be. The slim opening in the thick growth forced them to walk single file. When Sam stepped over rocks in the path, Georgia grabbed his belt. His upward movement pulled her with him over the rocks.

After Sam and Georgia spent a solid hour walking on a slight downward incline, the path turned toward a grassy meadow dotted heavily with dandelions. As they passed through it, Sam looked back and frowned at the trail they'd left across the dew-covered plants. He couldn't change it, so they plodded on, only to start another rocky climb. They stepped over rocks and around underbrush until they found a mountain stream.

"Let's fill our water bottles before we go over the mountain," Sam said.

Georgia handed him a protein bar. "That's the last of our food."

They trekked on, chewing slowly, determined to make their way to the highway. Their progress was slow. There were fewer handholds. They depended on one another for balance as they negotiated the narrow path along the cliff.

"It's about twenty feet to the top," Sam said. "We're almost there."

Just as Sam stepped up to get over a boulder, a gunshot reverberated across the canyon. His backpack flew off his shoulder and down the side of the cliff. Sam fell forward into the rocks, taking Georgia with him. He landed hard, with Georgia crumpling near his feet.

"Are you hurt?" Georgia asked as she lifted herself up. "Sam!" she cried as she saw the blood spreading across his back. She scrambled closer toward him. Another shot rang out and hit the rock wall above them. Shattered bits of rock rained down.

"Stay low, Georgia! Stay low!"

Georgia leaned in close to Sam to look at his wound. Blood was soaking the ground around his shoulder.

~~~

The van bumped along the two-lane New Mexico highway. Jenson was half listening to Hood's constant yapping. He'd concluded the job was too much trouble. He was getting out as soon as he could. He wanted to get clear of Gonzales. Then he'd be gone.

"Why do we have to go so far?" Hood complained. "We can drop the dog off anywhere. I want to sleep." He twisted around in the seat, trying to get comfortable. "Two hours on the floor last night! I was miserable. I'm tired. I'm hungry."

"Shut up," Jenson said. "You know why. This will throw off any search for those two. We'll be in Los Alamos in about twenty minutes." Jenson felt mounting fatigue as well, but he'd never let Hood know. Any sign of weakness was dangerous around his increasingly unstable partner. Jenson didn't want to be associated with Gonzales or Hood. Los Alamos was two hours from the crash site, and the tags on the dog would prompt a phone call to Waggoner. The authorities would be looking in the wrong place. He thought it was a good plan.

At midnight, Jenson rolled into a church parking lot and stopped. He turned off the lights but left the motor running and waited. Hood got out and opened the rear doors of the van. Gracie jumped out and disappeared into the night, leaving Hood staring into the darkness. He climbed back in the front seat silently. Jenson knew Hood thought the dog liked him, and he watched him grow angry.

"I should have just killed that damned dog." Hood's eyes widened and he gritted his teeth. "It would've made it easier on us. I was stupid to keep it."

Jenson wasn't going to encourage Hood with a response. He put the van in gear and drove off to find a motel.

~ ~ ~

Gracie found a puddle of water and stopped to drink. She looked around the parking lot, then crawled into a thick hedge of sage along the wall of the church.

The next morning, Father Mike found her sitting on the back porch. "Hello, girl. Where did you come from?" The priest bent down and patted her head and scratched her behind the ears. "You look like you're lost." While he petted the friendly dog, he heard her tags jingle. The priest ran his fingers through the thick fur and found her collar with her information. "Well, you're a long way from home, Gracie. How did you get here?" Father Mike continued to talk to Gracie as he stood and motioned for her to come with him. "You look like you could use some water and a bite to eat. After we get you fixed up, we'll call the number on your tag." The man walked through the door to a small kitchen and Gracie followed.

Chapter 30

Cox's pleasant evening at his ranch ended with the ringing of his phone. His screen flashed *Unknown Caller*, and Cox hesitated. He decided at the last minute to slide the red bar. "Yes?" He suspected he already knew who it was.

"Cox, you've had my guy out there way too long," Lee Kimball said. "I need him back here."

"Lee, how are you?" Cox asked, ignoring Kimball's smartass posturing. Kimball was his noisiest partner. His value came from his ties to a Colombian drug cartel. He had the type of dark resources Cox didn't, like Gonzales. Kimball's contacts over the years had proved beneficial to the Mallard Project. Where the rule of law couldn't apply and bureaucratic red tape got in the way, Kimball interjected his own rule of law. But Cox was no fool. He was aware of the capriciousness of his partner. Kimball was thirty years younger, and ambitious. Cox understood what it cost him to include the drug cartels in laying the groundwork for the project.

"Bill, it's time, man," Lee said. "What's going on there, anyway?"

"You're right, Lee. He should be finished soon and get back to you by the end of the week." Cox knew Kimball was under pressure from the cartel. He was informed—he and his Washington contacts had discovered Kimball's involvement in the drug trade at the beginning of the Mallard Project. The DEA had been watching him for some time. Cox was careful to build layers of protection and secrecy to guard their plan, but on occasion they needed the kind of force the cartel could offer. Kimball believed Cox's plot was to control water in the United States. He had no inkling of the global reach of the Mallard Project. Cox knew he'd have his project operational soon, and then he'd be able to break away from Kimball. They'd leave him something small, and only later would he realize the big picture. The drug cartel could be Cox's real problem, but they had so much money with no place to put it that Cox had dismissed them as an issue. The violence and the continuous wars among the five major cartels kept them busy with each other anyway.

"What's Gonzales into?" Kimball asked. "If you're trying to recruit him, forget it."

"It's nothing like that," Cox said. "He'll be on his way tomorrow, I'm sure. Pass that information along to your friends, Lee, and tell them we appreciate their help here."

Kimball was silent on the other end. Cox laughed and hung up, thinking that this was probably the last time he could ask his California connection for help.

~~~

Lynnette was sleeping deeply when her phone rang. She picked it up from her nightstand and stared at the display, wondering why James was calling so late. "Hello. Is something wrong?" she asked.

"Not a thing. I'm getting on the last plane to Dallas in a few minutes. Pack a bag and meet me at the airport. You're getting your chance."

Lynnette's mind raced. She could barely believe it. She knew she was ready, though. James was going to give her the details on the plane. She'd have time to ask him about the contact, and Cox, and the project. Hopefully, he'd be willing to talk.

She made her way to the airport and searched for James, shifting her black leather backpack from shoulder to shoulder. Lynnette had fifteen minutes to spare when she located him at the gate. She put the bag in her lap as she sat next to him.

"I'm glad you made it," he said. "We'll talk on the plane."

Lynnette noticed few other passengers waiting. It was a good choice of flights. She and James boarded in silence. A calm came over her. She knew she'd gotten inside the Cox organization. Even James looked different to her. He didn't seem so formidable. She knew she had the upper hand for the first time.

Lynnette and James spoke quietly for the first part of the flight. He was efficient, and Lynnette was so wired she didn't take any notes. She remembered it all.

"Call me immediately after the meeting," James said. "Cox

knows that I'm letting you go to Washington to meet with Sandra."

"Of course." Lynnette was pleased James and Cox had discussed including her. Now she could find out more information about Cox. While James gave her instructions, he unintentionally referenced the Mallard Project. He didn't realize the gem he'd revealed. Lynnette added another piece to the puzzle.

As the plane landed at Reagan International, Lynnette tried to focus on the job at hand and remain alert. Her earlier energy was fading. When James left her, she took time to recoup. Her meeting was at 11:30 at the Smithsonian Castle. She was to go to the Smithson Crypt, on the north side of the building. Since it was 8:15, she decided to eat breakfast in the airport and then take the Metrorail to the meeting.

Lynnette made it to the Smithsonian with time to spare. She wanted to blend with the tourists, so she ambled over to her designated meeting place. Though Lynnette sensed no movement, Sandra was suddenly beside her. They began talking quietly, appropriate for the chapel-like room.

"What's going on in New Mexico?" Sandra whispered.

"How did you know about New Mexico? Never mind. Everything should be taken care of by the end of the week." Lynnette understood that Sandra must have many ways of getting information, not just her.

"Some people worry you've started something you shouldn't have in Texas."

Lynnette knew Sandra was trying to establish power with the veiled threat. She'd used the tactic herself on occasion. "Who are these people, other than you, Sandra?"

"They believe it could jeopardize the whole operation. But now that you and Cox are in the middle of the fiasco, finish it quickly. I'm not putting my neck on the line just because of your inability to handle a few ranchers." Sandra stared forward sternly, without blinking. "I want to know as soon as it's over."

"Of course," Lynnette said. She'd hoped the meeting would have gone a little more smoothly. It certainly hadn't begun the way she'd wanted.

While the pair finished talking, Sandra slipped a visitor's brochure into Lynnette's jacket pocket. She disappeared from the room as quickly as she'd arrived.

Lynnette was worried. She'd have to deliver the message in the brochure as well as the veiled threat. James and Cox wouldn't like this. Lynnette waited until she was riding back to the airport to open the trifold Smithsonian brochure. Written in a blank spot on the back were the coordinates and the arrival times of several ships.

Chapter 31

Georgia gingerly pulled the bullet-shredded shirt from the wound atop Sam's shoulder. The warm, sticky blood covered her hand. "Be still, Sam. Be still," she said as Sam tried to roll over.

"How bad is it?" Sam stopped moving and rested his forehead on the back of his hand.

Georgia knelt over him and quickly assessed his wound. "The bullet grazed the muscle on the top of your shoulder. I have to stop the bleeding."

"Try to hurry," Sam said. "The shooter will be on us within a few minutes."

Georgia shrugged out of her jacket and tore the sleeves from her shirt. She folded one sleeve into a square and pressed it against the wound. She tied the other around Sam's shoulder to hold it in place. "Can you move, Sam?"

"Yes, I think so. We have to stay down until we get to the top."

Georgia and Sam crawled thirty feet before they could stand

and still remain out of sight. A trail of blood and prints clearly marked their path.

"Put your arm around my neck," Georgia said. "Try to keep your bad arm close to your body."

Sam reached across Georgia's shoulder and steadied himself. He kissed her fiercely on the forehead and nodded his head toward a stand of thick aspen. "We'll be safer in the forest."

With Georgia's help, Sam made it to the cover of the trees. He leaned against a trunk and felt his wound. "Stop here, Georgia. Let's see if my compass still works."

"How's your shoulder? The blood loss is going to make you weak."

"It hurts, but I can stand it. We're going to have to rest again soon, though." Sam pulled the compass from his pocket. "The face is cracked. That won't help us." He glanced at the sun and lined up an outcropping of three distinct rock formations to help keep them on track toward the highway. "Let's keep that landmark in sight."

The path ahead didn't appear clear, but Sam convinced himself they should hike to the highest point to get their bearings. He knew the chances of that working were slim. He held his arm across his chest and wished he had medicine to help with the pain. Unfortunately, the drugs had tumbled down the mountain inside his pack. They walked on, knowing they had no choice. Neither of them would ever give up.

"Sam, it looks like there's a blue diamond on that tree up

ahead. If it is, we may find a Forest Service yurt. Other people could be there, too. Look for the next blue diamond."

"The man behind us can find the markings just as well," Sam said. "Let's stay off the trail as much as we can."

"The yurt may have supplies. I think we have to risk it."

Sam and Georgia continued to follow the blue diamonds, hoping to find shelter before nightfall. They wouldn't survive the cold night without their gear.

"I see the yurt ahead," Georgia said as they came into a clearing.

It wasn't any too soon. Sam was feeling light-headed, wobbling along. His shoulder was bleeding again, and he felt feverish to Georgia.

The circular structure was on a platform with a deck around the outside. A dozen wide steps led up to it. Sam knew negotiating those steps in his weak state would be tricky. He wasn't sure Georgia could support him if he didn't have the strength to help.

"Can you make it, Sam?"

"I can make it." He saw the worried look on her face. "I may be dizzy, but not so bad that I can't hold the rail and pull myself up."

"I'll get behind you. Let's go." Georgia put both hands on the small of his back and pushed as Sam struggled upward. They rested at the top of the stairs.

"We'd better get inside," Sam said as he looked back down the way they'd come, half expecting to see the man with the gun emerge from the trees.

"Sam, here's a telescope. I'm going to point it down the trail. We can keep watch." Georgia adjusted the giant telescope to see if it worked.

"Can you see anything?"

"It's better than the naked eye, and I can make out movement."

Darkness had quickly engulfed the yurt, and they hurried inside. There, they found four bunk beds, a woodburning stove, and a rustic table and bench. The stove was even prepped for a fire. In a cabinet, Georgia found matches and a small first aid kit. In no time, she had the fire going and was boiling water to clean Sam's wound.

Sam rested his head on the table while Georgia moved about. Inside the first aid kit were a few adhesive bandages and some antibiotic ointment, but not enough for the injury.

"I'm satisfied the wound is clean," Georgia said as she attended to Sam. "But you need real medical attention." She examined the other cabinet in the room and found a can of stew. "A little food should make us both feel better," she said a few minutes later, handing a steaming cupful to Sam.

"I already feel better just resting and having some water. I'll be fine." Sam pulled the bench close to the stove for light so he could examine the map. "This shows that the trail beside the yurt is only three miles from the highway."

"Won't the shooter be going that way, too?" Georgia asked.

Fear showed in her eyes and on her face.

"Yes. But I don't know if he can track us at night."

"I'll check the trail through the telescope again," Georgia said as she slipped out of the door to the deck. "Nothing," she said as she returned a minute later.

"Georgia, we can't spend the night here. We can rest for a while longer, but I think we should move on tonight. He won't be expecting us to travel at night."

"I'm all right with that." Georgia sipped from the canteen, then handed it to Sam.

"I'll set the alarm on my watch for one hour, then," Sam said. He hoped they had that much time to spare.

Georgia pulled a mattress off a lower bunk, turned it over to avoid the mouse droppings, and hauled it over beside the wood stove. Their sleeping bag was torn and had leaves and twigs sticking to it, but Sam didn't care. By this time, the stars were out. His watch said eleven. Georgia looked through the telescope once more before she laid down next to an already sleeping Sam.

Chapter 32

Ray ran up the courthouse steps as the clock made a seventh tinny sound. It was a stretch to call the noise chimes. Still, Waggoner citizens were proud of the unusual noises that came from the historic courthouse tower, which was built in 1896.

Inside the cool Vermont marble walls, the sound was muffled as Ray turned the corner to get to his office. Frank had let him know a fax was coming with the latest information from the FBI. One document was a copy of Sam's EPA fine. Frank had already told him the fine was $20,000 a day.

Ray scanned the papers and realized he'd have to act quickly to keep the fine from going into effect. Joe, Sam's foreman, could help him, and Ray called to get him in as soon as possible.

Ray next checked the results from the bulletin he'd sent out on Jenson and Hood. There were no reports from Texas, and he suspected they'd moved out of state. He considered asking Frank Wade to send an FBI bulletin nationally.

Ray's phone rang, and he saw the call was from the vet, Dr. Thompson. "Hello, Doc. This is an early call. What can I help you with?"

"I just got a call from a priest in Los Alamos, New Mexico. He has Gracie, the Stanfields' dog, with him. He said she just showed up at his church. He called me from the number on her tags."

"Los Alamos? What's the priest's information? I'll call him right now." Ray copied the name and number while he looked at a New Mexico map. "Thanks, Doc."

Ray wondered what had happened to Sam and Georgia. Gracie being loose like that couldn't mean anything good. Now he had two reasons to talk to Joe. He was relieved when he walked in fifteen minutes later.

"Got your message, Ray. Have you heard from Sam yet?"

"Not yet. Have a seat. I've also found out more about that EPA letter. It's a fine, and it's a steep one. The other part is that Sam has two days to get the cattle off his land before it takes effect. I need your help."

"I can take care of that, Ray. Sam and Georgia have plenty of friends here who would be willing to help."

"How long will it take? There are still a lot of cows to be moved out there."

"I'll make calls today, and we'll have it done by tomorrow night. I'll call you when we're finished."

"I heard from Dr. Thompson just before you came in, Joe. Gracie has been found in Los Alamos. That's a long way from Mora." Ray spread out a New Mexico map and showed Joe the distance between the two towns.

"Ray, after we get the cows moved, I'm going to Los Alamos to get Gracie."

"Let's call the priest who found her," Ray said as he dialed his phone. When the priest answered, Ray explained who he and Joe were and about Gracie's owners, Sam and Georgia. "Father Mike, how did Gracie get to your church?"

"I found her on the back steps, Sheriff. I checked the videos of the parking lot from last night, and someone in a van dropped her off. I can e-mail you a copy."

Ray gave the priest his e-mail address and turned to his computer. Within a minute, the file had come through. "Bingo," Ray said as he watched it. "This is a real help. I recognize the person in the video."

"Is there anything else I can do to help?"

"Taking care of Gracie is enough. I want you to know that Joe will be there to pick her up in a few days, Father Mike. Thank you." He set down the phone and turned to Joe. "We've identified our suspects in the Bar S crime. You just saw one of the men in the video. I want to warn you that these guys are dangerous."

"If they had Gracie, what happened to Sam and Georgia?"

"Exactly." Ray pulled out a copy of the pictures of Jenson and Hood. "Take these posters with you in case you see them."

Joe studied the photographs. "What evidence did you find on them?"

"We analyzed that blood from the post and got a hit in the system. These guys served time in Huntsville together. I can't tell you enough times to be careful. If you see them, call the authorities in New Mexico right away. Leave them to law enforcement. I'm only giving you these pictures to help you be prepared."

"Don't worry, Ray. I have your number. I'm not a vigilante. All I want to do is pick up Gracie."

After Joe left, Ray called in Maureen. "I need to talk to Georgia's uncle, Harry Reynolds."

"I can get his number. I'll call a few people."

Ray was aware of Harry Reynolds's continued influence in Texas. He was one of the good guys, an actual politician who lived by his word. Ray was glad to have all the help he could get.

"Sheriff, Harry Reynolds is on line one for you," Maureen called in from her desk a few minutes later.

"Hello, Mr. Reynolds," Ray quickly answered.

"How can I help you, Sheriff?"

"I'm calling about Sam and Georgia, sir. I think they're missing. No one has been able to contact them."

"I knew they were going on a trip to the Panhandle. What leads you to believe they're missing?"

"Sam and Georgia said they'd call me, but they haven't. That's not like them. I can't reach them by phone, and neither can Joe, their foreman. The most concerning part is that their dog, Gracie, turned up at a church in Los Alamos, New Mexico. We have a video showing a known felon dropping her off around midnight last night."

"This is serious business," Harry said. "This must have something to do with those threats."

"We believe so. But that's not all. The EPA has imposed a large fine on their ranch. They claim the cows are polluting streams. And now the IRS has frozen their accounts. I went to the IRS office in Fort Worth, and they've informed me they're issuing a warrant for both of their arrests."

"What in the world for?" Harry asked. "Sam and Georgia have never done a dishonest thing in their lives. I'm astonished."

"The charge is for money laundering," Ray said. "Records show that large amounts of money were deposited into their bank accounts and then moved offshore into another account."

"That can't be. Someone is out to ruin them. What do you need?" Harry was fuming. "I'll be glad to help in any way I can."

Ray didn't hesitate. "Can you come to Waggoner so we can talk more?"

"I'll be there tomorrow."

Chapter 33

The only light in the yurt came from the potbellied stove and its smoldering coals. The dry wood burned quickly and let the dark, cloudy night creep in around them. It was a hard but fitful sleep for Sam and Georgia. They awakened at the same time, their internal clocks letting them know an hour had passed. Sam switched off the alarm on his watch and stuffed more wood inside the stove.

"How's your shoulder? You look stiff." Georgia spoke softly as she rolled up the blanket and tied it again for a pack.

"It's getting easier the more I move around." Sam filled the canteen and slid the strap over his good shoulder. "I can carry the water, at least."

Georgia crouched down when she went through the yurt door. "Let me look down the path," she said, adjusting the telescope. "I don't see anything out there."

Sam took Georgia's hand and drew her to him. "We're going to make it through this, my love."

"Yes, we are. We can do this together." She wrapped her

arms around his chest and kissed him, then rested her cheek against him. The top of her head tucked neatly under his chin. Sam put his arm around her, and they stood still for a moment, gathering strength from one another.

Slowly, they eased down the steps of the yurt, leaving plenty of white smoke trailing upward from the chimney. Moving quickly, Sam and Georgia crept behind the structure to find the trail to the highway. The crushed granite trail was lighter than the underbrush. They could follow it easily in the dark, but their steps made a loud crunching sound.

"We're making a lot of noise," Georgia said. "I wonder how far sound travels."

"It can't be helped," Sam said. "The moon is coming up soon, and we'll have light enough to find other places to step."

"How are you feeling, Sam?"

"I'm not as dizzy," he said. "Plus, I have some energy back. Hopefully the trail won't be as rough as what we've endured for the past two days."

The moon did light their way, and they quickly fled down the path that led to the trailhead and the main road. Together they set up a rhythm in their footsteps that conveyed determination. They'd left the yurt around 2:00 a.m. Sam figured that with the distance they had to walk and the time they'd been on the path, they should hit the highway well before dawn.

As they walked, they were silent, each thinking what to do

next. Who should they call? Who could they trust? They heard night noises all around them. With each sound they prepared for the worst. So many things were wearing them down. Sam wondered how long they could hold on. Often, they stopped and listened, fearing their enemy had found them, but all they heard were the animals scurrying into the underbrush.

Two hours passed and still there was no sign of a highway before them. They stopped to rest every few minutes and listen for road noises. The moon moved higher in the sky, and while it helped light their path, it also would show the way for the man behind them.

At the top of a ridge, they stopped to get their bearings. In the distance, they saw headlights.

"How far do you think that is, Sam?"

"About a mile, but it depends on how straight the trail is."

The sky showed hints of lighter blue in the east by the time Sam and Georgia reached the road. They rested on the guard posts and waited for the next driver.

Sam heard the truck before he saw it round the steep curve. He ran to the road and stood in the middle, waving. The eighteen-wheeler slowed down. Georgia joined him, and together they ran after it. For two hundred yards, the trucker applied his brakes. Sam and Georgia were nearing the back of the trailer when a loud clunk hit the side. Sam knew the bullet had struck close.

"Hurry, Georgia!" Another shot came in low and glanced

off the pavement in front of them. They'd reached the back door of the dual cab, and Georgia was climbing in when the third shot hit the frame of the truck.

"Is that gunfire?" the truck driver shouted, taking his foot off the brake.

The big eighteen-wheeler started rolling again. Another shot rang out.

"Take my hand," the burly man shouted, stretching his arm out to Georgia and pulling her up and onto the seat. Then she turned and tugged on Sam's jacket to get him inside. With his good arm, he grabbed the doorjamb and made it to the edge of the seat. He grabbed the door handle and slammed it shut. Another bullet hit the truck. The semi steadily gained momentum going down the mountain, and within seconds it was out of sight.

~~~

Jenson had his phone close. When it rang, he checked the time. Early. It was Gonzales, of course.

"You and Hood need to pick me up on the highway between Mora and Taos."

"What happened?" Jenson challenged. "Did you get 'em?"

Silence.

"You mean you missed them?" He'd known inmates like Gonzales back in Huntsville. You were a dead man if his kind came after you. It must have been a blow to him—two people he considered old. Jenson wanted to know what had happened, but he wasn't about to prod the other man any further.

"After you drop me off at my car, go into Mora and watch for them there," Gonzales said. "They're headed that way in a semi. They can't get far. If you find them, take care of business."

Jenson was wide awake. He threw a pillow at Hood. "Get up, man. We've got to go."

"What happened?"

"The Stanfields are still alive. Now come on, it's our time to go hunting. We're on our way to Mora again."

Chapter 34

Cox gazed at the sunset from his Houston tower, the same sun that sank over the Gulf and over his tank farm. If all went as expected, ten tankers from Pakistan would arrive in twenty-four hours. He raised his glass to no one but himself and nodded approval of his own success. Alone in his office, he enjoyed imagining the power he'd have over the Middle East oil countries that he'd battled through the years. They'd take notice of him now. His small oil company meant nothing to OPEC or any of the mega energy companies that existed today. That would change.

The refurbished storage tanks were full of water, and his crew in Mexico was ready to load the tankers. He wouldn't sleep until the ships were returning to Pakistan.

It had been two months to the day since he and Albert had met with the Pakistani in Mexico. They'd built enough trust for him to believe they could get the water as promised. However, the on-going negotiations would go through Lynnette. He wouldn't meet with the official again.

There was only one loose end—New Mexico. He hated unfinished business. He was so close to his goal, and this was an aggravation he wanted erased. The fact that DC voiced a concern had him wondering why. That morning the previously inconsequential issue moved up on his scale of worry. He wanted to leave this bit of "fly in the ointment" drama and move on.

Al walked in with a scowl on his face.

"What do you have?" Cox asked. He knew Al well enough to recognize when he had bad news.

"I spoke with James earlier, and he had lunch with the director of the Texas Department of Public Safety. He said the department has stepped up its investigations of the cattle deaths and the irrigation tampering. He's keeping me posted."

"We may need to cut our ties. Nothing can lead back to us."

"Your friend Harry Reynolds is snooping around, too. He's asking questions in Austin. His contacts are mostly outdated, but he may be trouble. We can't afford to underestimate Harry."

"I don't like this. Gonzales is on his way to Taos, and he's left Jenson there to finish the job. We can't leave the Stanfields alive. They'll cause a big stink if they get to the authorities." Cox thought that Gonzales would do what he said. After all, no one had suspected murder in the case of Buddy Gatwick.

~~~

Lynnette excused herself from the dullness of the training session in the small auditorium to check her burner phone. The meeting was one of several required by her firm each year. Not only was the speaker the same as the previous year, the topic was the same, too, the do's and don'ts of workplace harassment. It was an endurance test for everyone involved, but perfect cover for Lynnette to slip away and attend to other business.

She located a vacant restroom in the basement of the building and looked at the small screen. She had two voicemails, one from Texas with an update on the Stanfields, and one from Sandra confirming everything was on time. She sent James a coded text message that let him know to expect a call that evening. Then she used her time to contact Jenson. "I want an update on what's going on in New Mexico. We're getting pushback up the line."

"Gonzales is taking over here," Jenson answered.

"Is he as savage as I thought?" Lynnette shivered at his name.

"He hasn't done anything so far."

"What's he said?"

"He doesn't say much. But I'm tired of his orders, and Hood hates the guy."

"Where do you think he's from? Who sent him?"

"That's easy. I saw his tattoos. Seen them before."

"Well?"

"Drug cartel, Lynnette. Drug cartel."

"Holy shit."

"You bet your sweet ass, holy shit. I'm getting out of this. I don't want to do this anymore. Everyone is nervous, and so am I."

After the call, Lynnette felt ready to talk to Cox. She wanted to come face-to-face with the big boss. Her armor was information. She felt she had what she needed. She hurried back to the auditorium to make it to her seat before the training concluded.

"Are you okay?" her friend asked when she sat back down. "You sure did take a long time."

"Oh, sure, I just couldn't face coming back to this again," Lynnette smiled at her friend. "We're almost in compliance for another year."

Chapter 35

Sam relaxed for the first time in days as he leaned back in the big cab of the semi-truck. "Thank you," he told the driver. "You saved our lives." Sam turned his shoulder to ease the aching and watched Georgia lean back against her seat.

"What's going on here? Are you folks all right?" The driver was wide-eyed and asking questions on top of questions, not waiting for answers. Sam could tell he was nervous and excited at the same time.

"It's a long story, but you saved our lives," Georgia said. "We can't thank you enough. If you hadn't stopped for us, we'd be dead by now." She reached up and patted the driver's hand.

"The name is Stanfield. This is Georgia and I'm Sam. Thank you, sir."

"Just call me Forza. It's no problem, but what was that shooting about?"

"We ran into a bit of trouble on the trail back there, and someone was shooting at us. Do you think you could get us to the sheriff's office in Mora?" Sam wished he could give the man more explanation. He deserved it.

"Sure. I know the deputy there. I'd call him, but the reception is lousy here, and we'll be in Mora in ten minutes."

"All right," Sam agreed. He thought he could hold on that long.

"You don't look so good, man. What about getting that looked after?" Forza nodded toward Sam's bloodied bandage and shirtfront.

"Is there a doctor in Mora?" Georgia asked, nervously watching Sam. "Maybe we should go there first."

"There's a clinic across the street from the Mora Mercantile. I can drop you off there. It's not far from the sheriff's office. The doc might not be there, but someone can help you."

~~~

At least a dozen people were waiting already when Sam and Georgia walked through the clinic door.

"How much cash do you have?" Georgia asked. "I'll find us something to eat."

Sam fished out his wallet, found his insurance card, and counted his cash. "Take at least a hundred."

While Sam waited in the clinic, Georgia walked to the general store across the street and bought sandwiches and drinks. She picked up a clean shirt for Sam and a burner phone with a charger. At the checkout counter, Georgia looked out the window.

"Oh, no!" she cried as she watched the familiar van pull into the gas station two blocks away from the clinic.

"Is something wrong, ma'am?" the clerk asked.

"No, uh, I just forgot this," Georgia said, grabbing a canvas tote from the counter. She made her purchase, then stood behind a rack of caps to watch the van. One man walked into the gas station, but the driver didn't get out. Georgia decided to take a chance before the man reemerged from the station. She waited for a family to leave and hurried out the door at the same time. Then she worked her way back to the clinic. When Georgia walked into the waiting room, Sam was gone.

"Excuse me, have you called Sam Stanfield back?" Georgia asked the nurse at the counter. "I'm his wife."

The woman checked her clipboard. "Yes, he's in Room C. You can go back."

Georgia hurried down the hall and found Sam sitting on the paper-covered examination table. He looked up and smiled. "What did you find?"

Before Georgia could answer, a nurse walked in with a syringe of antibiotics. "This should help get you back on your feet." She quickly jabbed Sam in the arm, then handed him a small bottle of capsules. "Take these for the next five days. That should do it for now, but you need to come back in a week. See the nurse outside."

"What about my wife?" Sam asked before the nurse left the room.

"I don't have her papers. Talk to the nurse at the desk, and we'll get to her." She smiled at Georgia and walked out and closed the door.

"Sam, we can't stay here," Georgia frantically whispered. "The men in the van are here." She handed Sam the denim shirt she'd bought and helped him get his arms in the sleeves and button the front. Sam threw his old shirt in the trash.

"The PA took my information because of the bullet wound. She said I'd have to go to the sheriff's office. She called them, but no one's there now. I was going to head down there and wait."

"The men will see us if we go out the front."

"Then we'll go out the back." Sam opened the door and checked the hallway. They made their way to the back door and walked out of the building, heading away from the gas station and toward the Mora County Sheriff's Department. They hurried down the alley behind two vacant buildings and stopped near the sheriff's office. The jail was at the back of the building, but the entrance was on the side.

As Sam turned the corner to head for the door, he stopped and inched back around the corner.

"What is it?" Georgia asked as she backed up.

"The stocky guy is waiting right there. He's between us and the front door, and the van is parked on the street. They have us blocked out."

"Let's go back to the clinic."

"The door locked behind us when we left. We'd have to go

around the front. We don't know where the shooter is, either. Let's go down that dirt road." Sam pointed to the path directly behind the empty buildings.

They walked down the narrow, muddy road, which ran between two vacant lots. One had several goats penned inside, but the other was thick clumps of grass and prickly pear. Sam considered it a place to hide, if necessary.

They walked on for several blocks, passing a dozen stucco homes until they left the residential section of town. Farther down on the left side of the now-paved road, they found an auto repair shop. The garage had only one bay, filled with tools and tires, and a primered '70s VW bug resting on the rack. Outside, four vehicles were for sale, but only one had tires—a faded brown Ford pickup that had seen much better days. Spare parts rested in the bed, and bailing wire held the passenger door closed.

A woman walked up to them, wiping her greasy hands on a dirty rag. She wore baggy overalls that looked as though they belonged to someone else. "Can I help you?" she asked as she shaded her eyes from the noonday sun.

"Does this pickup run?" Sam asked.

"It did the last time I tried it. Let's see what happens." She got into the pickup and turned the key. It took a couple of tries, but the motor turned over and came to life. It sounded a little rough, but after the woman revved it a few times, it settled down into an almost regular purr. She climbed out and looked at Sam. "Beauty, eh?"

"How much will you take for it?"

"It says four hundred dollars on the windshield," she said, her smudged face unchanged.

"I have three hundred cash. That's all I have." Sam opened his wallet to show the woman the three hundred-dollar bills inside. It really was all he had. "Will you take three hundred for it?"

The woman put her hands in her pockets for a moment, thinking. "Let me call my uncle. This is his place. I'll find out." She walked back to the garage and disappeared inside.

A few minutes later, Sam and Georgia were driving the old truck down the highway toward Taos. They soon learned it wouldn't go faster than forty miles an hour and barely made it up the steep inclines. Sam drove as fast as he could going down the mountain so their momentum carried them up the other side. The woman had assured them the brakes were in decent shape, but their nerves were on edge until the road leveled out and they weren't tearing down the mountain. Then Georgia took the food out of the tote, and they ate while making their getaway.

Georgia spotted a tiny motel on the outskirts of Taos called Lost Canyon Resort. "Let's try that place. The sign says sixty dollars. I have that much left from what you gave me. We can't go on any longer without rest. I have a cell phone. We can plug it in the room and call Ray from there."

Sam turned into a one-lane drive-through. A sign directed them to a parking spot, and Sam left the motor running while Georgia went inside the motel office. Ten little box-shaped cottages made up the complex. Huge cottonwood trees towered above them, providing ample shade during the relentless summer days.

Sam was asleep with his head leaned back against the seat when Georgia returned. She carried an old-fashioned key on a ring attached to a wooden disk with the number seven burned into it. She touched Sam's shoulder, and he startled awake, then followed her in the truck to the cabin. He drove around to the far side of the cottage and backed the truck into the parking spot. Sam had spotted another exit toward the back by the motel garbage bin and had an escape plan.

Their room was simple and clean and had a view of the one-lane entrance. Sam checked the windows and closed the drapes. He sat down on the bed and moved a pillow so he could lie on his uninjured side.

"I'm going to shower, sweetheart. It won't take me long," Georgia said. She noticed Sam was already in a deep sleep atop the bed covers. She took the edge of the bedspread and pulled it over her exhausted husband. A few minutes later, she crawled in beside him and closed her eyes.

Georgia awoke before dawn as Sam thrashed and threw off the blanket. She reached across and felt his forehead. He was burning up with fever. Without waking him, she retrieved the antibiotic and Tylenol from the clinic. Sam was delirious. His eyes fluttered. He pushed her away, but he managed to awaken enough to swallow the medicine. She turned on the ceiling fan and sponged his face and neck with a cool cloth, giving him sips of water until he settled down.

All through the ordeal, Georgia talked to Sam. He could hear her voice and knew when she peeled back the bandage on the gunshot wound. He tried to talk to her, but the words wouldn't form.

"The wound is healing. Rest some more." Georgia patted him on the chest and changed the dressing.

Finally, he relaxed again.

She stretched out beside him and fell asleep, still holding his hand.

Chapter 36

Ray met Frank at the door of his office and invited him to sit inside until he finished his morning briefing with his deputies in the conference room. Ray smiled to himself. He knew there would be no glancing at papers or case materials on his desk. Years ago, he'd formed the habit of putting his files and any evidence under lock and key, no matter what the rush. His mentor and partner had instilled this daily routine into Ray. It was a good habit, and he'd never forgotten it.

Ray found Frank sipping coffee when he returned a few minutes later. Frank sat in the old wooden captain's chair in the corner, looking out the tall courthouse window at the street below.

"Morning, Frank, I see Maureen has taken care of you. I hope you have some information for me."

"This isn't a bad place, Ray. I envy you."

"I like it." Ray walked around his desk and sat down, waiting for Frank to talk.

"I can help you with this case," he finally said.

"Can you? How about Sam and Georgia Stanfield? The IRS

has frozen their assets. The EPA has levied hefty fines. If that's not enough for a sixty-year-old couple who have been the foundation of their community, let's throw in the FBI investigating them on terrorism charges." Ray's voice boomed through the halls of the old courthouse, and Maureen quietly crept up and closed the office door.

"I know how you feel," Frank tried to soften his words. "Can we put that aside for a moment and get all of the evidence on the table? Can we just look at them as though they were any other suspects?"

Ray walked behind his desk. "You remember meeting Sam Stanfield. How did he strike you? Did he seem like a man who was about to begin a crime spree?"

"No, he didn't." Frank shifted in his chair and looked out the window again.

Ray decided to push his point, despite Frank's discomfort. "Sam and his wife, Georgia, left for a meeting in the Panhandle with a lot of unhappy ranchers. Many of them have been victims of this so-called vandalism. No one has been able to contact Sam and Georgia since. They've been missing four days. The last time anyone spoke to them, they were in the New Mexico town of Mora." Ray unlocked his bottom desk drawer and retrieved a file folder marked *Stanfield*. He placed it on his desk.

"Is this the information you have on them?" Frank reached for the file, but Ray kept his hand on it.

"Before I show this to you, how about some information from your side?"

"Very well. You'll need to ask me some questions, though."

"All right, I'll play along. Are you still investigating the Stanfields as potential terrorists?"

"Their activity is still being followed on the blog, but they're not suspected of any terrorism activity at this point."

"Good. Why is the EPA involved here, and why did they issue a fine without exercising their normal notice protocols?"

"We're still considering the EPA issue. We've hit some roadblocks that we're trying to work around."

"What kind of roadblocks?" Ray wondered who could get in the way of the FBI. On second thought, he'd learned to be open-minded.

"Nobody is talking to us right now, but we'll find someone who will."

"That leaves the IRS. I know that according to the laws of civil asset forfeiture, the IRS can seize money derived from suspected illegal activities."

"That's true."

"The IRS depends upon banks to report suspicious activities, to prompt investigations. So who reported the Stanfields?"

"It would have to be an officer of a bank. I can't give you a name, but you have a few people who could have turned them in. It could have been anonymous."

"Good enough. I can find out." Ray knew Buddy had to have been behind it. The Stanfields only banked at the Oak National Bank, and Buddy was the only one there with the kind of authority to make a report like that. His death was now officially too much of a coincidence. Ray was sure this was all connected. "What kind of money are we talking about here?"

"I can't tell you that." Frank uncrossed his legs and turned toward the desk. He leaned in toward Ray. Ray knew Frank had more information. He just had to ask the right questions.

"Let's say this person had a lot of money to move. Would the money be moved to an offshore account?"

"Probably." Frank unconsciously gave a slight nod.

"Can the FBI find out who else was involved with the off-shore accounts?"

"Sometimes." Frank leaned back and relaxed.

"Do you know anyone else involved?" Ray wanted to see what else Frank would share. Even a word or two might point him in the right direction.

Frank folded his arms and stared at Ray. "You don't think it's even a remote possibility that the Stanfields are trying to get out of the country so they can access that money?"

"No, I don't." Ray frowned as he picked up the manila file folder and stood. "Follow me, Frank. I want to show you something." The men walked out of the office and down the hallway in the basement to some stairs that led to an even lower level.

Ray's phone rang, and the screen showed Joe's number. "Excuse me, Frank. I need to take this call." He swiped his phone and said, "Joe, hold on for a minute."

Ray unlocked the door for Frank and pointed to the table and rolling evidence board. Ray walked back upstairs and outside to get better reception. "Now I can hear you. What did you find out, Joe?" Ray stood on the granite stairs and covered the mouthpiece with his hand, blocking out the wind.

"I have Gracie. I just need to check with the Western Union in Taos to see if Sam and Georgia have been there to pick up the money. It won't take long."

"I'll call the Taos police and background them. They may be able to help."

Ray finished the call and returned to the basement. "I have someone in New Mexico and no word from the Stanfields."

Frank looked up from the pictures on the table. "You have quite a lot of information here, Ray. Talk to me about these two thugs connected to the cattle killings." Frank walked to the board and traced the black lines that connected Jenson and Hood to the Stanfields. "This doesn't look good for your friends."

"I know. Joe, their ranch hand, picked up their dog in Los Alamos. She's the only proof we have they were ever in New Mexico. They were in Mora when I last talked to them. The dog ended up in Los Alamos, two hours away." Ray slumped down in one of the metal chairs and fixed his gaze on the board, as if to will the answers to reveal themselves. Frank screeched the other chair across the cement floor and joined Ray in sifting through the evidence.

Chapter 37

Jenson and Hood left the Taos diner where they'd eaten breakfast and found Gonzales leaning against their van. The two rumpled thugs nodded acknowledgement as they climbed into the front seats. Jenson didn't like the way Gonzales looked at them as he pulled the side door and got in the back.

Gonzales sat behind Hood on the passenger side. He slid the door closed, latched the handle, and slid back into his seat. Jenson felt the air simmer inside. He looked at Hood, whose face was flushed.

"Get going," Gonzales instructed. "Make a right turn here and head west to the Rio Grande."

Jenson turned the key and drove out of the parking lot. He didn't hurry. He was thinking. He saw Hood begin tapping his foot and rubbing his hands on his thighs. He started to say something to calm the friction, but Hood spoke first.

"The Rio Grande," he said with a smirk. "Like the river? That's in Texas, man. Don't you know nothing?"

"Shut up, Hood," Jenson said. "You don't know what you're talking about."

No one spoke for a minute, then Hood laughed. "What's the matter? Too dumb to answer me?" He turned to grin at the Mexican but couldn't see him in the darkness of the van. Hood glanced at Jenson when he shifted back to the front with a sneer on his face as though saying, "I told him." Hood shrugged his shoulders.

"I told you to shut up," Jenson said, trying to sound more intense so Hood would understand the danger he was in. "The Rio Grande starts up in Colorado and goes all the way to the Gulf of Mexico. The one in Texas. So just shut up." Jenson gripped the steering wheel and stared forward.

Jenson drove west under Gonzales's directions until they spotted a break in the terrain, indicating a ravine. He turned left and drove south, following the river's meandering path. They were on a dirt road, the river at least a hundred feet below them. The silence was a comfort to Jenson. He relaxed and concentrated on driving.

"Turn here." Gonzales leaned forward to point to a small dirt road that headed down into the canyon, closer to the river.

Jenson slowed and drove down the switchbacks. He didn't like the steep, narrow road, so he slowed to a crawl as he descended into the gorge.

It wasn't long until Gonzales issued another order: "Park over there."

Jenson stopped on a small pullout on the edge of a cliff. The semicircle looked as though it could have been an observation look-out at one time. The view to the west was unimpeded, highlighting the high desert landscape.

Gonzales began barking commands from the backseat. "Check all of the motels in Taos and look for a tan pickup. One of you stake out the police station in case they make it there. If they do, we'll have to get to them quickly."

"We wouldn't be in this situation if you'd done what you were supposed to do out there in the forest," Hood barked back. "You dumbass! You never knew about the river, either, just like you didn't know how to kill those two in the woods." Hood's rant stretched into a shriek. The more he talked, the more enraged he became. "I can't believe they sent someone like you." Sprays of saliva fell with every word. "That old couple beat you. They are still winning. Loser! L—" Hood's scream filled the van. His eyes bulged. Blood streamed down his chest.

Jenson heard a loud click, and two side blades sprang outward from the center of the dagger and created a three-pronged weapon. Gonzales had reached around the seat and stabbed Hood's torso over and over. Jenson watched Gonzales's hand grow slick with Hood's blood. The trifecta stiletto barely made a sound as it moved in and out.

Hood struggled for breath. He stared at the knife as it plunged in and out of his body. He tried to lift his arms, but Gonzales pinned them back. The thrusts moved to his gut, to his genitals, to his ribs, above his collar bone.

Jenson heard gurgling. *How can he still be alive?* he thought. He was still staring at his partner's blood-covered chest when Gonzales jerked open the passenger door and dragged Hood from the van. Jenson felt frozen. He couldn't do anything. Hood was still trying to scream when Gonzales cut out his tongue and threw Hood to the ground. Jenson gripped the steering wheel hard.

Gonzales turned toward him. "Get rid of the body, and then go watch the jail. Burn this van. Get another car." Gonzales handed Jenson a roll of bills, turned his back on Hood and walked down the dirt road a half mile, where he washed his hands in the Rio Grande.

Jenson peeled his hands from the steering wheel. He rubbed his palms across his jeans to get the circulation going while his mind raced. He knew what he had to do. He had no choice. He stepped out of the van and walked around the front bumper. Then he dragged the still-choking Hood to the edge of the cliff. Jenson stood there looking down into the darkness below. Hood's eyes focused on Jenson one last time as he rolled his partner over the edge, down the incline into a pile of rocks.

Afterward, Jenson searched for Gonzales but found no trace of him anywhere. Jenson shook his head. His ears were ringing. He held his palms up and stared at the crimson stains. He drove to the river to clean himself but realized the steering wheel was covered with Hood's blood as well as his own fingerprints. There was nothing to do except set the van on fire.

He drove toward Taos and left the vehicle parked in a ravine a few miles north of the city. He'd come back later to burn it. He pulled out the wad of bills from his pocket. He had to get new transportation and a can of gasoline.

On the road back to Taos, Jenson picked up a vehicle for sale by a house. The man took the cash, no questions asked.

An hour later, Jenson sat in his latest ride, a black 1979 Jeep, keeping an eye on the Taos police headquarters. He'd been there only a few minutes when a tow truck drove past, hauling his van into the police parking compound. He fell back against the headrest. He was dead. His blood and fingerprints were all over the van.

He thought about breaking into the compound and setting the van on fire, but the fence surrounding the lot was ten feet high and topped with stainless steel razor wire.

Now that the police had the van, he knew he had only a short time before they made him. The minute they saw the blood on the passenger seat, they'd go through the van and find his bloody clothes. He sat there frozen to the seat. He didn't know what to do. They'd go out there to look for him. As long as he was here, he wouldn't be found.

Daylight came before he decided to drive away.

Chapter 38

The night before the delivery was restless for Cox. He spent less than an hour in his bed before he gave up on sleep and started making calls. He was sitting in his leather desk chair wearing his headset when Al arrived shortly before dawn. Cox waved his partner inside. He pulled out the earbuds and poured a celebratory drink.

"Congratulations to us, Al. The first transfer is complete. The money is in the bank." Cox raised his glass and saluted the other man.

Al downed his Pellegrino. "We have countries that will pay even more than Pakistan did."

"I have a conference call set up with James. He and Lynnette are in DC." Cox picked up one of his cell phones and dialed a comparable one in Washington.

James and Lynnette were sitting in a hotel room with the phone on the desk between them. They leaned in to hear Cox.

"You did it!" James said.

"Yes, as we planned," Cox said. "Everything went well. Not one glitch."

"That's great news, Bill," James said.

"We're ready for the next contract," Cox said, standing and beginning to pace. "What have you heard from Sandra?"

"Lynnette will meet with her later this morning. She's built a rapport with Sandra. She's doing well and is about to turn another contact in the EPA."

Cox was still irritated with the Stanfield situation and couldn't restrain from bringing it up, even during the success of the project. "We still have that problem in New Mexico. Our California people aren't happy. I haven't heard from Gonzales. See what you can find out."

"I'll get back to you within the hour," James answered.

"See that you do." Cox abruptly hung up. Turning toward Albert, he drained his celebratory glass, then poured another.

~~~

Lynnette looked at her watch. Cox was up early. She stood at the hotel window and watched the river of red taillights feeding into the city. Their brightness was beginning to fade with dawn. She had her back to James, but she could hear him rustling papers on the desk and crumpling them into his briefcase. She whirled around to startle him.

"Did you get it recorded?" she asked.

"Yes, but I'm not sure about this. You take it and keep it. I don't want to get caught with it."

"We're the ones taking the risks," she pointed out. "You deserve more money for what you're doing. Recording Cox is just insurance. I don't think we'll have to use it, but at least we have it."

"I have to catch a plane soon. But it's essential we find out what's going on in New Mexico. You get in touch with Jenson. See what you can find out."

"I thought Cox was getting a direct report." Lynnette was nervous about getting in touch with Jenson. She hadn't heard from him in a while, but she wanted to know firsthand what was going on in New Mexico.

"Just do it, Lynnette."

She heard the exasperation in James's voice. He was tired. The pressure was weighing on him. But she was close to getting what she wanted, so she kept asking questions. "When can I go to Houston and meet with Cox? I can fill him in on DC and New Mexico. Let me do this for you."

Lynnette watched his expression soften. He was considering the idea. He slipped on his suit coat and pulled his cuffs down over his wrists. She waited. She held back.

"I'll talk to him," James said at last. " The trip to his ranch is inevitable. It's quite an experience."

~~~

Lynnette and Sandra met on a busy side street in the middle of Georgetown. Cars filled every parking space and blocked every driveway. People scurried past. Lynnette kept halting their conversation. There were too many people around them, and they'd been on the public street together for too long. She felt eyes from every direction. One pair could be the wrong ones. Why wasn't Sandra more aware?

Lynnette took control. "Follow me and stay about fifty feet back. I'll find us a better place to talk." She walked east, continuing for half an hour before she slipped into a bar set back from the sidewalk. She stood at the door, waiting to adjust to the darkness. Stale cigarette smoke burned her eyes, and a thin cloud hovered above the high-backed booths. Lynnette quickly scanned the dark interior. There were only three other people inside—a young male bartender, a woman leaning on the far end of the bar, and a man sitting by himself in the first booth, reviewing a stack of receipts. Lynnette walked directly to the last booth.

"Nice," Sandra said a minute later when she scooted into the seat across from Lynnette.

"Isn't it? It's the best I could do considering the circumstances. At least I don't think we'll run into any of your colleagues from the State Department in here."

A waitress walked from the bar over to them, her heels clicking. "Order?" the woman asked. She stared at her feet.

"Do you have coffee?" Sandra asked.

"Sure. I can make a fresh pot," the woman answered. She sounded disinterested. Lynnette thought her demeanor was practiced. She was used to not noticing the clientele. She was dressed so no one noticed her, either.

"Make that two coffees," Lynnette said.

As the waitress disappeared, Sandra began to chatter away, to fill the void.

Lynnette raised her palm to silence her. She had to bring the conversation under control. She would carefully choose her words. "Hold my hand." Lynnette stretched her hand across the table, and Sandra took it. "We need to look more like lovers than conspirators. This already looks like a clandestine meeting." With the other hand, Lynnette covered her phone on the table with a thin paper napkin and pushed the button on the side.

They released their hands and sat back when the woman set the thick white cups in front of them. The rich aroma briefly cut the odor of stale beer. Lynnette held her hot mug close to her face while she recorded Sandra's words.

"I have three sub-Saharan countries that are ready to sit down and discuss water purchases—if you can deliver within the next six months."

"We can do that." Lynnette didn't hesitate. She was confident.

"I have to be sure when I sit down with them." Sandra's voice was watery, giving Lynnette the impression she was faltering on the deal.

"We're aware of your important part in this, and we're grateful," Lynnette reassured her.

"Just how grateful? I won't be able to spend this money for

a long time, and when I do, I won't be able to go to work anymore," Sandra was breathless. "I don't want to wait to enjoy my life."

So, there it was. Sandra wanted her cake now. Lynnette couldn't really blame her. How long could she do this and not get caught? "Let me see what I can do. I know you couldn't have put away too much cash working for the government. But the more successful we are, the more generous he'll be." Lynnette wanted to sound sympathetic and gain Sandra's trust. She hadn't known Cox's name for very long, and she was counting on the fact that Sandra didn't know much about him, either. Lynnette was building confidence with Sandra. She wanted more information from her, and if she had the country contact names, she could prove her worth.

"We'll be successful," Sandra said. "Don't worry about that. I know more, and I'm smarter than anyone else in the department—and my contact is smart."

Lynnette leaned back. Sandra was underestimating people. That was sure to get her in trouble. She and this partner of hers were on their way out. They just didn't know it yet. "Are you sure you can trust him?" Lynnette asked.

Sandra nodded. "I've known him for a long time, since college."

"How can he help us? What kind of power does he have?"

"He has people under him who can issue fines and push land into foreclosure. It can be very profitable for someone who can afford it."

Like Cox, Lynnette thought. *He could afford it.* Surely Sandra knew of Cox's land purchases. Lynnette stopped short of asking her partner's name. Sandra had given her enough information to identify him anyway. There was no need to make her suspicious.

Chapter 39

Sam felt Georgia's absence as soon as the door clicked shut behind her. He propped himself up on the edge of the bed and looked around the tiny room. Sam saw the bottle of water on the nightstand and realized his throat was horribly dry. He forced himself to take small sips.

"Georgia?" he called.

Then he saw the note. She'd gone into Taos. He was relieved at first, then worried for her safety. He decided to clean up, but when he tried to stand, he fell against the nightstand. He'd been in bed too long. His muscles needed activity. He had to move.

Sam struggled up and shuffled across the carpet toward the bathroom, holding on to the furniture as he moved. He couldn't believe how weak he was. He had to stop several times before he finally managed to get into the shower.

The hot water eased Sam's soreness. He stood in the steamy room and felt warm for the first time in days. They'd been so cold on the trail. When the water became tepid, Sam turned off the faucet and hurried to dry and dress. He almost felt normal as he sat in the small room. He opened the phone Georgia had purchased in Mora and plugged it in to charge. He wasn't sure how long it would take before he could make a call to Ray. He propped himself up on the bed and rested.

Sam jumped awake. He was panting, and he could feel his heart throbbing in his throat. He searched his mind to remember where he was. Then he realized Georgia still wasn't there. He grew sick with worry. Had something happened?

He surveyed the room to try to think what he could do, and his eyes stopped on the phone charging on the chest. He realized he should be calling for help. He sat up quickly and was flooded with nausea and dizziness that took several minutes to subside. Sam breathed deeply, then stood slowly, intent on retrieving the phone. He knew only an instant before he blacked out that he was going to fall. He couldn't stop it. His body betrayed him. He fell forward onto the floor.

~~~

When Georgia opened the door to the cottage, she found Sam on the floor beside the bed.

"Sam!" Georgia rushed to kneel beside him. She dropped her packages and felt for his pulse. "Sam, what happened?"

Sam moaned and opened his eyes. "Georgia," he whispered.

"Don't try to move." Georgia lifted his head and slid a pillow underneath.

"I think I blacked out." Sam tried to remember. "I got up to get the phone and call Ray."

"We'll take care of that. Don't worry." Georgia sat on the floor and held his hand.

"I was worried about you," Sam said. "Even after I found your note. That was risky."

"Maybe, but I made it to Taos and found everything I needed. I was tired of running and hiding. I think being around people made me feel better."

"I'm glad you're back safely."

"Are you feeling better? What about your shoulder?"

"Not so bad, but still tired. I believe I can sit up." Sam made it to the bed and sat down hard. He felt like his heart was beating out of his chest. "I'd better rest a bit more."

"Here, it's time for you to take this." Georgia picked up the bottle of water for him, and Sam took the antibiotic she offered.

"Did you have any trouble?" he asked as he lay back against the pillow.

"It just took longer than I thought it would." Georgia sat gingerly on the bed beside Sam. "Ray did send the money to Western Union. He thought to send pictures of us and copies of our driver's licenses. I showed the clerk your driver's license, and she gave me the money. Then I bought groceries and fresh clothes."

"We need to call Ray."

"I know, but you need something to eat, so let me get that first." Georgia opened a can of soup and began to heat it in the ancient microwave.

"Did you find the police station or notify the police?"

"I was going to, but I was afraid to leave you alone too long." Georgia handed Sam the steaming mug and a spoon. "I had no idea how long they'd detain me before I could get back. I thought we were safe here and could call Ray to see what we should do."

"Let's call now. Unfortunately, his cell number went over the cliff with my phone and the truck. We'll have to dial information."

"Right. We also need to call Joe." Georgia opened the phone.

"I think this is the best chicken noodle soup I've ever had in my life." Sam managed a smile, then listened as Georgia left messages for Ray and Joe.

"Let's hope they call back soon," she said, smiling.

Chapter 40

Ray pinned a photograph of Buddy Gatwick to his evidence board. It was the one Beth had used in his obituary. He looked boyish and innocent. Buddy had been naïve, but he'd hurt Sam and Georgia as well as his wife before he died.

Ray was convinced Buddy's death wasn't an accident. Frank had learned that Buddy was the one who'd turned Sam and Georgia in to the IRS. They had suspiciously large sums of money coming into their account and immediately going out again. The fact that the Bar S crime and the deposits occurred around the same time wasn't a coincidence.

Maureen stuck her head in the door. "Ray, there's a call for you on line one from a detective in Taos, New Mexico. It sounds urgent."

Ray pressed the button for line one. "Sheriff Collins here."

"Sheriff, my name is Bronson, Detective Bronson. Some kayakers here found a man's body at the bottom of a cliff by the Rio Grande River. We've identified the body as J. D. Hood, the man you're looking for. His fingerprints match, and we recognized him from the picture you provided."

"Was it a homicide?"

"It's definitely murder," Bronson said. "He has seventeen stab wounds in his abdomen, chest, and groin area, and he had his tongue cut out. We found the kill spot near the cliff. Someone dragged him and shoved him over the edge. We don't have the coroner's final report, but we think he bled to death, and they threw him over the cliff to get rid of the body."

"Any sign of his partner, Jenson?" Ray asked. "He has to be in the area. They were working together."

"Evidence is piling up fast. We found the crime scene yesterday, but we didn't know it at the time. The Taos Pueblo Tribal Police found a van across town from where the stabbing occurred. Someone had abandoned it on tribal land. They towed it to the police yard. That's when we discovered all the blood on the front passenger seat. We also found dozens of prints from both Jenson and Hood inside the vehicle."

"Jenson and Hood are suspects here in the Bar S Ranch crimes as well. We have video of them together here."

"We did receive your inquiry about the Stanfield couple. We don't have anything on them."

"I'm afraid something terrible has happened to them."

"We have a statewide APB on Jenson," Bronson said. "He may have headed south, and if he stops in Santa Fe or Albuquerque, we have a good chance of hearing about it."

"Let's hope he doesn't take the back roads and disappear into the desert," Ray said. He was concerned that if Jenson disappeared, he'd never hear from Sam and Georgia again.

"We collected a box of items from the van. We have a machete with blood, but it's not the murder weapon. Hood was killed by a knife with a slim blade."

"That could be what they used to mutilate the cattle," Ray said. "Was there anything else?"

"We found two sleeping bags, and we have the usual assortment of cups and food boxes, but one thing is a little strange," Bronson said. "We have a bag of crosses."

"Crosses? Can you send me a picture of the crosses?" Ray asked. "There may be a connection to one of our churches here."

"Sure. I'll send it from my phone as soon as we hang up. We'll let you know if we find out anything about the Stanfields."

"One more thing," Ray said. "They may show up at the Western Union. They'd be picking up money there."

"I'll ask an officer to go by and check. We'll tell them to call us if they show up there."

Soon after he hung up, Ray's phone dinged, and he glanced through twelve pictures of different crosses. After he printed the pictures, he'd take them to the Methodist church.

Ray walked over to the rolling evidence board and wrote *deceased* across Hood's picture.

Chapter 41

The little black phone plugged into the wall charger at the Lost Canyon Resort kept ringing. Sam struggled through a haze to come awake, as Georgia jumped awake and sat up in the bed. Sam finally reached the dresser and answered.

"Sam! Are you and Georgia all right?" Ray asked. "Joe and I have been searching for you. We've been worried."

"Both of us are fine now, Ray, but we haven't been." Sam felt for the bed with his free hand. He had to sit down. He didn't want to black out again. He felt better but was still weak. "We've had some trouble, but we're safe now."

"What happened?"

Sam rubbed his forehead as he sank into the soft mattress. "After we talked to you last, we were driving to Taos when a man ran us off the road. Our rig went down the side of the mountain. It was a miracle we survived. The rest is a really long story." Sam paused, waiting for another wave of dizziness to subside. His heart was beating fast and his head was throbbing. His voice sounded weak even to him, and he leaned back on the pillows for support.

"Ray, talk to Georgia for a minute. She can fill you in on the details."

"Ray?" Georgia asked as she lifted the phone.

"Georgia, tell me what happened. Is Sam okay?"

"We've been on the run. Someone has been trying to kill us."

Ray could hear the desperation and fear in Georgia's voice. "Can you describe them or tell me anything you remember? Take your time."

"Sam and I heard them talking where the truck went over the cliff. We heard one call the other one Hood. They both talked about a man named Gonzales. He's the man who shot Sam."

"Shot? You didn't say Sam was shot! Is he okay? Will he be all right?"

"Sam has been through a lot. I was worried about him for a while. But I think he's mending." She stepped around the bed and started digging through the groceries while she talked to Ray.

"You both need to get to the hospital."

"That would help, but we've been afraid to leave the room." She handed cheese sticks and an apple to Sam. "We can recognize this man, Gonzales, and I don't believe he's given up looking for us. The other two men in a van have been following us since Oklahoma."

"Stay there, Georgia." Ray was insistent. "I'll call and get the Taos police to come and get you. They've been looking for you. Promise me you'll be there."

"We will, Ray." Georgia set the phone on the nightstand,

then leaned on the bed beside Sam. "The Taos police are coming to get us. Ray wants us to stay where we are."

Georgia began to put their things back into the sacks from her shopping and get ready for the police to pick them up. After a few minutes, she sat down again to rest, but Sam was anxious. He went to the window and glanced outside. He saw a man walk out of the cottage next to them. Sam stepped back quickly and closed the gap in the drapes. He was glad their room lights were off.

"Did you see them?" Georgia sat up. "Are they here?"

Sam put his index finger to his lips to quiet Georgia. The front door was their only way out. The window in the bathroom had been painted shut long ago. Gonzales would see them if they tried to leave.

"What is it, Sam?" Georgia whispered. "You're scaring me."

Sam returned to the bed and put his arm around Georgia's shoulder, drawing her close. "I believe I saw Gonzales outside. He didn't see me, but we have to be quiet while we wait for the police."

"No!" Georgia said. She buried her face in his shirt. "What are we going to do? What if he finds us?"

"We'll stay alert. We'll keep our movements to a minimum."

Georgia crept quietly back to the window, peering through the slim ribbon of light. Then she saw Gonzales's boot hit the first step of his cabin. "Sam!" she whispered in terror. "He just went into the cabin next door!"

"Are you sure?" Sam struggled up from the bed. He returned

to the window and stood beside Georgia to keep watch.

"Absolutely. I'll never forget him. How did he find us? Why hasn't he come for us if he knows we're here?" Georgia felt frozen.

"If you're sure it's the same man, then we have to see what we can do to protect ourselves. There's only one way out—the front door." Sam dragged the desk chair along the dusty carpet and angled its metal back underneath the doorknob.

"Maybe he doesn't know we're here." Georgia watched at the window.

"We can hope for that, but let's be prepared. The window leaves the bed exposed to the outside. We shouldn't sit on it. We could be shot through the window."

"What else can we do?"

Sam looked around the room. "This place isn't particularly substantial. If he has weapons that can pierce metal like with the eighteen-wheeler, these thin wooden doors and walls won't protect us. We'll have to use the bathroom for protection. Come help me move this chest, Babe."

Sam and Georgia managed to squeeze the chest into the small bathroom, but they had to balance it on the edge of the tub and the toilet to be able to close the door. After they moved into the tight space behind the door, they shoved the chest over so it stood upright again.

"If he shoots, we can both climb into the bathtub," Sam said. "I believe this old girl is cast iron and will protect us a bit." Sam was in survival mode, thinking ahead for every possibility.

"What about someone coming to get us? Shouldn't the Taos police be here by now?"

"I hope they come soon. We could use some help."

The couple sat on the edge of the tub, listening and waiting. The sun had passed over the roof of the cottages and cast a shadow on the front doors. The boards on cabin seven's front porch creaked in the quiet afternoon. Something brushed against the stucco walls. Sam and Georgia heard him coming. Sam wrapped his arm around Georgia and cupped her elbow to pull her back into the tub. They crouched together in the long, narrow tub.

The doorknob rattled once, twice. Then all pretense of stealth evaporated, and the intruder began banging on the door. He splintered a panel, but the metal chair held. The door wouldn't move any further.

Georgia reached for Sam's hand. "It has to be him—the man who shot at us. He knows we're in here."

"Call 911. It may be our only chance." Sam kept watching the bathroom door, expecting someone to burst through at any moment.

Another crack echoed around the cottage as Gonzales pounded on the front door again.

"He may be able to break in and just come over the chair," Sam said.

Georgia had the 911 dispatcher on the phone. She gave the

address. "Lost Canyon, cabin 7. Someone is trying to break down our door. We're hiding in the bathroom. Please hurry. Yes, I'll stay on the line."

"Let's lie down in the tub," Sam said. "He can shoot through the walls, but he doesn't know where we are."

Sam and Georgia were shifting to lie down in the tub when the small square window high on the wall above the toilet burst into pieces. Shards of glass flew across the room and shattered against the chest at the door. Georgia dropped the cell phone, and it skittered across the floor and under the chest. A 9 mm followed the glass through the open window and pointed in their direction.

Sam thought the elevated window would be even higher on the outside wall of the cottage, making firing into the room difficult. He pushed Georgia behind him, close to the back wall where the gun couldn't be angled at them. They watched the pistol inch into the room and methodically fire in an arc. Gonzales fired and moved, and fired again. The bullets missed them but ricocheted when they hit the old tub. Bullets riddled the chest. Glass from the medicine cabinet and plaster from the walls flew across the bathroom at Sam and Georgia. They covered their faces while bits and pieces of the old bathroom peppered them.

Sam decided he had to grab for the gun, but it was hard for him to get in a position for leverage. If he leaned forward, he'd be in the line of fire. Sam picked up the plunger from beside the toilet. He raised it above his head and brought the wooden handle down on the gun. It rattled to the floor.

"You did it, Sam!"

Sam sat back down in the tub, but within seconds, Gonzales began firing through the walls of the bathroom with a rifle. Sam's move had given away their position. Sam and Georgia lay down as flat as possible. Georgia fit, but Sam had to bend his knees. They thought the barrage would never end. Gonzales fired, reloaded, and fired again. During the lull of a reload, Sam and Georgia heard sirens in the distance. The firing continued another minute, then stopped.

Sam opened his eyes, staring in horror at their surroundings. The room was annihilated. "How did we survive?" He looked at Georgia. She was covered with shards of glass and debris. Small trickles of blood dotted her arms and face. He didn't dare touch her for fear of making it worse. "Are you all right?"

Georgia nodded as Sam touched his own face, realizing he'd fared about the same. Sam picked the splinters and glass from his hands and pushed on the sides of the tub to climb out. The sirens grew louder.

"Be careful getting out. Do you think it's safe?"

"I think our help has come."

Four Taos police cruisers raced into the one-lane entrance of the Lost Canyon Resort and surrounded cabin 7.

Chapter 42

Lynnette leaned closer to her computer, reading for the second time a substantial article about the more than three billion people who suffer from a lack of potable water, all of them potential customers. This latest research would help the EPA prove that irrigation practices for high-maintenance crops around the world were big contributors to the water shortage. Like all impactful research, it could be manipulated to suit the needs of those who would profit the most from the data.

Lynnette had learned that Sandra and her partner had come up with a plan to use the EPA system to their advantage. Agents would be directed to target water runoff offenders. Then the steep fines for violations of the Clean Water Act would force foreclosures. Then the land could be acquired cheaply.

Lynnette pitched the plan to Cox over the phone, and he loved it. He asked her to visit his ranch.

Lynnette soon discovered that Cox was an old hand at manipulating information. He had teams that launched trends and anti-farmer propaganda on social media to turn the general sentiment against farmers. Food growers of America would soon become the resource-consuming fat cats hated by the very people they fed. What irony, and how easily the regular citizen believed intentional misinformation. The EPA could move forward and force the federal regulations on state agencies, too. Some states had written laws to block individuals from consuming water runoff from their homes and barns. Lynnette's mind drifted to the real, life-threatening water issues and how Cox's plans were working out.

The data she'd collected on him was damaging. Lynnette clicked send, and the information arrived in seconds, safe on a distant server. She wanted to be sure she was protected by proof. She knew how dangerous this game of intrigue was, but she didn't regret the path she'd taken. Extra safety measures just made her feel better.

During lunch, Lynnette called James on her safe phone and told him about the meeting with Cox. She could always get a feel for what was happening just by talking to him. He revealed too much through his voice, especially on the phone.

"Bring your information about the Mexico and the Rio Grande water theft. I think we'll have a chance to set up a deal with Cox and still use his Mexico port."

She kept their conversation short and focused. Even if their phones were safe, she took no chances. Precautions had become second nature to her, but Lynnette worried that even her vigilance might allow a mishap. She was always worrying about someone cracking her hard-edged exterior and exposing her.

Lynnette flew to Austin with her Mexico file. She arrived at the apartment first and busied herself making coffee.

James arrived while the pot was still perking. He opened the door with an enthusiasm she hadn't seen in months. "That smells good," he said. "Pour me a cup, will you? Then tell me what you have."

"I have contacts and meetings with officials from Mexico, and we're going to specifically address the Rio Grande water issue. I'll make my pitch to two of the delegates, separately, of course. Both have ties to different cartels, and I think they'll want to get in on this as soon as they understand the true significance for exercising control over certain regions in their territory."

James stood behind the sofa and crossed his arms. His mouth disappeared in a grimace. "We have to be careful, though, or this could backfire. They could decide to take off on their own when they understand how this works. They could take over the water network in Mexico."

"Yes, they could begin to run operations themselves. It could be business as usual with the cartels."

"Be ready for these questions from Cox. He'll ask you for your contacts."

"Why? Do you think they're different from the one he's working with in California?"

"He wants to know everything. And how did you know about California?"

"Well, now that you've asked that question, I know for sure." Lynnette smiled. "I made the connection when you brought in Gonzales. Who else would be that willing to kill someone that easily? Jenson knew right away."

"You're right, but I don't know what cartel. Cox is pretty closemouthed. I'm not sure I want to know, anyway."

"How will the water shortage affect the US, James? Will part of the United States become desert?"

"I know what you're asking, Lynnette, but if we don't do it someone else will. How long do you think the world will play nice when millions of people begin to die of thirst? This political game will turn into worldwide domination."

Lynnette walked to the kitchen counter and poured a cup of coffee as she listened to James justify his and Cox's actions. She wrapped her hands around the mug to steady trembling hands. "I understand," she said.

"I'd rather be in power than standing in line for water," James said. "There are parts of the world much worse off than you can ever imagine."

"So, for the United States, the more arid parts of the country will have the shortages."

"Yes, that's true," James admitted.

Lynnette watched his face change ever so slightly to bewilderment and back to arrogance in a split second. It was as though he'd thought about having a conscience but dismissed it quickly.

"But if we can get some hype going against Mexico, we can blame the lack of water on them."

"That's the idea. We must take any attention away from the Mallard Project."

"It shouldn't be hard. Mexico has broken the agreement, if they ever intended to keep it in the first place. They're already taking more than their share of the water flowing into the Rio Grande."

James nodded. "They are. The diversion dams they have in the Sierra Madre Oriental Mountains south of the river are no secret to the US government. US citizens are the only ones who don't know what's going on."

"We can use the information about the Mexico dams to distract news about increasing water shortages in the southwestern states. The media will jump all over this. Public opinion will be directed toward Mexico and the cartels."

"Exactly. That's my girl. Cox will be impressed."

James finished his coffee and left in a hurry for the Capitol. As soon as Lynnette closed the door behind him, she walked to the window and watched him drive off in his silver Mercedes. Then she removed the scarf from her phone on the table and pushed the stop button. She was pleased. James had implicated Cox and revealed the true purpose of the Mallard Project.

Chapter 43

Sam's ears rang with echoes of the gunshots and the wails of the ambulance siren, but he didn't mind the noise, nor the rough ride to the hospital. He watched the medic adjust his IV. Sam didn't like lying down. He moved to sit up.

"Sir, you need to be still, so you won't pull out the needle in your arm."

"What happened to the man shooting at us? Did they get him?"

"I didn't see anyone. You'll have to ask the police."

Sam found it bizarre to watch the hospital staff rush around taking care of Georgia and him. For a week, they'd driven themselves to the limits of their endurance. Sam wasn't comfortable having others take control. It was hard to relinquish being in charge.

Sam and Georgia stayed together in the hospital for two days while a police officer kept watch outside their room. Sam learned they were in protective custody until law enforcement could straighten out their predicament. He wanted to know what their predicament was.

Then Ray called the hospital room. "Sam, I'm glad to hear you and Georgia are all right."

"What can you tell us, Ray?"

"I've been keeping in touch with the police there. You can trust them, so tell them everything you can."

"We have. But what's really going on? The officers here are so vague."

"They agreed to let me tell you."

"Tell me what?"

"I'm afraid you and Georgia have warrants for your arrest for tax evasion. That's why your bank accounts are frozen."

"That doesn't make sense. Why? This is wrong, Ray. Who's behind this?"

"Let's get you home, and we can work on it together. Until then, we must follow protocol." Ray just wanted them back in Waggoner as soon as possible so he could control the investigation. "I'm sending two deputies to meet you at the Texas border and bring you back. I think that will be the safest way."

"But Ray, we don't understand," Sam said. "Georgia and I have been struggling to stay alive. Someone wants us dead. And we're talking about tax evasion?"

"I agree with you, but you and Georgia must get back to Waggoner. You'll be safer here."

"All right. I think the doctor will dismiss us soon. We'll leave then."

"Sam, I have more bad news. The EPA has ordered you to remove your cattle from your land or else be fined. They say the cattle are polluting the waterways on your ranch. Joe brought the letter to me, and I got permission to open it. They gave you two days to move your cattle."

"That's impossible. Where would we move them to, even if we were there?"

"You and Georgia have a lot of friends, Sam. They've already made it possible. People came from all over the county to help. The cattle have already been moved, and you have folks taking care of your cows until you get back."

"I don't know what to say. I'm overwhelmed."

"There are lots of good people here. We are going to solve this."

There was a time of silence on the other end as Sam caught Georgia up on everything.

"I do have some good news for you. Gracie is back here at the ranch. A priest in Los Alamos found her and called the number on her tags. Joe drove there and picked her up."

"How did she get to Los Alamos? We lost her in the wreck. We thought she was dead."

"Another part of the mystery."

~~~

Sam watched the squad car pull up in front of the hospital. He guessed it was their ride to the state line. He was dressed and

ready to walk out the door. Georgia was packing their few belongings in the tote from Mora. Neither of them sat in the wheelchairs
that had been brought for them. They were ready to go home.

Sam turned from the window when the Taos police chief
knocked on the door.

"You've been medically cleared, Mr. Stanfield," the chief
said. "The doctor says you and Mrs. Stanfield are fit for travel."

"We're eager to get home, Chief," Georgia said, joining Sam
by the door. "Are we leaving now?"

"The deputies driving you have the extradition papers. The
warrants will be served when you get to Texas. I'm sorry it has to
be like this."

"We'll be fine, Chief, and we can get everything straightened
out when we get back home," Sam said. "I'm sure of it." He wasn't
sure it would be easy, though.

The two deputies interrupted the conversation and stood
shoulder to shoulder just inside the door. "We're here to take you to
the squad car."

The older of the two smiled and mock-scolded Sam and
Georgia. "Okay, you two, let's get the cuffs. That's the only way I'm
letting you out of here."

"I don't know," the other one said. "She looks pretty tough.
I give up."

Georgia smiled as she and Sam left the room. The chief
walked along with them. He was their official escort.

"We're going to take you as far as the state line and meet the

Texas deputies there," he said. "They'll take you the rest of the way. It will be five hours to the border, and as you know the longest leg will be the one in Texas. The trip will take you twelve hours."

Sam and Georgia sat in the back of the squad car and waited for the second deputy to climb in the passenger side. Sam took a deep breath of the cool, dry air, leaned back, and relaxed against the seat. "Quite a different trip going back," he said.

"Yes," Georgia said. "It's as though I've never seen this country before."

Sam searched for familiar places as the officer drove them through the mountains. The bright, sunny day and safety of the car changed everything. Georgia was quiet, and Sam didn't want to disturb her peace. He saw the forest road. They slowed passing through Mora, and the miles melted away on the road to Texas.

The Texas deputies were waiting for them at a gas station on Interstate 40. The exchange was made, and New Mexico and Texas law enforcement shook hands and went their separate ways.

"Do I know you, Deputies?" Sam asked, trying to engage the men in conversation and find out news from Waggoner.

"Probably not," the driver said. "We're new."

"How long have you been in Waggoner?" Sam pressed.

"Why don't you sit back and keep quiet?" the man snapped. "This is a long trip, and I don't like talking."

Sam did as instructed. *We must be in more trouble than I thought.* He needed to talk to Ray. He reached over and patted Georgia's hand. She had been silent, but now she looked distressed. When Sam caught her eye, she just shook her head and nodded slightly at the men in the front seat.

After a few miles, the deputy turned off the highway and headed north.

"Why aren't we going through Amarillo?" Sam asked.

"We're taking the roundabout way," the driver answered. "We don't want to get caught in traffic."

Sam and Georgia knew the country well. They weren't going around Amarillo. The squad car kept heading north into the Panhandle. Georgia looked at Sam with wide eyes. They were both alarmed.

Looking more closely, Sam saw that both men wore leather jackets that covered up insignias or county identification. They were in uniform, so he hadn't thought much of it earlier. Now they'd passed through two small towns and were still headed north.

"Where are you taking us?" he demanded. "This isn't the way to Waggoner. In fact, this is completely opposite of Waggoner."

"Is that a fact?" The other deputy spoke for the first time. "We have other business to attend to. If you don't be quiet and sit back, we'll have to put cuffs on both of you. Now shut up." Then he pulled out his handgun, turned in his seat, and pointed it directly at Georgia.

Sam leaned in front of the gun and pushed Georgia behind him. "Wait a minute. There's no—"

The man hit Sam in the face. The barrel left a red streak across Sam's jaw and knocked him back against Georgia.

"Sam!" Georgia screamed.

Sam threw up his arm to stop another blow, and the man cocked the pistol. "Shut up, both of you. Put these on him. Maybe that'll settle him down."

Sam encouraged Georgia to put the cuffs on him. Tears streamed down her face, but she finally fastened them on Sam's wrists. She scooted closer to him and buried her face on his shoulder.

"That's better. Maybe now you can behave until we get there."

Sam wanted to know where "there" was. He'd known for a while that these men weren't law enforcement. They were part of this conspiracy that Ray and he had talked about.

Eventually, the driver slowed and turned down a gravel road. He drove about five miles and pulled up in front of a deserted farmhouse. Sam studied every detail. If he and Georgia survived, he wanted to remember this place. An old wooden barn with a shed stood several hundred feet from the house.

The driver pulled the squad car into the barn. Before it even stopped, the deputy in the passenger seat swung his pistol back and forth between Sam and Georgia. "Don't try anything," he said. "Now get out of the car slowly."

The driver got out and opened Sam's door. He and Georgia climbed out and walked at gunpoint through a barn and into another barn that was used as a hangar for a crop-dusting plane.

"Keep going. You're not there yet."

The next building was smaller and obviously hadn't been used in a long while.

"Open that door and get in," the man with the gun ordered. "Go on."

Sam opened the door. The small space had been a tack room in another time. Even though sunlight filtered through the graying boards, it was hard to see.

"Stop there," the driver said. He took the cuffs off Sam while the other man pointed the gun at him. The gunman shoved the couple inside and locked the door.

Sam and Georgia heard a wooden bar slide into place. They waited and looked around the ten-foot square cell.

"There's a case of water," Georgia said.

"They've put in an empty bucket and a mattress," Sam said. "They don't plan to kill us right away."

Sam and Georgia heard the car drive away. Georgia sat down on the dirty mattress and spread out an old quilt she found beside it.

Sam shook the door to test it. It wouldn't budge. He crawled over to look through the slits between the boards. "This is definitely a large farm in the Panhandle. I can see the corn growing. Enormous crop fields surround us. Since we're on the back side of this building, we can't get a good look at the house or the other barns."

"They didn't take my tote," Georgia said. "I had it strapped across my shoulder, and I guess they didn't notice. I have medicine and a little food in it." She sighed and leaned back. "Sam, I'm totally drained."

"Lie down." Sam picked up the quilt and covered her with it.

"I'll rest a little." Georgia lay down but didn't sleep. She watched Sam look through the cracks in the door and study the walls. Slivers of light filtered in the tiny room, and the prairie wind whistled through the weathered boards of the little shed, reminding them of their isolation.

Chapter 44

The officer led Jenson to the phone bank in the back of the Taos Police Department. Jenson knew he'd messed up. He hadn't made it back to burn the van, and he'd stayed in Taos too long. He should have gone to Santa Fe before he got something to eat. The girl in the drive-through window had looked at him funny. He had to wait a long time for his order, and then the police had surrounded him. All he could think of was to call Lynnette. If they could send a man like Gonzales, they could get him out of this fix.

"Get me a lawyer, Lynnette! They're not going to pin Hood's murder on me. That crazy Gonzales did it." Jenson was unravelling.

"Okay, Jenson. Let me make some calls. Try to stay calm."

"My fingerprints are all over that van." He knew it looked bad for him.

"Just let me find out what we can do. Don't say anything. Do you hear me? Don't say anything to anybody."

Jenson hoped he could depend on Lynnette. He could be on his way back to Texas, if he was lucky, but not before the Taos boys questioned him. Maybe they wouldn't connect him with Hood's murder right away. Maybe they'd just get him on the parole violation. But that wasn't what worried him. He figured Lynnette wasn't reliable, but he didn't have anyone else to call. He'd keep his mouth shut for a while, but in the end, he'd take the best deal for himself.

Jenson was normally calm. He had to be the calm one. That lunatic Hood had gotten himself killed. His crazy behavior was what put fear in people. It had worked most of the time when they were together at the Wall in Huntsville. Hood would get that look in his eyes, and the guys believed he'd kill them without blinking. He was the muscle, and together they'd managed to survive that hellhole. One thing he knew for sure, he wasn't going back to that place. He'd made it before, but another stretch in any prison, he wasn't so sure, especially without Hood.

Jenson paced in his cell. In a few minutes he'd be answering questions, and he already had his deal planned. His face was flushed. He kept popping his fingers and balling his fists while he paced. When someone walked by, Jenson turned and grabbed the bars and glared at them. He knew he was worked up by the time the guards came to get him to consult with his public defender.

A few minutes later, he sat handcuffed to a table. His eyes followed the man who was supposed to help him.

"Mr. Jenson, I'm your attorney, Dalton Robb." Robb walked into the holding room and sat opposite Jenson.

Jenson could smell the fear on the diminutive man. *I could snap him like a twig*, he kept thinking. "Now, Robb, you listen to me. I'm going to make a deal. I know things that the feds would like to know." Jenson wasted no time issuing his orders, and he could see the look of terror radiating from his lawyer. Beads of sweat had broken out on the little man's upper lip, and drops of panic slid down his temples. Jenson wanted to stomp the weakness out of him. He'd done it to many others in the past, but he controlled his urge and concentrated on getting out of jail.

Robb bent over his briefcase and pulled out a yellow legal pad. "I'm sure we can do that, Mr. Jenson."

Nelson Orville Jenson cleared his throat and began to rattle on about cattle and irrigation systems, following people, a Mexican assassin, and the stabbing. Robb wrote down everything he said.

~~~

Ray drove north on Highway 287 with Frank Wade in the passenger seat. The Taos police were holding Jenson. He'd asked to speak with someone from Texas. It was obvious to Ray that Jenson was scared of facing murder charges in New Mexico.

With the disappearance of Georgia and Sam now officially labeled a kidnapping, he could call in Frank and the FBI. "Are we getting any more FBI help for Sam and Georgia?" he asked.

"A team is coming in from Dallas to question your deputies today."

"They can't say much," Ray said. "They never saw anyone. They waited at the state line for two hours, and then left. The Taos officers have the only information."

Ray couldn't sit still in the Waggoner courthouse and wait for anyone else to bring him bits and pieces of his case. It had been three days since Sam and Georgia had disappeared. He wasn't optimistic about their situation.

"Tell me again what Taos said about the suspect exchange," Frank said.

"They saw county deputies. They had uniforms, a squad car, and sidearms. They both had on jackets that covered anything with a name. The Taos guys just assumed they were from the correct place."

"Any markings on the transport car?"

Ray shook his head. "None."

"What direction did they go when they drove off?"

"They headed toward Amarillo on Interstate 40, but there are several county roads they could have taken. It will take awhile to investigate each one. We'll stop at the exchange location on the way."

"Anything new today?" Frank asked.

"We've alerted all counties in Texas. Nothing has come of it."

"These guys could have been actual police officers."

"It's possible, and that may be the reason we haven't gotten any leads from the Panhandle," Ray said. "These are mostly small towns, and if they're out there, and we have it on the news, someone will notice something."

"My Dallas team will conduct investigations in the towns. They'll talk to the police departments, too. It might turn up something."

"The question I have is, how did someone know where to intercept them and at that particular location? The Taos police knew, I knew, and of course my office knew." As soon as Ray said it aloud, he suspected he knew the answer already.

"Wait a minute, Ray. The leak could have been in the FBI office. We really haven't kept this a secret. At least a dozen agents in my office know about this, and people in administration as well. Let's work backward from the kidnapping time. What if the deputies were real? Who could have contacted them?"

"We're back to the 'why.' If we can figure that out, we may have a direction to go. I think we'll get some answers from Jenson."

~~~

It was late afternoon, but the sky was still white waves of heat when Ray and Frank pulled into the Taos police station. Both road-weary men glanced around when they withdrew from the car, but neither noticed the dark man hunkered down behind the steering wheel across the street. Ray was looking into the sun and couldn't see how the man's black eyes fixed on him.

"This won't take long," Ray said. "We'll introduce ourselves and come back in the morning."

When Ray and Frank emerged from the station, evening had fallen, and the night air felt comfortably cool. A pleasant desert fragrance drifted around them, and the lingering cooking aromas reminded them that they hadn't eaten since 10:00 o'clock that morning.

"Let's find something to eat and get a room," Frank said. "I want to get an early start tomorrow."

"Jenson may be ready to talk to us," Ray said. "If he's convicted this time, he'll spend the rest of his life in prison. He doesn't know the Taos police have connected him to Hood's murder yet. He may still think he can make a deal with us."

"It could become a federal case."

"Of course, Taos will want first dibs on Jenson since the murder took place in their jurisdiction. I can't say I blame them. I'd want the same thing. They can have him, if they'll just let us question him about Sam and Georgia."

~~~

It was 9 o'clock the next morning when Ray jerked open the door to the interrogation room and walked inside, taking the only vacant chair. Frank followed and moved to the corner behind the public defender. Jenson sat beside his lawyer, Dalton Robb. Robb kept flipping through the yellow legal pad he held. Ray could see the pad was filled. He waited for the little man to find what he was looking for.

"Sir, what do you want from my client? He's basically not talking to anyone."

Ray raised his brows at Jenson, as if to say, *You're letting this guy speak for you?* He wanted Jenson to break his silence.

"I'll talk to them," Jenson said. His voice was a growl.

Ray had succeeded.

"Don't say anything. Let me . . ." Robb tried to break in.

"I'll tell you when I want you to say something," Jenson said to his attorney. Then he turned back toward Ray and Frank. "I've got a lot of information that would be useful to you. But before I say anything, we have to talk deal."

"We already know about Hood," Ray said, "about what happened in the van."

"I didn't kill Hood."

"Then who did?"

"I'm not telling you that." Jenson crossed his arms, and Ray believed he wouldn't reveal Gonzales. He'd save that for later in the interrogation.

"All right, I get it, you want a deal," Ray said. "How about this? Tell me who pays you, and we'll see what we can do."

"Really, you expect me to believe that?"

"You haven't told us anything so far, except that you didn't kill Hood. I don't think you have anything. You're trying to get out of a murder charge, that's all." Ray fairly spat out the words. "You tell us something that will make us believe you have something to trade."

"I've got plenty, you hick cop." Jenson was shocked they weren't willing to talk about a deal.

"You've got nothing. Let's go." Ray stood and motioned to Frank.

Frank walked around the table. "Look, Jenson, you tell the sheriff the information he needs, and we won't send this to federal court." Frank turned toward Robb. "We'll leave the room, and you talk to your client. Help him understand why he doesn't want this to go to federal court."

"All right. I'll talk to Mr. Jenson."

"I told you I'd tell you when to talk, Robb," Jenson shouted. "You two sit down and listen to me. If you leave now, I ain't talking, ever. Nelson Orville Jenson is not going back to prison."

"Just talk to your guy here," Frank repeated.

Jenson bowed his head, and from deep inside his tattooed body he began to let loose a primal wail. He shook his head back and forth, his eyes traveling past each of the men in the room, one to another and back.

Ray turned back. He recognized the change in the man. "All right, Jenson, it's okay. Let's talk about a deal." Ray hoped to calm the man, but he'd disconnected from everyone. He didn't hear Ray at all.

Jenson began a slow chant. "I ain't goin' back! I ain't goin' back! I told this worm everything, and we're gonna make a deal. I ain't goin' back." Jenson's voice crashed against the walls and bounced around the four men, growing louder with every "I ain't goin' back." Jenson began pounding on the steel table as he continued his chant.

Ray saw Robb's slender hand reach up to touch the giant forearm of Jenson as it smashed down again on the table. The physical contact, though light as a feather, enraged Jenson even more. He threw his arm upward and turned in his chair to stand. Jenson's motion caught Robb under his chin and slammed him by the neck against the cinder block wall behind him. The thud against the cement was sickening, and Ray and Frank watched in disbelief as blood dripped down the wall. The blow had crushed the back of Robb's head. Jenson stared at the lifeless form that crumpled to the floor.

Frank called for help from the guards in the hallway, and it took all four of them to drag Jenson from the gruesome scene. Jenson was quickly moved to solitary lockdown. The police station was still in an uproar hours later when Ray and Frank left after giving their own statements.

Chapter 45

Lynnette dialed James Baxter again after she landed at Dulles. She had to leave him a message. She and James would have to concoct some acceptable explanation about the Stanfields for Sandra. Even if Lynnette had to make it up, Sandra had to be placated, at least for now.

Things had been quiet since Sam and Georgia had been locked up in the Panhandle. Gonzales would be there soon. Jenson knew the two deputies who had taken the Stanfields, but she'd never met them. They had done several jobs for them.

Lynnette couldn't get any information from Taos. She knew the public defender was dead, and Jenson was accused of killing him. She couldn't hold on to this news. She had to tell James about Jenson killing his own lawyer. The information would eventually get to Cox anyway, so she was better off telling James now.

Lynnette checked into the hotel near the Capitol and purposefully delayed calling Sandra. It was an advantage for Lynnette if Sandra got angry. Emotion clouded judgement. If Sandra didn't get angry, Lynnette would know what kind of person she was dealing with.

Lynnette ordered dinner through room service and settled in to wait for James to call. She stood at the open drapes and sipped wine as she watched the sky change colors around the Washington Monument. Lynnette jumped when James finally called. She hadn't realized how rattled she was.

"Austin business kept me tied up longer than I thought," he said. "Are you set for tomorrow?"

"Yes. Don't worry, James. I'm not the girl I was when we met. I've grown up considerably since then. Reality is a bitch, and I'm facing it head on."

"You have stepped up to the challenge lately, Lynnette," James said, his voice seeming melancholy. "I'm not sure I want you to be so independent. You've always needed me before."

"I still need you, James." Lynnette felt mixed emotions—regret, anger, and determination. "But I had to grow up sometime."

~~~

The next morning, Lynnette initiated a strategy that hopefully would net her a huge win. She found that a little fear kept her alert and cautious. Her first move was to set up a face-to-face meeting with Sandra, at her own hotel.

"I'm in room 1439," she told Sandra.

Sandra hesitated. "I can't be there before 6:00 tonight."

"That will work. I have several other meetings today. That should give us plenty of time to discuss our business." Lynnette closed the call and dialed James to let him know the meeting was set.

She left quickly for her appointments, scattered across the city. She made it back to the hotel room only a few minutes before Sandra's knock.

"Right on time, I see," Lynnette said as she stepped aside to let her in.

Sandra breezed silently by and placed her briefcase on the desk chair. Lynnette sensed the other woman's defensiveness. Sandra turned to look out the window at the Capitol, shrouded in scaffolding. Sandra folded her arms and took a few moments before she spoke.

Most of Lynnette's negotiations began with meaningless conversation. Occasionally, opponents wanted to be direct and go straight to the bargaining points. She pegged Sandra as the "get to the point" type of person, but Lynnette would direct the discussion tonight. Sandra had grossly underestimated her. Lynnette dealt with that misconception easily now. In the past, it had infuriated her. Much of the time it came from men, and simply because she was a Southern girl from Texas. She'd learned to use it to her advantage instead of spending time swimming in anger. She busied herself fixing a drink from the minibar while she waited.

"You can fix me one of those," Sandra said as she turned and faced Lynnette.

"Certainly," Lynnette smiled. She wasn't intimidated.

As she reached for her drink, Sandra began. "I want to make a deal with you."

"What do you propose?"

"We can take over the Cox operation, and we'll make ten times the money we're making now."

"If not more, but again, Sandra, how?" Lynnette pressed her. "I'll listen, but it has to be a good, well-thought-out plan."

"I'd want you to meet with me and my partner. If you can't agree to that, then it's no deal."

"I'll talk to you both, but I name the place and time."

"I can live with that." Sandra sat down for the first time since she'd arrived.

Lynnette joined her. *This couldn't have gone better*, she thought. "Mexico may prove to be a problem because of the politics there, and the power of the remaining cartels."

"We've thought of that and have already started an alternative route," Sandra said. "My partner and I have always thought going through Mexico would be fraught with problems."

The discussion continued for another hour, until Lynnette finally cut it short. She didn't want to be late for her 8 o'clock meeting. "I'll call you with the meeting place." Lynnette handed Sandra a piece of hotel paper. "Write your burner number for me."

Sandra left the room and left the hotel the back way, the same way she'd arrived. Lynnette picked up the phone and instructed her driver to meet her in front of the hotel.

A few minutes later, Lynnette opened her own door and hopped inside the limousine. The chauffeur took off, already knowing his destination. She poured a drink and prepared for the next meeting in Maryland. She ticked off her meetings for the day. She had made it through with success. She was still exhilarated from the sparring with Sandra. She leaned back, kicked off her shoes, and stretched her legs across the back seat.

She considered the issues she needed to smooth out. She'd worked her way into the organization, but the Stanfield kidnapping complicated everything. Cox wouldn't let it go. That was his weakness. He'd kill two people to get his way. He would leave a gap open for someone else to step in and take over. James believed he could do that. Sandra and her partner believed the same thing. She had to choose sides and how far she would go to get to the top.

The car pulled into the drive, and Lynnette quickly walked down the curving walk to the classic Georgian home. The door opened.

"Come in, Lynn. We've been waiting for you."

Chapter 46

Sam's sleep was fitful, and he thrashed about often. He felt Georgia shivering in the dark under the threadbare quilt. They had to lie on their sides to fit on the twin mattress, so when one turned, the other turned, too.

Sam finally sat up and folded the quilt over Georgia. "Sleep for a while, and I'll keep watch." He stretched out his legs and leaned against a wall, then shifted to look through the cracks outside.

He thought about their chances of survival. He remained hopeful their captors wouldn't kill them. Two days ago, they'd gone to the trouble of tying and gagging them when someone came to take out the crop duster in the other barn. It had been painful to sit in one position all day while the plane was out, but Chris, one of the deputies, had come that evening and untied them. They'd heard the deputies talk about having to move them if the pilot came out here on a regular basis to fly the plane.

That was when Sam had decided he could fly the plane out, and they could escape. Georgia was willing. They were making their plans.

Sam and Georgia had settled into a routine that began with one of the deputies making a delivery each morning. The deputy called Randy came most of the time. As Sam stared through the cracks, he could see the squad car speeding down the road already, leaving a cloud of dust behind it. Unless it rained, any approaching vehicle could be seen from miles away. The only time they couldn't keep an eye out for the car was when the deputies parked out front. Each day, they counted how long it took for someone to come to the barn and unlock the door.

"Good morning, Randy," Georgia called.

"Don't call me that, Miss Georgia. You know it can't be good for you to know too much."

"Why are we here, Randy? I still don't understand why you're holding us here. You need to let us go." Georgia continued to press him, as she did each time he came.

"I'm gonna give you the same answer I have every other day: I don't know."

"Who gave you the orders to lock us up here?" Sam asked.

"I don't know that, either. I told you already. Now stop asking questions and take these supplies." Randy pushed forward a sack of items Georgia had requested. "Everything is in there you asked for." He pitched the sack on the dirty mattress and hurried to close the door.

"Wait! Randy, wait!" Sam shouted, but all he heard was the board slide into place. Soon afterward, tires were slinging gravel against the side of the barn.

After the brief visit, Sam and Georgia continued working on their escape plans. They'd loosened three wall boards. The ground had to be broken up at the bottom of each, and their only tools were the toothbrushes from the hospital. One brush had broken in the hard-packed earth, and the other had worn down to the point that neither could get a grip on the handle.

That morning Randy had delivered two more toothbrushes in the supplies. He also had included soap, wipes, and candy bars, a random selection, but useful. Sam and Georgia moved together and pulled the ends of the flimsy mattress away from the wall so they could continue to dig the trench under the loose boards.

Hours later, Georgia sat back on the mattress and rubbed her hands. "Let's rest some. We've worked all morning, and we can treat ourselves to a candy bar at least."

"We're almost there, and I want to get out by tomorrow night. We can use the darkness as a cover." Sam looked up and smiled. "But we can rest awhile."

"I think one more board and we'll have enough room to crawl out. Let me see your hands. Just what I thought." Sam's hands were bleeding, and the blisters had broken and were oozing. Georgia reached for her tote and took out some gauze she'd packed for Sam's wound. She began to wrap it around his palms instead.

"That helps." Sam leaned over and gave Georgia a peck on the cheek. "I'll have to unwrap them when the deputies come, or they'll ask questions but this will help me with digging this afternoon."

"I don't know how you can stand it." Georgia winced and looked away.

"It's painful, but I'll do whatever it takes to get us out of here." Sam turned around on the mattress and stabbed the ground with the handle of a new toothbrush.

"Will your hands interfere with flying that crop duster? I know you're confident in flying an airplane, but the crop duster is different."

"Don't worry, sweetheart, I'll be all right. That plane is the best way out of here, wherever *here* is, anyway. I just hope the duster isn't a single-seater. Then we'll have to implement Plan B."

"You mean walk to a farmhouse and get help?"

Sam nodded.

An hour later, Sam tested the last grayed plank and was shoving it outward when the board splintered about three feet above the dirt floor. They were so engrossed in their task that they'd failed to notice the white patrol car rumbling down the county road. The dust was a thick tan storm hovering behind the speeding vehicle. It would be upon them in less than five minutes.

"They're coming!" Sam shouted. "Quick, let's get this board back together!"

Sam stuck the broken piece back together and set it in place, then they dragged the mattress so it covered the trench and the loose dirt. They sat on the mattress and peeked through the crack to watch the police car slow and approach the farm.

"It looks like two more cars are coming down the road. It could be the crop dusters again. Oh, no! I don't want to be tied up again." Georgia moaned.

The squad car stopped next to the farmhouse and parked there instead of proceeding to the area between the barns. This was different from the deputies' previous visits. They worried that this kind of change couldn't be a good thing.

"Oh my God," Sam said. "Look who's in the backseat."

Georgia sucked in her breath, alarmed. The man who had shot Sam and tracked them through the forest was sitting there, staring at the barn. The three men opened the doors and got out.

"What are we going to do, Sam?"

"Wait . . . they just spotted the other cars."

Gonzales returned to the backseat and closed the door, and the deputies stood so they blocked the view of him inside. Sam and Georgia listened as a Suburban and a pickup stopped and the occupants spoke with the police officers.

"Howdy, Larry. You going out to dust some crops this late?" Randy asked.

"Not today. I just brought my mechanic out here to do some work on the plane. I brought my brothers along. What are you boys doing out here?" Larry looked over at the car.

"Just on patrol," Chris said. "You know how this vandalism has everybody nervous. We're just trying to cover as much territory as we can, making our presence felt." Chris smiled and patted Larry on the back. The men walked together toward the barn where the plane was stored.

The drivers of the other vehicles drove on and parked in front of the hangar barn. Chris walked back to the patrol car. Sam watched both deputies stare at the barn again. After the others had gone into the hangar, Randy sauntered toward their cell, carrying ropes in his hands.

"Let's sit back-to-back with our hands behind us," Sam said quickly. "If he doesn't see our hands, he may forget to tie them."

The pair were ready when Randy appeared, and their trick seemed to work. He wrapped the rope around their torsos, gagged them, and tied their feet, but he ignored their hands.

"You make a sound while that other bunch is here, and you won't live another day. I'll be back later. Understand?"

Sam and Georgia both nodded.

"We're moving you tonight. Don't think about trying to get those other guys to help you. They'd just as soon shoot you as look at you." Randy left quickly and walked back to the car. "They'll be all right for a few hours," he assured his partners. "Get in, Chris. Let's go."

Almost as soon as the car began rumbling down the road, Randy began worrying. "We are not going to kill those folks here. Larry and his brothers have seen us. We would be the first ones they would question. I know another deserted place, and you can do your work there. We'll come back before dawn to pick them up and take them to the new location."

Chapter 47

Ray studied the people hustling about the town square through the slit in his wall he called a window. The atmosphere was subdued in his office. He'd found his leak—Maureen. What a disappointment. If he hadn't heard her mention Harry Reynolds as he passed her desk, information about his cases would still be flowing freely on the phone lines. He'd learned that many in Waggoner depended on Maureen for their latest information. It hadn't occurred to her that the news she was sharing was going all the way to Austin.

While he watched the busy streets, Ray saw Frank's unmarked car pull up in front of the courthouse. It was the first time he'd seen Frank since their trip to Taos. He didn't like admitting that the leaks had come from his office. He was still standing when Frank walked in.

"Good morning," Frank said. "I have some news."

"Stop, Frank," Ray said as he held up his index finger to his lips to alert Frank to possible bugs. Ray looked around the room at the ceiling and the furniture and walked around the office searching.

Frank nodded his understanding, and Ray walked to the door, motioning for Frank to follow. They left the courthouse, crossed the street, and walked down the sidewalk off the square.

"I have leaks in the office," Ray said. "It isn't safe to talk there. It was more for gossip rather than malicious intent, but detrimental nonetheless."

"I noticed it was quiet in there this morning. Is it bugged?"

"I won't know until we do a sweep. I'm assuming it is until I find out otherwise."

The men turned south and continued walking passed the Methodist church.

"Let's talk in here," Ray said as he opened a gate to a small courtyard. The shade was plentiful, and no one was around at that time of the morning. The men sat on a concrete bench, a nearby fountain muffling their voices.

"My investigative unit received unexpected pushbacks from its probes into the EPA's activities," Frank said. "After my guys mentioned the Stanfield case, no one would talk to them. There was a total shutdown, and we couldn't find out who was behind the order to stonewall us."

"Have you found where the order came from yet?"

"It had to be from high up, but we still don't know. Now that this EPA action has halted the FBI, we're on full alert. We will find someone to talk to us."

"I thought other agencies usually cooperated in kidnappings."

"They do," Frank said. "I'm not sure who I can trust since this EPA order is coming from the Department of the Interior. There are cases already in court, and even now one rancher won his case against unfair fines. They can use the excuse that the Stanfield case is an ongoing investigation and not cooperate with us."

"The IRS is my concern," Ray said. "Sam and Georgia still have warrants I need to deal with."

"I'll get the evidence from the IRS inquiry. I want to know how that came into play and see if we can trace where the money came from. I understand how you feel about Sam and Georgia, but if both the IRS and the EPA investigations are bogus, then there's obviously a connection."

"I can tell you who started the IRS investigation—Buddy Gatwick. He reported the large Stanfield transfers to the IRS. Then the IRS was here looking into the Stanfield business just days after the report was filed. You and I know the IRS doesn't move that fast. Someone had to be pushing them into it."

"What do we know about Buddy Gatwick?"

"The team should be through checking by now," Ray said. "Let's go back to the courthouse, and I'll show you my new evidence. The bank sent a box over that was delivered to Buddy Gatwick after his death, and they just remembered this week to let me know about it. The box is unremarkable on the outside—no fingerprints or marks or writing. I wanted you here when I opened it, to get your opinion on what's inside. Of course, it could be nothing at all."

Back in the basement, Ray showed Frank the names and pictures he'd added to the link chart on the rolling bulletin board. The lines between them were multiplying.

"We haven't used this technique in a while," Frank said as he looked at the board. "It makes it clear something is going on here. The Stanfields got tangled in a big net."

"The county doesn't have any analysis software," Ray said. "I have to use something to track this case."

"I kind of miss this, actually," Frank said, running his hand across the board. "It puts you in the middle of it."

The men stared at the pictures of Jenson and Hood where the names and pictures ended. There were no pictures of Gonzales or the kidnappers.

"Sam and Georgia gave me a description of Gonzales when they were in the hospital," Ray said. "His tattoos were his only distinguishable characteristics. His looks are fairly general in nature."

"Cartel?"

"That's what I think. We know Jenson made a phone call from Taos. It was an 817 area code. That's Fort Worth. Do you have a name?"

"We do. That's one of the reasons I came over this morning. Jenson's records mostly show calls to disposable phones. We did get one viable number, though. It belongs to a Lynnette Wilkerson." Frank pulled out a picture of Lynnette that he added to the link chart, running a string to Jenson.

"What do you know about her?"

"She's an attorney in Dallas. We also know that early in her career, she worked for a lobbyist in Austin named James Baxter."

"This is powerful, Frank. We have a lead."

"I thought so. We're already checking out Baxter."

"Let's open the box," Ray said.

He pulled on blue latex gloves, then carefully removed the lid. Inside were dozens of papers, neatly clipped together. When Ray lifted the documents out of the container, a picture of Buddy in his drunken state stared back at them. It was the same picture that had been inside the FedEx envelope. Ray turned the picture over.

Gatty, a reminder for you, was written there.

Ray pulled out stacks of 100-dollar bills. "That threat won't do them any good anymore." He passed the photograph to Frank. "I have an even more incriminating picture of Buddy Gatwick stored in my safe."

"Ray, this looks like a setup to me. Buddy was obviously being blackmailed. Then he died suddenly."

"Blackmail and murder," Ray said, nodding. He reached into the box and pulled out the final item: a plain white envelope. Inside, a typed page showed bank deposits and withdrawals from Sam and Georgia's accounts. Ray turned the papers over and read them closely. "This shows bank names and lists of deposits and withdrawals, none with the Stanfields' names on it. This could clear them of the IRS charges."

Frank examined the paper. "We have enough information here to follow the money and find out where it came from. Someone had to know what they were doing to give us this much information. I don't think Jenson sent this."

"I have a hunch." Ray picked up his phone and called Beth Gatwick. After a few minutes, he turned to Frank, who was taking time to make some calls of his own.

"What is it?" Frank asked, covering his receiver.

"We have an interview with Buddy's wife, Beth."

~~~

An hour later, Ray and Frank walked into Beth Gatwick's neat living room. They sat in overstuffed chairs, flanking Beth, who was dwarfed by the enormous matching sofa. Her clothes hung on her small frame.

Ray took the lead. "Beth, we may have information about Buddy's death. I need to ask you some questions."

"I'll answer them if I can, Sheriff." Beth twisted the tissue in her hands and looked at both men with a weak smile.

Ray wanted to be gentle with Beth. She looked frail. He made small talk for a while before he began his questions. "Do you remember anything else about that trip Buddy took to Dallas?"

"I know he changed after that day. He wasn't the same happy person."

"Did he mention any names or who he saw that day?"

"He wouldn't say. He looked scared all the time."

"How was he the day he went hunting?"

"Well, that day he seemed more relaxed. I thought he was excited about going hog hunting."

"Beth, have you ever heard the name Lynnette Wilkerson before?"

Beth sucked in her breath and burst into tears. She reached for another tissue and continued to cry. "Sheriff, is she involved? I knew it."

Ray and Frank gave her time to recover.

She stood up and walked to a bookcase, taking a Longhorn yearbook from the shelf. She sat back down and flipped through the pages. When she found the one she wanted, she turned the book around and tapped her finger on a photograph. "There she is. Buddy was in love with her in college."

"She was a pretty girl," Ray said. "Still is, I'm sure. How'd she feel about Buddy?"

Beth shook her head sadly. "Buddy thought she was in love with him, too, but from what he has told me, I know she was just stringing him along."

Ray nodded. "Can we take this annual with us, Beth?"

"Take it. Keep it. I don't want it. It's just a reminder of her."

"One more question, Beth. Did Buddy have a nickname in college?"

"They all called him Gatty."

~~~

Back in the evidence room, Ray connected Buddy and Lynnette on the board. "How fast can we get Lynnette's phone records?" Ray asked.

"My team is already on it. I was texting as soon as I heard Lynnette Wilkerson's name in there. They'll let me know as soon as they have anything."

The phone rang. "Collins," Ray answered.

"Sheriff Ray Collins?"

"Yes, who is this?"

"This is Harry Reynolds. I have some information for you. Can we meet?"

Minutes later, Ray and Frank were locking the evidence room and hurrying to meet Harry at the Bar S.

"Sheriff, news of the transfer of Sam and Georgia from New Mexico was common knowledge in the Department of Public Safety office at the Capitol," Harry said. "The radio transmissions alone could have been picked up and given to anyone. The department has a few people under surveillance."

"We had some leaks of our own," Ray said.

"Lawmakers from the Senate and House are in and out of their offices. They have DPS staff as well. It could be anyone who helped set up the kidnapping, but there's one person who might know something. He's a lobbyist and always knows what's going on around the Capitol. Talk to him, Ray. His name is James Baxter."

Chapter 48

Lynnette fastened her seat belt and accepted a glass of merlot from the flight attendant. She was nervous. She'd been so careful not to be seen in DC with anyone connected to the Mallard Project. Now here she was on a plane headed directly to Houston to see Cox. He'd insisted that she come to him. She saw no way around it. She'd be at Cox's ranch in six hours, and she was going to sleep on the plane if she could. The meeting had gone as expected with Sandra. She was satisfied. The negotiations hadn't been easy in the beginning, but Lynnette had given in at the end so Sandra felt she had a decent deal.

Lynnette carried a backpack over her left shoulder as she walked up the gangway. It was her only luggage. Her long blond wig, jeans, and T-shirt made her look more like a college student than an attorney. She needed to blend in with the masses. Without baggage, she slipped through the crowded airport to the taxi line in minutes.

It was still early morning when she arrived at the Houston skyscraper. She approached the security desk and gave a false name to the uniformed attendant.

The security guard rose from his seat. "Follow me, please."

They walked to the elevator, then rode down to the parking garage to a waiting SUV. Lynnette had a two-hour ride to Cox's ranch. Along the way, she removed her wig and applied a bit of makeup. She changed into a Valentino blouse and jacket and four-inch Gucci heels. Then she turned the backpack inside out and carried it as a tote. Her transformation was remarkable. Lynnette knew how important perception was. The outfit she now wore gave her added height and a sense of power. The T-shirt and backpack had made her appear vulnerable and defenseless.

She was a stunning example of femininity as she emerged from the vehicle and walked onto the enormous wraparound porch of the Cox ranch house.

A muscled giant opened the door before she had the chance to knock. He motioned her inside and led her through the foyer and down a wide hallway to a magnificent library. A fire burned in the massive stone fireplace despite the summer heat outside. She noticed the air was still cool inside, with a hint of pine.

She was examining book titles—all related to the oil business—when Cox entered from another door at the back of the room.

"Hello, Mr. Cox." Lynnette spoke in a smooth, calm way that implied she was the owner of the surroundings, rather than the man who had entered.

Cox greeted her with a slight look of surprise, but quickly regained his composure and showed her to a chair facing the fireplace. "We finally meet," he said, oozing charm. "Please be seated." Cox reached out to shake her hand, but she felt his intent change as his left hand covered hers. He drew her toward him slightly, a motion that conveyed instant intimacy. When he let go of her, Lynnette realized she'd been briefly mesmerized by his intense masculinity. Her resolve subtly changed without her realizing the tables had turned.

She and Cox spent the morning together. They rode across the magnificent ranch in an open Jeep, stopping to watch his token herds of longhorn and buffalo. They walked along spring-fed streams and finally stopped to have lunch in a splendid grove of pecan trees.

By noon, Lynnette had shed her jacket and replaced her heels with tennis shoes. The hot weather and wind had destroyed her hair, her face was red, and she was sticky with sweat. She endured lunch, but as they returned to the ranch, Lynnette called a halt to the tour. "I must go, Mr. Cox, or I'll miss my flight back to Dallas," she said. " I only have a short time for us to discuss our business. While this has been interesting, I must insist we talk about what I came here for."

Without a word, Cox turned off the road, and the four-wheel drive vehicle bumped and jolted across a field of sorghum Sudan grass. He headed down the rows, his tires leaving tracks between the half-grown stalks. "Hold on," Cox shouted from the driver's seat while he sped down the green roadway. At the end of the row, they bounced over a dip and landed in a thicket of young mesquite trees. Cox skirted the thorny branches for a time and ended the trek when he entered a path with only two ruts to guide their way.

Lynnette felt bruised from the wild ride, but she looked up to see the back side of the ranch house.

"Here we are." Cox slammed on the brakes and cut the ignition.

Lynnette sucked in air after holding her breath for too long. She released her hold on the door handle. She was furious, but she knew she had to get control of her temper. The crazy ride had been intentional, and the planned effect had worked. She was thinking more of her outrage and physical condition than the deal they were supposed to discuss.

"Why not take time to shower and refresh yourself, Lynnette? My staff has already taken care of your flight reservation. We'll have plenty of time to discuss our business. You can follow Joyce, and she'll show you the facilities."

Lynnette looked toward the back door of the house to see a middle-aged woman holding the door open for her. Lynnette was wary, but the shower would be welcome, plus it would give her time to think about how she should handle the rest of the day. She walked into the ranch house without a word. She was beginning to fear that Cox knew about her recent actions. She was on his ranch. He could kill her, and her body would never be found. She was afraid to even make a call.

~~~

Lynnette smoothed her hair and breathed deeply before she entered the library again. She couldn't be sure Cox wasn't watching her every move in the house. She tried to look confident.

"Better now?" Cox asked in a fatherly way.

Lynnette knew he was trying to establish dominance. She ignored him and walked to the fireplace, where he sat in a worn leather chair. She sat opposite him.

Cox watched her. He placed his drink on the side table and folded his hands in his lap. "We both know Sandra is a liability, Lynnette. And you want to make a deal directly with me, don't you?"

Lynnette thought about the proposal and tried to evaluate how much Cox really knew. But she hesitated too long.

"Drink?" Cox reached for his glass and offered her one.

Lynnette took the drink, symbolizing her acceptance of his deal. She decided to tell him about the arrangement with Sandra. She sipped the whiskey. "I saw Sandra last night, and we made a deal to cut you out. She wants to build the clientele on our own. I'm not confident she can deliver."

"We have other ways to contact foreign governments. We don't have to go through the State Department."

"Sandra has another partner, someone high up in the Department of the Interior, and her loyalty is with him. We'll have to be smart about cutting her out. I don't trust her. If she's turned on you, then I can't be sure she won't turn on me."

"Smart girl. Let me handle Sandra and her partner. You and

I can deal directly. It will take a few days for me to set things in motion." Cox looked at her, evaluating her and the deal. "You've turned things around, Lynnette. Not long ago, you were only James's girlfriend. You still have a lot to show me before I trust you, but telling me about Sandra is a good start."

"You won't regret letting me be part of your organization, Mr. Cox."

"As much as I like having you here, this will be the last time we can meet at the ranch." Cox abruptly rose from his chair and left the room.

The hulk Lynnette had encountered that morning came in the hallway door and nodded in her direction. "This way, miss."

Lynnette placed her glass on the table, picked up her tote, and walked out to the waiting SUV. The driver handed her an airline ticket and closed the door.

Chapter 49

The fading afternoon sun deepened the shadows that curled around Sam and Georgia. Their muscles were cramping, and the rope was cutting into their skin.

Sam kept talking to keep their minds elsewhere, to escape the strain they were under. "We have to get out of here," he said. "They're just going to come back and take us somewhere to kill us. I've been thinking about who would want us dead, and all I can come up with is the government. We must have hit a real nerve with our blog and the water shortage. It has to be the feds. Why would the EPA and the IRS bother with us? We're nobody."

"Who are these men?" Georgia asked. "Someone is paying them. Someone with a lot of money."

"Listen. The cars are leaving. It won't be long, and we can get out of here."

Sam and Georgia listened as all the vehicles left. When they were positive the cars had gone, they started working on their restraints. Georgia managed to slither down and push the rope over her head. Sam grabbed the rope and tossed it to the side. Then they untied their ankles. At first, they could barely stand. Sam looked out of the cracks and saw nothing. They stretched and rubbed circulation back into their legs while they stood in the dark.

"We have to get on the offensive," Sam said. "I refuse to be a victim."

"I'm with you."

The couple pulled back the mattress and crawled over to the loose boards. Sam tore them from the wall, and the couple pushed through the hole they'd made and soon were standing outside for the first time in a week.

They stayed close to the barn wall. Their vision adjusted to the evening light, which was more than they had inside the barn. Sam inched his way to the edge of the building and motioned Georgia to follow him. They hurried across the barnyard to the hangar doors.

"Just as we thought," Georgia said as she rattled the locked door handle.

"Let's go around the sides of the barn and see if there's another way in."

The urgency drove them harder and made them less cautious. "Sam, I found a side door. It's locked but loose."

Sam searched in the dark for something to break the lock, finally finding a large stick in the grass. He weaseled the dried branch through the narrow opening and bore down on his lever. The stick cracked but not until the last push shattered the old doorframe and created an opening large enough for them to get through.

They'd discussed this moment for hours. Sam had tried to remember as much as he could from his pilot's checklist. Georgia had assured him she could evaluate the cockpit, and he could check the outside of the crop duster. She'd watched him many times when he'd checked his own plane. He trusted she knew what to do.

Sam walked along the side of the fixed-wing, yellow-and-red aircraft. He was relieved to find it had an observer seat. He estimated the time to be close to midnight, and the deputies and Gonzales could return at any time.

The pilot and his brothers had been in the hangar for several hours. Sam hoped they'd been working on the duster's mechanics rather than its chemical operations. He prayed the plane was in good enough condition to fly. Sam checked the props, then he worked his way around the plane, inspecting each section for damage or leaks. He was relieved to find everything was in good working order.

"The fuel tank is full," Georgia said as she climbed out of the cockpit so Sam could finish his review.

He scrambled up on the plane and made sure the electrical system and flight controls were operational. Sam tested the controls for freedom of movement, then started the engine and revved it until he was satisfied. Then he quickly cut the engine. The next challenge was getting the barn doors open.

Sam had noticed a work area in the corner of the barn and began to rummage through the tools. With any luck, he'd find something to break the lock on the large sliding doors. A drop-cord light-bulb hung over the workbench, and more tools hung on a pegboard wall mounted behind it.

The dim glow from the overhead light illuminated the area enough for Sam to find what he needed. "Georgia, here's a crowbar. I can use it to tear out all the screws behind that metal plate. It shouldn't be too difficult, considering the age of the wood."

Georgia held a flashlight while Sam wedged the crowbar behind the metal plate where the thick iron staple held the padlock. It only took seconds to force the hasp and lock from the barn door. Then the couple pushed the enormous sliding doors to the side.

The grass runway was behind the hangar and ran parallel to the road into the farm. A ribbon of road led away from the barn to the entrance on the far side of the airstrip, but the entirety of the taxiing area couldn't be seen in the dark. Sam couldn't determine how far they'd have to travel before even getting to the takeoff strip. He pointed the flashlight toward the runway.

Before Georgia could respond, Sam headed off through the tall grass directly behind the barn. "I don't see a road here, but I know it goes toward the runway." He stopped and surveyed the area. "If we don't know what's out there, we can't take the chance. We'll stick to the road."

"Let's go back. The sky is getting lighter."

"Just a few more feet," Sam said.

Headlights suddenly flickered across their faces, and Georgia pulled on Sam's arm. "They're coming!" she yelled.

From the far part of the road, headlights clearly shone through the subtle beginnings of daylight. Sam and Georgia ran to the plane. Georgia scrambled inside and climbed into the observer's seat while Sam removed the blocks from the wheels. At last he climbed into the cockpit. The engine started with a smooth purr. The lights came on, and Sam moved the aircraft forward. He eased it out of the barn and down the small road he hoped led to the airstrip. The squad car was nearing the farm road when he turned to look behind them. It would only take the deputies minutes to realize Sam and Georgia were in the crop duster.

The road ran away from the barn and wound through mesquite trees along a barbed wire fence. They made a loop to the left before Sam found the entrance to the airfield. He taxied through the wide gate and had to climb a small knoll before the plane emerged at the end of the prairie runway.

He was turning the plane into position for takeoff when lights flashed on the windshield from the patrol car. Their captors were now at the spot in the tall grass where Sam and Georgia had been standing only minutes earlier. The police car took the shortcut behind the barn. The vehicle bounced through the field on its way to the runway. Sam watched them and calculated the car would be at the airfield as he passed by them in the plane. He had no choice but to continue forward for takeoff. They had to take their chances.

The car below sped up, but suddenly the headlights were

tilted upward toward the sky. Randy's sedan had sped over the wide irrigation ditch and hit the opposite bank with a thud, leaving the trunk and back tires lodged in the muddy ditch. Georgia watched as three men poured out of the wrecked car. To her horror, she saw them draw their guns and begin firing.

"Get down, Georgia!" Sam shouted into his headset. He kept pushing the little plane down the runway, past the three gunmen. Georgia heard the bullets hit the side of the plane, and her observation window shattered.

As the plane continued, the men ran forward, chasing it. The deputies continued to fire their handguns, and the other man lifted a rifle to take aim. Georgia whispered a prayer. There was nothing Sam could do but fly. The takeoff seemed to take forever. He concentrated only on getting the plane off the ground.

Finally, they felt the little plane's tires lift off. Georgia heard the scratch of the treetops underneath the duster as it rose into the pale light. She looked back and saw the headlights still shining upward.

Chapter 50

It was late when Lynnette made it back to Dallas. Her flight was on Southwest into Love Field, closer to her apartment than DFW. Every detail let her know that Cox had information on her. She'd used the ticket he'd given her. She had no choice. He'd know if she changed the flight. She'd only spoken with James briefly before her flight had taken off. He'd be waiting for her tomorrow at their secret flat near Austin. She'd called his home phone and also used her cell to make the call in the airport. She wished she hadn't. It was the kind of mistake amateurs made.

Lynnette left Dallas at 4 a.m. to make it to James by 7. He'd picked up bagels on his way over and had eaten his half before Lynnette walked in the door.

"You look like hell," James greeted her. "Here, get some of this coffee down and tell me all about your encounter with Bill."

She gratefully took the mug of steaming coffee and sank into the sofa, glad it was Sunday and she didn't have to worry about the firm. "Where do I start?" She swallowed a mouthful of the strong black brew. Then she began the tale of her visit to the Texas ranch and the powerful man she'd crashed into the day before.

"It sounds like you've made the deal," James said.

"Yes, I guess it does. I think Sandra is clueless. If she thinks she and her partner are going to outsmart this man, she's sadly mistaken. I was handled and then turned loose. I finally decided to go with the flow and see what I could learn. Especially if we're going to continue dealing with him, I need to be able to at least keep up. Then we'll see if we can get ahead of him."

"You really are rattled." James looked at her with concern. "Maybe I need to consider our relationship as well."

"I tried, but I have to tell you, Cox is scary."

"What did Cox say about Sandra? How did he react when you told him about the double cross?"

"He didn't react at all. I think he already knew about her and was waiting to see if I'd tell him about it. I'm glad I did. He said he'd take care of her."

"What does that mean?"

"I think you know what that means." Lynnette believed James was frightened. He'd known Cox all his life. Surely James understood how dangerous he was.

"I'm afraid I do. I've felt immune all these years, and I've become complacent. He plays me, calls me Jimmy, and treats me like his son. I get it. I guess I believed it."

"Don't worry, James. It won't have anything to do with us." Lynnette tried to calm him. She understood Sandra was a target because she'd made the wrong choice. Lynnette also knew that meant death. There was no other way for Cox to deal with a traitor in his organization. Since she'd met him face-to-face, Lynnette understood the kind of man he was—ruthless, without remorse.

James and Lynnette left their apartment separately later in the day. She left first, stopping to polish her sunglasses while she surveyed the parking lot. She spotted two men sitting in a parked car. They were watching the entrance. She suspected Cox was having her followed. He didn't trust her.

She walked to her car and called James. "We're being watched," she said. "There are two men waiting outside in a white, late-model Kia. I think Cox is suspicious of us. It must be him. You can see them from the patio door. When I leave, let me know if they follow me."

"You go ahead. I'll call you."

Lynnette drove away and watched the white sedan follow. Her phone buzzed.

"One man stayed. The other took after you. They already know about the apartment, so I'm going to stay and get rid of anything we have here that would incriminate us."

"Good. I'll call when I get back to Dallas."

Lynnette had three hours of drive time going north on Interstate 35. The white Kia stayed with her. She'd left herself too open by going to the ranch. Cox had seemed too quick to agree to her offer. Either he already knew about her, or he was getting rid of those who knew about him. Lynnette knew she needed to disappear.

~~~

The car followed James to his home, a coveted old rancher by a stream in the center of Austin, the hilly city. Ancient live oaks with branches two feet thick stood above a dense carpet of ground-cover that surrounded his home. The house was hard to see from the road and difficult to approach on foot.

"Were you followed?" Lynnette asked as soon as she called.

"I saw the guy a few times in the mirror. It's no secret where I live. If this is Cox, we're screwed. But who else would be following us?"

"You know lots of people, James."

"Are you home?"

"Not yet, but I will be soon," Lynnette lied.

It was the last time she'd talk to James. She was at her office scanning her files on Cox. She didn't know how deep his tentacles were. Someone in her office could be his informant. When the files were secure on the remote server, she began shredding. She estimated she had about two hours before anyone showed up for work.

Lynnette looked around her office. She hadn't packed any of the personal items she'd collected through the years. She'd known this would happen one day, and she'd planned for it, both intellectually and emotionally. On her way out, she left her office keys and a letter of resignation on her assistant's desk. She took two bags of shredded paper and her laptop with her.

Lynnette skirted the front reception area and took the stairs. The elevator dinged as she made her way down the first flight. Early birds. Ambitious youngsters wanting to make their place in the world. She remembered when she had such dreams. Her life had been wildly exciting, but not the one she'd planned.

Outside, the streets were coming to life. A light rain peppered down, and the headlights blinded her as Lynnette walked briskly, still carrying her shredded paper. She turned the corner and saw her car waiting. A door opened before she'd reached it. Someone took the bags and the computer. The day was beginning, and in a few more hours, she'd be safe.

~~~

Lynnette stepped out of the hotel shower and examined her clothes. She'd slept hard for three hours, and now she was ready. She dressed quickly and strode into the living room of the suite, where two armed men waited. She surveyed the room, settling her gaze on the recording equipment the men had set up. They were going to tape her.

This was better than being dead. She'd made the deal with the FBI months ago, and she'd been living in terror ever since. She'd survived spying on James and Bill Cox by her wits alone. She didn't have any training. She wasn't an agent. Her instructions had come from an anonymous source. She had called the source on her way back to Dallas, and agents had come for her as they'd promised. She was ready.

"Would you like to eat something first, Ms. Wilkerson?" The younger agent pointed toward some fruit and eggs on the table.

Lynnette felt robotic. She had trouble focusing, but she ate. She moved, she tasted, she spoke, and she wondered who she was. Her eyes were wet. She put her fork down and placed her hands on the arms of the chair to stop shaking.

"You're safe now, ma'am. Would you like to sit for a while before we start?"

Lynnette said nothing, but she sat for a time, staring at the Dallas skyline. She finally turned toward the agents. "I can start now."

Two more agents entered the room, and the questioning began.

"For the record, state your full name, please, ma'am . . ."

Chapter 51

Ray was halfway to Austin and eager to talk to James Baxter. Baxter's secretary had told Ray he was in town, but he'd be at the Capitol all day. Ray wanted the element of surprise. He knew suspects revealed more when they were off guard. He wanted to get to Baxter before anyone else. The investigation was moving fast, but he didn't want to wait around for the FBI to feed him information. He picked up a cup of coffee in Waco and continued south on Interstate 35.

He was passing through Hewitt minutes later when Maureen called. "Ray, the Taos police are calling you, urgent. There's a homicide sergeant, Jonathan Ramirez, on the line. Do you want me to patch you through?"

"Yes, go ahead."

"Sheriff Collins, this is Ramirez. We talked when you were in Taos."

"Sure, I remember you, Ramirez. Do you have something from Jenson?"

"Jenson is about the same. He's not talking. But we have

some information I think you may need for your case. It's from the files from Dalton Robb's computer and what was in his briefcase. Officially, it's evidence in Robb's murder case, but I can send you copies if you get a court order for it."

"I think I can do that. If not, maybe I can get some help from the feds."

"Just remember, you won't be able to use the evidence against him. He said a lot about the crimes in Texas and mentions some names."

"Is there anything that would help us find the Stanfields?"

"Jenson mentioned some deputies in the Panhandle who were vandalizing farms and ranches to try to drive them out of business. He didn't have any names or an agency. Sorry it's not more, Ray."

"It's crucial information for the case. I'll get that court order as soon as I can."

Ray talked to Maureen again and set the process in motion. She knew how to get a court order in Waggoner County. Ray wasn't sure the county had enough clout to get an order for papers from New Mexico. To ensure he got the information from Ramirez, he called Frank at the FBI office and caught him up on the details. "Can your guys get that court order?" Ray asked.

Frank put him on hold to check, returning momentarily to tell him the FBI was already working on it.

"So, what's the timeline then?"

"Always impatient, Ray. It won't take long. I'll get back with you."

Ray knew he was close to unraveling the case. The numbers on Lynnette Wilkerson's phone records belonged to James Baxter. The FBI had already begun investigating Baxter. They'd get him if he was part of the conspiracy. Ray knew that. His biggest worry was that it was too late to save Sam and Georgia.

~~~

Ray walked through the Congress Avenue entrance to the Capitol. The building was constructed from the same pink granite he saw every day in Waggoner, though it was older and much larger than his county courthouse. Ray stopped and picked up a brochure for a self-guided tour. He walked by legislative offices and talked to whoever was willing. His uniform gave him access to places he otherwise might not have been able to enter. Some people didn't know Baxter's name, but he finally got lucky.

"Good morning. I'm looking for James Baxter," Ray said to one young man. "I was told he'd be here today."

"He was supposed to be here this morning, but he hasn't come by yet."

"Are you working for Senator Hepner?" Ray read the name on the door.

"Yes, sir. I'm his intern." The kid was eager to help Ray.

"You should know then. When do you think the senator will be here?"

"It's close to lunch," the intern said. "That means he won't be here until later this afternoon."

Ray walked into the reception area and looked inside the other office. No one else was around. The kid was alone. "That's too bad. I was hoping to talk to him before he met with the senator. I have some information for them."

"Maybe I could help you. I take notes at all the water meetings."

Ray pointed. "Your office?" Ray went in and sat down, forcing the intern to follow. Bingo. He was in the right place.

The young man sat down behind his desk as if to protect his territory.

"What do they have about the Panhandle incidents?" Ray asked.

The young man fumbled with his papers. He finally looked up at Ray, who held his gaze. "They've been helping those poor people who are losing their farms." The man seemed defensive.

"How's that? How do they help them?" Ray leaned in and looked interested.

"They get buyers for them." The intern leaned back in his chair. Ray could see he was trying to back off from Ray's intense scrutiny.

"That must be hard for the ranchers with equipment and wells gone." Ray tried to sound sympathetic. "I have some leads for them. I think they'll be interested in the property, but I can't wait around until after lunch. I've got to get back."

"I could help you," the man said. "You could leave the information with me."

"I don't know," Ray said. "I was supposed to talk directly with Mr. Baxter. By the way, who buys the land, anyway?"

"It's supposed to be anonymous, but I send repossessed land information to Albert Martin at First Anderson Bank in Houston. He gets the buyers."

"Do they really buy all that land? Are you sure they want more?"

"Yes, sir. I've seen the paperwork. I just know the land has to be connected with the other pieces they have already."

"Okay, thank you." Ray heard a woman's voice in the reception area. People were returning from lunch. The kid wouldn't be alone. Ray had more information than he'd ever expected to get. He stood and walked out.

The intern looked startled. "Wait! What message did you want to leave? I didn't get your name."

Ray heard the woman ask, "Who was that?"

Ray walked down the hall and worked his way through an oncoming guided tour group. The young man might not even tell anyone about their conversation since he didn't get Ray's name or a message. He'd want to keep his job.

Ray jogged to his car and checked the meter. He dropped some quarters through the slot and made a short hike to the University of Texas campus. He found a quiet place in the LBJ library and searched for information on First Anderson Bank in Houston. There was none. But he found plenty on Albert Martin, financial wizard.

Ray read article after article about Martin's relationship with Bill Cox. He found Baxter's name in a few press releases. He e-mailed links to every article to Frank and to himself.

The conspiracy was making more and more sense. He'd found the head of the snake. Ray had to get back to Waggoner.

Chapter 52

Albert Martin and Lee Kimball stood by the fireplace inside the Cox ranch house.

Cox was pouring drinks at the bar. "How was your trip from California?" he asked. "It's good to have a partner here to celebrate our success." He handed them each a drink and joined them around the fireplace.

"To the tankers," Albert said. "They docked this morning."

Cox lifted his drink to his mouth but stopped as he watched Lee down his. He wanted his wits about him. He planned to bring up Lee's involvement with the cartel. "Thank you, Lee, for sending Gonzales to help us out. We're grateful."

"He has to go back soon," Lee said. "When will you be through with him?"

Cox was mildly surprised that Lee didn't know the latest. Gonzales must only be informing the cartel of his actions. Cox worried that Lee had gone too far or had been too careless with the cartel and wouldn't be around long. He was a liability to them. It was time for him and Al to distance themselves from Lee. "He should be back in about a week." Cox tried to satisfy Lee for the moment. They needed to take care of James first.

"Evening, gentlemen." James walked into the library as if on cue.

"Good. You're here," Cox said. "We've been waiting for you."

Lee handed James a drink. The four men stood for a moment, then Cox directed them to a row of chairs that formed a semicircle in front of the roaring fire.

"Sit here, James," Cox said, motioning toward the center chair. Cox sat next to him on the left, and Lee took the chair on the right. Albert sat next to Cox as expected, but the fifth chair beside Lee was conspicuous in its emptiness. James considered its significance for a moment before the conversation turned to Sandra.

"What do you think of her?" Lee asked to the room.

James took a deep breath. "I think she's greedy, but we need her. Money will keep her in line."

"Ah, but she has a partner," Cox informed the group. "His name is Brian Appelt. We found out his family has old money, and he and Sandra have been friends since they met in college. Here's the best part. He works for the EPA, fairly high up, too. We're having them followed around the clock."

Lee turned toward James. "Did you know about this Brian fellow?"

"I didn't." James loosened his tie and unbuttoned his collar.

"That's too bad," Albert said. "It might have given you more insight into what was going on with her."

"What have you found out about the Stanfield situation?" Cox asked James.

"That should be taken care of by now," James said.

"Is that so? It's just this one little thing," Cox said, "and you still haven't been able to take care of it."

"I thought Gonzales was taking care of it." James's voice edged higher.

"What about Lynnette?" Albert asked.

"She's a great asset," James said.

"Is she? Exactly what does she know?" Cox asked. "Did you know she resigned her job today? She hasn't been to her apartment, and no one has seen her since she left your secret place in Austin." Cox could see James was shocked. The man looked to be shrinking in front of his eyes. Cox let his words settle, knowing for sure now that Lynnette had left James in the dark. Cox decided he'd let James check out Lynnette's disappearance for himself. They'd been together for several years, and Cox expected James would try. "Why don't you try to reach her? Call her now."

James took out his cell. The other men sat and waited as he dialed. Cox turned in his chair to watch him. Finally, voicemail picked up. "Lynnette, this is James. Give me a call. It's important. Call me now." He hung up the phone and looked at Cox.

"That's done," Cox said. "Let's take a break and have some

dinner. We can continue business after we've eaten."

Cox ushered the men to the adjacent dining room, settling them at a banquet table meant for sixteen. Cox sat at the head with Albert to his right. Lee and James sat side by side on Cox's left. The lopsided island of men left the vacant end in darkness, a quirky twist that matched the mood.

Conversation was minimal through the first course. James's lesson from Cox dampened the celebratory atmosphere.

After a while, Cox asked, "How many properties do we have up for purchase in Nebraska, Albert?"

"We have nine farms now. The central line will expand by five hundred miles in two months. The pipeline leases are already in place for the land not up for sale."

"We need to increase our storage capacity before the central line is complete," Cox said. "We can send new tanks to Mexico by train, but we'll have to make a deal with the cartel there. Lee, can you set up a meeting?"

There it was. Cox had exposed Lee's dealings with the cartel. They all watched as Lee put his fork on his plate and looked from face to face. "How long have you known this?" he finally asked.

"From the beginning, Lee," Albert said. "We've always known."

Lee put his hands in his lap. "I don't know if they'll meet. I'll try. There's no controlling them. Getting involved with them isn't a good thing."

"We'll stay out of their drug business," Cox said.

"That's not it," Lee said. "It's more like, will *they* stay out of *your* business? It's not like doing business with the people you're used to. I'm in too far. You don't have to do this. Find some other way."

Cox nodded. He knew he couldn't go into Mexico without talking to the cartel. They'd take notice when he started increasing the size of his tank farm. He believed he needed their protection.

"We're aware of the dangers," Al said.

"If I can meet with them, then I'll be able to decide if we can do business," Cox said. "Until we can increase storage, we won't be able to expand our markets."

"What markets?" Lee asked.

"Sub-Saharan. We have Liberian tankers coming in next week."

"I'll try to set up the meeting," Lee said. "Be prepared that they'll know everything I know—and more."

"Ask them to come to Houston," Cox said. "Meeting on our turf might help."

"Don't count on it. They have people everywhere."

Cox turned toward James. "I want you to go to Africa in a couple of weeks. You may be there for a while. Make arrangements at your office."

"Of course, Bill."

The men discussed details until one in the morning. They

were leaving the dining room when Bill's bodyguard walked in with a phone. "It's Gonzales."

Chapter 53

Ray had driven straight from Austin to his office. He'd either been in the evidence room or printing articles for the past few hours when the Taos e-mail had come in. Ray walked through the outer office to the printer and collected the pages from the Taos police. Ramirez had e-mailed Frank and faxed copies to him.

Ray had his documents organized and in stacks on the table. He picked up statements from Jenson to Robb. Jenson talked a lot about Lynnette and his jobs. He said the big boss wanted to get rid of Sam and Georgia because they were causing problems. Jenson mentioned Gonzales several times. He said Gonzales killed Buddy and was sent to kill Sam and Georgia. Gonzales killed Hood.

Ray put the papers down. No wonder Taos let him know about the papers. Gonzales was still out there.

Ray heard someone rattling the door to the office. He found Frank outside.

"I thought you might be here," Frank said. "Are you going over your evidence?"

"Organizing it," Ray said. "What are you doing here?"

"You found some incredible evidence today. I've been looking over what you sent me. I took it to my boss. The information caused such a disturbance in the Dallas office that we got the attention of special investigations."

"I'm listening." Ray thought it had to be really big if Frank had come all the way to Waggoner to give him the news.

"You uncovered something the FBI has been trying to nail for three years—a direct connection between Cox and the land grabs. You gave them the pieces they needed."

"I'm glad I could help, but exactly what connections?"

"Linking the state senator to James Baxter and on to Albert Martin. The unit is obtaining search and arrest warrants as we speak."

"But what is Cox trying to do? I've read about him. He's made a lot of money in oil. Is he trying to control the water in Texas?"

"Yes. But it goes way beyond that. He's selling US water to foreign countries. He's using gas pipelines to transport the water across states and export it. Some countries are desperate and will pay big money for it."

"When are you making your arrests?"

"Tomorrow. I wanted you to know before it hit the news. I'm going to Houston to help with the operation. Some of the detectives and uniforms in your old department are helping out."

"I wish I could be there with you, but I have to keep trying to find Sam and Georgia."

"I'll let you know if we find anything about the Stanfields. But, Ray, you know it doesn't look good."

"I know." Ray lowered his head. He knew his friends were probably dead.

~~~

Ray walked back to the evidence room. He couldn't get Sam and Georgia off his mind. He thought maybe there was something he'd missed in all the files, some clue that would tell him where they were.

The papers in Buddy Gatwick's box from the bank had given Ray all the evidence he needed to clear Sam and Georgia of the IRS charges. They showed Buddy and his partners had set up the Stanfields. Buddy had given the blackmailers Sam's and Georgia's account numbers. The false deposits triggered an IRS investigation that implicated Sam and Georgia in money laundering. It was also obvious to Ray that poor Buddy was a pawn in the scheme. His murder would be hard to prove, but Ray had Jenson saying it was Gonzales.

Ray stared at the papers, then lowered his head to rest for a minute.

~~~

The next morning he woke to find himself stretched out on the sofa in the front office, listening to the sound of Maureen unlocking the door.

"Sheriff!" she said in surprise. "Did you sleep here?"

"I must have." Ray sat up and rubbed his face. He walked down to the evidence room and picked up his cell and put on his hat. The phone on the table rang, but Ray decided not to answer it. He locked up and went for coffee at Woody's Café. He was there with the late crowd. "Are you still serving breakfast, Marcie?"

"We sure are, Sheriff."

Ray realized how hungry he was. He'd been so focused on the case and reviewing the evidence that he'd forgotten to eat. "I think I'll have a full breakfast."

"You got it," Marcie said as she grabbed empty plates to clear a table.

Ray sat alone and imagined Jenson sitting at one of the barstools in the tiny café. Ray's back was against the north wall so he could see the front and back door of the old rock building. His phone buzzed, but when he answered, he couldn't hear anyone. It buzzed again and still he couldn't hear anyone.

JoAnn yelled to him from behind the counter. "Sheriff, you know you can't get any reception in here. You have to go outside if you want to make a call or get one."

Marcie walked up to his table, balancing three steaming plates. She set two down at his table and walked over to the next table to leave the third.

Ray stood to go outside to check his phone. He hated leaving his hot cakes and eggs, but he tore himself away and strode out of the café. Maureen had called him three times.

He was dialing when he looked up to see a black Taurus racing into the parking lot. Maureen jumped out. She started running across the street, waving her hands and shouting something Ray couldn't understand. She skidded to a stop in front of Ray and bent over at the waist, breathing hard, trying to catch her breath.

"Take your time, Maureen," Ray said. "Talk slowly so I can understand you."

"Sheriff, the airport called, and they think they have Sam flying a plane home." Maureen gasped. "You've got to get out there. Now."

"Get in the squad car, and tell me what all you know on the way," Ray said.

They both scrambled into the car and headed north to the airport, lights flashing.

In the mirrors, Ray could see that the entire café had poured out behind them. Everyone had their phones out. Within minutes, the whole town would know what was happening at the airport.

Chapter 54

Checkered fields of green and brown slipped past Sam and Georgia, but they still couldn't make out any recognizable landmarks. Georgia searched the countryside from each window in the back and through the three panels in front of Sam.

"I'll help look as soon as I'm a little more familiar with this plane," Sam said. "They took us north from Interstate 40, so I'm setting the direction southeast. We should find something familiar before much longer."

"The larger highways will be obvious even if we can't distinguish the small towns," Georgia said into her headpiece.

"I love you, Georgia, and we're going to make it home. How are you holding up?"

"You are still the love of my life, and I am fine."

The excitement of the escape had subsided. They both felt slightly dazed.

"What about your ribs?"

"My side hurts, but I can stand it. Don't worry about me, Sam."

Sam felt in control for the first time in weeks. He smiled at Georgia's remark. She was always thinking of him first.

"I see a highway," Georgia said. "It could be 287."

"I see it, too. I need to try the radio to see if I can raise anyone." They'd written down the aircraft tail number to use in just this moment. "Read that ID to me, Georgia. Mayday, Mayday, Z802NH calling any ground airstrip," he said, repeating the tail number. "This is Sam and Georgia Stanfield. I am not sure of our location. We have just escaped from kidnappers, and we need a safe place to land. Mayday, Mayday, over. Z802NH calling any airport, over."

They waited, but no response came. Even though they heard static, neither Sam nor Georgia could hear a responding voice.

"I'm afraid the radio isn't working," Sam said after several more long minutes. "I'll try again in a minute. Keep looking."

Sam followed the larger highway, keeping it on his right. He didn't know he was flying across the corner of Oklahoma until Georgia spotted a muddy river.

"Sam, that's the Red River!" Georgia said. "I'd recognize it anywhere."

"Yes, it is." Sam banked to the right to find familiar roads.

"That must not have been the 287," Georgia said. "We've been in Oklahoma."

"I know this area." Sam tried the radio again but heard no one.

They crossed the Red River, still looking for a familiar highway.

"The weather is changing. My visibility is shrinking." Low clouds forced Sam to bring up the plane, and they missed the four-lane highway that would have led them home.

Sam tried the radio again. Static. Then suddenly a voice broke in.

"Nocona City Airport calling Z802NH. What is your position? Over." Nora, the woman working at the small airport, had picked up the radio communication from Sam. She scribbled the information on her notepad. She could hear Sam repeat his information, and she wrote it down a second time. She could hear him, but he couldn't hear her. She shouted for help from Lois, the desk clerk in the outer office.

"Lois, see what you can find about these people. They're in trouble. The pilot says they just escaped from kidnappers. We need to get hold of the police department. Call the chief. Hurry. I have to stay here and see if they call again."

Nora stayed by the radio and every few minutes tried to raise Sam on the same frequency he'd used. She heard a commotion, and Lois rushed in the control room with the chief.

"Have they called again?" he asked.

"No. I think we've lost contact."

"I've put in a call to the sheriff in Waggoner to see if he knows anything."

The radio crackled. The three turned to listen.

"Mayday! Mayday! This is Z802NH. We must land. We are

a yellow-and-black crop duster. Over." Sam's voice came through clearly.

"Nocona City Airport to Z802NH, what is your position? Over." Nora tried again.

"I hear you, Nocona! We don't know exactly where we are. We don't have a GPS, and we don't know where we started. We passed over the Red River ten minutes ago. We're heading southwest. Over."

"What is your fuel situation, Z802NH? Over."

"The gauge shows half-full. I think we're okay there. Over."

"Describe what you see on the ground. Over."

Sam only heard the word "describe" and the radio went out again, spewing static into the tiny cockpit. He continued to transmit his message, hoping the Nocona airport could hear him, even if he couldn't hear them.

"We are experiencing low visibility, but the clouds are thinning. I will continue to transmit as possible." Ten minutes later, nothing else was going through.

"Sam, there's a lake on your left. I can see the water, quite a lot of it."

"I'll fly lower, and maybe we can get out of these clouds." The crop duster was made for low flying, but Sam didn't want to go so low that he hit a building or power lines. He could fly the little beauty, but he wasn't one of those crackerjack crop duster pilots.

When the clouds cleared, they were flying over water, but not for long.

"Sam, this is Cow Creek Lake. I recognize the docks by the Lagoon Bar and Grill."

Georgia's voice was soft, and Sam could barely hear her, but he recognized the area, too. He heard her say Cow Creek and felt relief. He knew where they were. "I'm afraid we've gone south of the Waggoner airport. There's a landing strip about five miles from here that I know. It's at a plastic pipe manufacturing plant. They have an airstrip there, if we can find it."

~~~

Ray rushed into the Waggoner airport tower, Maureen trailing close behind. For each step of Ray's long stride, Maureen took two, trying to keep up. He bounded up the stairs to the control room and was greeted by Craig Forrest, the man who managed the airport for the city.

"Sheriff, here's what we know so far. Sam and Georgia are headed southeast in a yellow-and-black crop duster. The Nocona airport said they talked to them about thirty minutes ago, but they never got a sighting of the plane. It's the cloudy weather."

"Where do you think they are now?" Ray asked.

"Sam didn't give us his airspeed—either his instruments were faulty, he didn't know how, or the radio didn't work. We've made an estimate based on the plane he's in, the weather, and typical speed patterns." Craig walked the sheriff over to a map and pointed at a wide area from Waggoner to a hundred miles west and south. "We haven't seen them in our airspace, so we're guessing they missed us because of the cloud coverage."

"I'll notify the surrounding counties to be on the lookout," Ray said, picking up his phone to alert his deputies. "Maureen, a deputy is picking you up in five minutes. I need you to go back to the office and coordinate this from there."

Ray could see Maureen's disappointment and was torn. He knew she wanted to be where the action was, but Ray needed her at the office. She didn't get to choose. She returned with the deputy.

~~~

The phone was ringing when Maureen walked into the courthouse. "Waggoner County Sheriff's Department," she said.

"Hello, Maureen, it's Steven over here at the lake."

"Hey, Steve. What do you need? It's real busy around here."

"Yeah, well, I saw a plane flying low over the lake, and I think it was the Stanfields. You need to tell Ray. They're headed west."

Alert to the news, Ray and Craig searched the map to find possible landing locations.

"Here! The plastics plant," Craig said after a few minutes. "They have a nice little landing strip."

Ray grabbed his hat and told Craig to call the plastics plant. "Tell them to look for a yellow-and-black crop duster."

The plant was about fifteen minutes away, but Ray could be there in ten. He flipped on his lights and siren and headed toward the airstrip. He hoped it was the right one. He radioed Maureen to send a deputy and an ambulance to the site.

Maureen also called the Bar S and told Joe and Harry Reynolds.

~~~

The duster flew west from the lake. Sam strained to find the runway.

"There's the plant, Georgia!" Sam buzzed the area twice to give them the idea he was going to land. The second time he flew low enough to see people emerging from the buildings. They were waving. He wasn't sure if they were trying to send him away or to invite him down.

He circled again, taking his time so he could watch the sky for other planes. The skies were otherwise empty. Sam was making his approach when he saw several vehicles with flashing lights speeding down the road toward the facility.

"I think it's the cavalry." The people below had formed the word "GO" and a giant human arrow pointing to the runway.

Ray skidded into the parking lot just as Sam began his descent. Ray had driven to the end of the runway by the time the wheels touched down. His deputy made it in time to hold the crowd back and direct the ambulance to the runway when the duster finally came to a stop.

"We made it, sweetheart!" Sam shouted as he killed the engine. "I'm so thankful. Let's get our feet on the ground."

Sam took off his headset and shoved the door open. He climbed out and stood on the wing. He saw Ray running toward the plane, and the ambulance pulled to a stop nearby.

"Georgia, Ray is here. I see Joe and Uncle Harry, and they have Gracie."

Gracie pulled on the leash when she heard Sam's voice. Joe let her go, and then he started running to the plane himself.

"Back the ambulance in here." Ray pointed to a spot near the wing.

Sam bent down to help Georgia out of the plane, but she'd leaned back against the cracked observation window. She didn't answer him. She looked asleep. He got on his knees so he could reach in for her.

"Georgia! Georgia! Wake up! We're here!" Fear struck Sam in the gut. He felt for a pulse. She was alive.

Ray could see that Sam was in anguish. "What is it, Sam?" Ray climbed onto the wing to get near Sam.

"Someone help her!" Sam looked Georgia over, and realized her side was covered in blood. "Please hurry! She's hurt."

"Sam, let the medics in. Come on back." Ray took Sam's arm and guided him off the plane. Gracie ran over and licked Sam's hand. She sat by Sam and looked on while the medics worked on Georgia.

Neither Sam nor Gracie would budge until Georgia had been taken from the plane. They walked alongside the stretcher until the medics placed it inside the ambulance. "I need to go with her, Ray," Sam said.

"Why don't you get in my car? I promise we'll follow the ambulance in to the hospital. They need room to do their work."

"Take Gracie." Sam handed the leash to Ray.

"Wait a minute, Sam."

Sam told the medics, "I'm coming. You can't leave me behind."

He stepped up into the back of the vehicle and sat beside Georgia. The woman in the back scooted over close to the monitors and continued working. Georgia's eyes were closed. She had an oxygen mask over her mouth and nose, and Sam could hardly see her face.

Carefully, he picked up her hand and put it between his two giant ones. He knew she could hear him. "Georgia, you're all right now. We're on our way to the Waggoner hospital. Hang on until we get there. I love you." Sam stared at his wife tenderly, noticing how her slender body looked even thinner than usual. She looked barely there. Sam gazed at the monitors. He patted Georgia's hand. "After all we've been through, you can't leave me now. Hold on."

Sam felt Georgia's hand move, and her eyes fluttered open. Immediately, she closed them again.

"She's just asleep, sir," one of the medics said.

Sam nodded to the young man and leaned back against the side of the ambulance. He still held her soft hand. He rubbed his thumb across her palm. He shut out the siren and the clicking and beeping of the emergency equipment. He watched Georgia breathing.

Sam knew that life didn't let you get comfortable. But for now, they were safe and would face their tomorrows together.

www.ingramcontent.com/pod-product-compliance
Lightning Source LLC
Chambersburg PA
CBHW020653110726
47901CB00001B/180